# THE GHOST OF Fannie Guthry-Baehm

*A Murder Mystery*

JONATHAN FAULKNER

VAN GILDER, INC.
Homer, Alaska

**Cover Photo:** Van Gilder Hotel in the 1920s, reversed to negative.

**Book Editing and Design:** Kenneth Guentert, *The Publishing Pro*, LLC, Colorado Springs, Colorado.

**Contributing Author:** Ashley Imlay of Homer, Alaska provided much of the research and text appearing as Dr. Strayer's "story within a story" in Chapter six. Ashley's story is a fictional account of Fannie's last day at work and her shooting at the Van Gilder Hotel and is based on actual police reports and trial documents.

Copyright © 2010 by Jonathan Faulkner. All rights reserved. No part of this book may be photocopied or otherwise reproduced without written permission from the publisher.

Published by:

Van Gilder, Inc.
4786 Homer Spit Road
Homer, AK 99603
www.vangilderhotel.com

ISBN: 978-0-9845595-0-3

Printed in the United States of America.

The Ghost of Fannie Guthrie-Baehm
*is dedicated to my wife, Sara,
who has endured my flights of fancy
and episodes of neglect for nearly a lifetime.*

*While inspired by actual events, the characters and events described herein are entirely fictional. Any resemblance that the names or characters created by the author have to actual people—either living or deceased—is coincidental.*

*With one notable exception.*

*Fannie Guthrie-Baehm was an actual person and a victim of homicide at the Van Gilder Hotel in 1950. She is not fictional. And while events surrounding Fannie's death are dramatized here, the storied encounters with her ghost are not.*
*The Ghost of Fannie Guthrie-Baehm is very real to some, including several who have contributed to the following story.*

# Chapter I
*Friday, January 18, 5:35 P.M.*

"NONSENSE, I DON'T BELIEVE IN GHOSTS," responded the portly woman with a thick German accent, "so I'll take the room."

The two-room corner suite facing Resurrection Bay was the last available room to rent at the Van Gilder Hotel, so the desk clerk was quick to prepare the folio, issue the key, and to provide directions to room 202. He glanced down at the names of his walk-in customers: Inga and Ellen Windemuth.

"But I am curious, how did the room get its name?"

James Van Oss, the young manager, was fatigued from a twelve-hour shift of fielding phone calls from stranded winter travelers and cleaning rooms. Typically, the story about Fannie's murder and her ghost was a promotional story, rendered with enthusiasm and carefully crafted to avoid upsetting a potential customer. But today the question annoyed James. The hotel's twenty-three rooms were fully occupied, a most unwelcome intrusion into his typically quiet and undemanding winter solitude.

Most of the day's arrivals were Alaskans who were in Seward to attend the Polar Bear Jump-off Festival but who had been stranded by the weather, not the typical summer tourists who inquired about the history of the nationally registered landmark. However, James was totally unprepared for the emergency circumstances of the day. As the lone winter caretaker, he shouldered the entire burden of cleaning rooms, checking in guests, and answering endless inquiries about everything from road conditions to internet access. The hotel's themed dress code consisting of pressed white shirt, black bow tie, and arm garter was one among several formalities James had dispensed with this January day. He was exhausted. Contrary to his normally outgoing and service-oriented disposition, James regarded Inga Windemuth's question as almost impertinent.

"Fannie was a young woman in her early twenties and was living here at the time she was murdered," described James. "She was staying in room 202 when her jealous ex-husband calmly walked into the hotel and up the stairs to her room and shot her point blank with a .22 caliber pistol. So we call it 'Fannie's Suite,' in honor of her, of course, not of a ghost. We have the story here if you would like to purchase a copy for one dollar. A local eighth-grade girl wrote the story, so we donate all proceeds to the Seward Middle School."

"Thank you, young man, maybe later," said Inga. "But if I could trouble you for help with our luggage, I will gladly donate a dollar to the cause."

"My honor, Ma'am, follow me!" replied James.

James grabbed the two heavy suitcases and lumbered up the stairs.

"Be sure you take time to look at these historic panels on the walls. They detail the history of Seward and the hotel back 100 years," said James.

Inga and Ellen, her daughter, labored up the steep stairs with obvious stress and paused at the first landing to look at the panels.

"What is the significance of that one?" Inga asked, stalling to catch her breath.

"That is a presidential motorcade coming down Third Avenue on the Fourth of July in 1922. President Harding is on the rear platform dedicating the Northern Railroad connection to Anchorage. In fact, he stayed here that night in room 201, which we call the 'President Harding Suite.'"

Inga was near-sighted and had thick, black plastic-rimmed glasses that she lowered onto her bony nose as she focused her eyes closer.

"Quite something, actually. It all seems so formal for such a frontier town. Who is that standing next to him?"

James dropped the bags and edged in closer. He had never studied the photo in any detail and actually had little interest in history aside from a general affection for old buildings. Nonetheless, he felt obliged to respond.

"I have no idea. I never noticed the woman before. They seem close; I assume it's his wife."

"More likely his mistress, Carrie Fulton Phillips, the first person in U.S. history to successfully extort a national party over an extramarital affair."

"That would make for an interesting footnote."

"You should read *The Shadow of Blooming Grove* by Francis Russell."

James rolled his eyes. The last thing he needed was a book referral. He pushed the bag up the two remaining risers to the second floor and deposited the bag at the threshold of room 202. At the moment James was less concerned with guest service than he was with his duty to return to the front desk, which is how he rationalized his hasty retreat. In truth, he was superstitious. Intruding into Fannie's domain was more than a casual concern to him. James would matter-of-factly recount stories of inexplicable occurrences around the hotel, but he would always stop short of admitting fear. But during the dark winter months when he was alone in the four-story hotel, he would avoid remote areas of the hotel and never venture into room 202.

"Your room may be hot since I turned up the heat," stated James hurriedly. "One thermostat activates the entire system from the ground floor so it can be hard to control. Normally, I would recommend you open a window, but tonight that would not be a good idea. The windows are still caulked shut. I'm the only staff person here tonight but the phone rings through to a cordless phone when I'm not at the desk, so you can always reach me by dialing zero."

"Thank you, young man," said Inga. "Here's a donation for your budding author."

James smiled and turned, thinking to himself that she probably expected a copy of "Fannie the Ghost" for the two-dollar gratuity.

"Live to serve, serve to live," said James in his trademark refrain.

"Our continental breakfast will be ready at 8:00 A.M," he shouted back over his shoulder as he disappeared down the stairwell.

Resurrection Bay is long and narrow, rimmed with 6,000-foot glacier-clad peaks that create a perfect wind tunnel. Warm, moist low-pressure systems from the Japanese Current roll north into the Gulf of Alaska during the winter months and collide with the cold, high-pressure air masses formed over Alaska's interior, creating violent weather. Today's storm was the worst James had ever experienced. But as the general manager and winter caretaker, James was expected to do whatever was necessary and to generate revenue whenever the opportunity presented itself.

Days of heavy rain-laden snows and high winds had forced periodic road closures of the only road leaving town. The small, short-field airport was closed, as were most of the downtown shops and restaurants. Forty-knot winds and snow buffeted Seward in a whiteout that encased the town in a tomb of cement-like snow.

James was more than a little anxious about taking on a full house in such extreme conditions. The sudden power outage that Friday morning was a sobering reminder of the hotel's complete dependency on electricity, and local radio stations were broadcasting warnings of more prolonged outages at any time. With temperatures hovering at freezing and high winds penetrating the poorly sealed doors and windows, James knew the indoor temperature would drop rapidly without his circulation pumps. With only a few hours of obscured daylight and limited battery backup for the emergency lighting system, a total blackout was more than likely. To make matters worse, his six flashlights and handful of candles were inadequate, and Seward's only hardware store was closed.

Since moving from Nashville, Tennessee, two years earlier, James embraced the prospect of an Alaskan adventure, a Jack London survival tale that Alaskans would regard as a right-of-passage. If he survived, James mused to himself, he would brag to his friends of a harrowing night in Alaska's oldest and most haunted hotel.

It wasn't long before Inga returned to the front desk with her daughter Ellen. James had taken the intervening time to properly attire himself, partly out of duty but mostly out of desire to impress his guests. He loved a party and being the center of attention. The opportunity for quick cash from tips also occurred to James as he went to work resurrecting the lobby bar for a planned reception later that evening.

"Where do you recommend we take a late dinner, Watson?" Inga asked with attempted humor.

"Christo's is two blocks away and may be the only place open. Try their Mama Mia pizza or their Greek salad. We also have a fully equipped kitchen down the hall if you want to prepare something here."

Inga turned and craned her neck down the hallway.

"Really? We might take advantage of that later, but tonight we'll try Christo's. By the way, the light bulb in the bathroom is burned out. Could you replace it while we're out?"

"It would be my pleasure," replied James.

Inga and Ellen pulled what looked like plastic bags over their heads, reluctantly inched out into the wet streetlighted darkness of Adams Street, and sloshed their way down the hill toward the waterfront.

Trained to react to such matters promptly, James grabbed a light bulb and spare key, locked the lobby gate, and dashed to the second floor suite. Curiously the door was open, which did not strike James as unusual. The Van Gilder is an intimate hotel, and guests often forget to lock the door or do so intentionally. The 100-year-old building is always settling and shifting, causing the doors to stick or the strike plates to become misaligned, which was likely the cause. Nonetheless, it was precisely the ominous sign that made James uncomfortable as he knocked lightly on the door.

After a trained announcement of his presence, James entered the bathroom and hit the light switch. Instantly the light came on. He then went to the vanity light above the new sink and flipped that switch. The light worked there as well. He then checked every light in the room with the same result. In a muffled voice, he said defiantly, "OK, Fannie, I'm not coming up here again," and hurriedly exited the room.

The new owner had remodeled every room in the hotel, extending some of the wiring circuits himself. Through the years, he had complained frequently about the old, illogical wiring scheme that prior owners had installed without regard to codes or engineered load limits. James recalled that the bathroom in 202 had been completely remodeled by a licensed contractor, which all but erased deficient wiring from the list of potential causes. Nonetheless, James left the room feeling confident that he would hear no more about it.

# Chapter II
*Friday, January 18, 9:05 A.M.*

"MARCUS, THIS IS WALTER CALLING. Do you have a few minutes?"

"Sure, Walter, what can I do for you?"

Walter Hayes had recently fallen from grace as Alaska's most prominent lobbyist, indicted by a federal grand jury on multiple charges of bribery, extortion, and ethics violations. The mere mention of Walter's name caused immediate recoil among Alaskans, thanks to constant media reports about his role in illegal fundraising schemes and vote buying among Alaska's legislators.

Walter had placed the call to Marcus Coble, a partner in Brady & Coble, Alaska's leading law firm on oil and gas leases. Marcus was chief counsel for Alaska's largest independent oil company, Beaufort Oil Company, which for more than ten years had used Walter Hayes to lobby the Alaska legislature.

Beaufort Oil Company had made Walter a powerful man. But it was equally true that BOC's meteoric rise had been substantially abetted by Walter's shrewd political maneuvering. Eighty-five percent of Alaska's $3.5 billion annual budget is derived from oil taxes and production royalties, giving Alaska's oil industry a huge stake in local and statewide elections, as well as tremendous power. The astronomical consulting fees paid by BOC to Walter Hayes every year included a substantial slush fund that was expected to secure political favors and to sway elections.

Like most successful attorneys, Marcus was less intent on passing judgment than he was in learning the angles to every case. These were dangerously unpredictable times, and Walter instantly commanded his full attention. He also knew there was a distinct possibility that Walter's phone conversations were being recorded by the FBI.

"I need some legal advice, Marcus. Given the conflicts involved and that you have your own personal interests to look after, I'm not asking you to represent me. But I'm hoping you can recommend someone, given our circumstances."

As a veteran lobbyist, Walter was versed in the art of coercion by suggestion, and Marcus recognized the warning signs. He understood that Walter's reference to "our circumstances" might have meant that he was including his family in his predicament. Another possibility was that "our" was an extension of the royal "we," which would be consistent with Walter's egotistical manner. The circumstances Walter alluded to were equally vague. It could be a reference to Walter's financial situation, which was dire, despite his track record as Alaska's highest paid lobbyist. His profligate lifestyle was legendary in Juneau.

But the spin that alerted Marcus the most was the implication that their fates were inextricably linked and that it would not be wise for Marcus to think otherwise. Walter was not seeking legal advice, Marcus speculated, but was warning that if he was going down others would too and that he expected help.

"I'm not sure what circumstances you're referring to Walter," Marcus replied. "I'm aware of your indictment, if that's what you mean."

"Mostly, yes, but let me put it this way: Is it possible a good criminal lawyer would take a high-profile case like mine on some kind of contingency basis? I'm not exactly flush with dough, Marcus."

"Not in my view. You're going to want to look out-of-state. You need an experienced criminal-defense attorney, a trial lawyer who can handle the media and knows the federal justice system. I'm happy to give you a referral."

"How much will it cost?"

"You're looking at three-to-four hundred g's, minimum, if you want the best effort, with 25 percent up front."

"I'll need all the help I can get."

A long and awkward silence hung in the air like a forgotten name, but Marcus did not take the bait.

"I would appreciate the referral," Walter continued. "But the pressure from the feds is so intense that I can hardly think straight anymore. I'm wondering if I wouldn't be better off striking some kind of deal."

The sudden suggestion was not rendered flatly or with the cold calculation of a man weighing his options. The resignation in Walter's voice was alarming to Marcus—and signaled the need for a deeper probe into Walter's stability.

"How are you holding up, my friend? You have a heart condition, and you can't let this get to you. You have friends who can help you through this. Are you sure you're OK?"

"I don't think you're hearing me. Do I sound OK?"

"Are they pressuring you to negotiate a deal in exchange for testimony, Walter? Is that what's going on?"

"I've got screws on my thumbs and my eyelids sewn open under a heat lamp, for Christ's sake. I'm hardly in a position to negotiate." Walter's voice was beginning to crack. "They want everything: names, dates, computer files, communications, sworn depositions, help with wire-taps, all that shit. I was sure you would have guessed this was happening."

"Well, I'm glad you called me first; let's get to the point. How can I help you, Walter?"

"You said that I have friends, but I don't know who they are or what I can expect from them. The truth is, I'm not even sure I fully understand the charges against me let alone how I can wage a defense. I'm not seeing any upside at the moment, only people running from me and plugging their ears whenever my name is mentioned."

"I can help you with a defense strategy, Walter."

"When I came to you last week with the invoice from Van Fleet, you sent me packing. I was trying to tell you that there's some shit out there, and when it all starts getting flung around, some is gonna stick. I can see clearly where this is going. You have been a close friend, and I understand that you have to look after Beaufort and your law firm. But what the hell would you have me do?"

"Don't do anything impulsive. Stay in control; you have options. Give me the weekend to develop a plan, OK? One thing you *must* do is secure legal counsel. Don't engage anyone in direct negotiation, do you understand?"

"Sure."

"Alright, I'll get you a name. How much time do you have?"

"I'm leaving town for a couple days to clear my head. I don't know if I have much fight left in me. Could be a day, could be a week. Get back to me soon. You're the only person I can turn to for help."

The call ended with a sudden "click," with no sign-off. Walter was being pinched; this was a distress call, a clear warning that something was about to break. Marcus grasped the urgency of the situation and located his Blackberry. An e-mail from Jack Randolph, CEO of Beaufort Oil, flashed in his in-box:

> Call me now re: Walter Hayes. He's a loose cannon. I am counting on you to contain Beaufort's exposure in this matter.

Marcus hit speed dial, and Jack answered on the first ring. "Where are we at, Marcus?"

"I just got off the phone with Walter. He called looking for legal advice, but there's more to it. He's feeling the pressure from the feds. He's not broken yet, but he's cracking. He's thinking hard about striking a deal. They're chasing the big fish, so they could go easy on him. He's looking for some upside to a fight and it's not all posture. Whatever deal the Justice Department is ready to offer Walter we need to beat."

"Christ, where's this going to end? Did you see the headlines today? Guilty on all counts in Representative Van Fleet's trial. I can't believe it. What the hell are you going to do about this guy?"

"Keep in mind Van Fleet's case was completely different and unrelated to us."

"What the hell do you mean 'unrelated'? He was convicted of taking penny-ante bribes disguised as ad buys in a bogus newsletter that a jury determined influenced his vote on a prison plan he would have supported anyway. Now he's looking at ten years in prison! If nothing else, it proves the jeopardy of a jury, and public opinion that's out to hang us all. I'm really starting to worry, Marcus. What are we going to do? The word I'm getting is that Walter's already turned."

"I'll tell you what we're not going to do: trust Walter or get in any deeper. We pay Walter to consult and to lobby for Brady

& Coble, that's it. We don't direct his activities or have specific knowledge of his client dealings. We pay for results. How he achieves them is neither our business nor our problem. The immediate plan is to find him a good trial lawyer so I can monitor his situation better. If Walter believes we're helping him, we should be able to prevent him from folding."

"Get on it, Marcus! Have you spoken with the governor yet, or his chief of staff, Elliot Lawson? They have more at stake than we do. We should compare notes before we get too far down the road with Walter."

"No, I haven't, but I agree it's a good idea. We need to move fast. Elliot is feeling the heat too and is expecting an indictment any day."

"Let's get a tail on Walter until we know what he's up to. If he's striking a deal, I want to know about it. Elliot thinks that you're the only person who can turn him. What do you think?"

"Every option carries risk. He could be wired and working with the Justice Department already. A wiretap is what sunk Van Fleet, remember? On the other hand, he hasn't turned yet. It wouldn't make sense. I know Walter; he's shuffling the deck, looking at his hole card, and getting ready to play his best hand. It makes sense that he would come to me for an offer before he folds."

"I agree. So what's our move?"

Marcus outlined his plan to contact a defense attorney and to arrange himself as co-counsel. "You call Governor Thompson. Find out how much Walter's testimony will hurt Elliot Lawson. Maybe we can silence Walter and gain some leverage along the way. You know what I'm saying?"

"I do. In fact, I've been looking for something I can use to nudge the governor along on our Endicott lease extensions."

In spite of the recent warning shots from the FBI, and Alaska's heightened sensitivity to scandal, the politics of Alaska's oil industry was still very much alive and in play.

☙❧

When Jack hung up the phone, his wife Rachel was standing over his shoulder.

"That sounded ominous. What's going on Jack?"

Jack knew he could not keep a secret from his wife, nor did he really desire to. Theirs was an open if somewhat distant relationship based on mutual respect and common interest. Rachel was what many called a "trophy wife": young, vibrant, shapely, and a former Miss Alaska. Her prior marriage ended in a bitter divorce, and Jack Randolph was the handsome, amiable, and seemingly self-assured person she needed at the time. He promised her a life of ease and independence without too many strings. She was sharp-minded, sharp-tongued, and curious of Jack's affairs, often to the point of being intrusive. Jack rarely turned to her for advice, and yet he privately valued her opinions, which Rachel was never short of and frequently volunteered. Although they had only been married six years, theirs had largely been a marriage without significant issues.

When it came to BOC business, however, Jack was not one to volunteer information to his wife. Also, these were difficult times and each day brought worse news and a cascade of calamities that robbed the opportunity for thoughtful discussion.

Jack hen-pecked Rachel on the cheek and pretended to be in a hurry. "Business, dear, nothing terribly important, just more meetings."

"I heard you mention Elliot Lawson's name. How much trouble is he in?"

Jack was thankful to divert the topic away from Walter Hayes and away from the private detective he had ordered to follow him.

"To be honest, he's in a lot of trouble. How much is hard to say, but it's pretty clear he'll have to resign at some point. All I know is what I've read, which is that he used the governor's office and very inappropriate means to strong-arm legislators into voting for his agenda and to raise funds for Governor Thompson's re-election. I'm meeting him tonight in Juneau, returning tomorrow sometime. How would you like to join me?"

Rachel knew that her husband did not entirely trust her to be home alone, but she also knew he had little reason to doubt her fidelity. His question was more obligatory than sincere.

"I would have nothing to do there, Jack. Just stay in touch. You know how anxious I get when you don't call me."

Jack retreated to his home office and sunk deep down into his leather sofa. He looked at his watch: 9:40 A.M. He called his secretary and directed her to purchase a one-way ticket to Juneau on the 11:40 A.M. flight from Anchorage and to alert the Juneau office to have the company jet on standby.

Jack Randolph was one of Alaska's most prominent and powerful oilmen. He began his career as a roughneck for Atlantic Richfield when they first struck oil on the Kenai Peninsula in 1969. A high school drop-out of unusual ambition, Jack realized at a young age that oil was big money and that the oil companies would pay well for two things: reliable field support and partners in the political arena. Alaska's regulations and oil tax structure cost the oil industry billions of dollars annually, and the person who could keep the reach of government in check would be well compensated.

Assembling local materials and crews to manage everything

from field camps to waste disposal, Jack Randolph made himself indispensable to big oil—and a fortune in the process. While his buddies bought fishing boats and expensive vacations, Jack invested in politics by hosting fundraisers and dinners for Alaska's business elite. His affable character won friends easily, and his energetic storytelling was as entertaining as it was accurate. He was plain spoken, crude in many ways, and blunt—endearing attributes to the field crews and laborers he hired by the thousands. In short, he was "one the boys" with a rough-edged charisma that was perfectly suited to the back-slapping, tobacco-spittin' oil fields and to the halls of the state capitol.

Hand-picking a team of well-connected investors, Jack set himself up early as a "straw-buyer" for a major oil company bidding on the original Prudhoe Bay state oil leases. In exchange, he received exclusive development rights on several small but high-value tracts. His legendary reputation as a "wildcatter" was controversial for other reasons though. He was accused of obtaining secret seismic testing data from the BLM vault prior to the Prudhoe Bay lease sale through questionable means, charges that were never proven. Still others believed his success was based entirely on luck. It was universally accepted, however, that Jack Randolph was Alaska's most powerful self-made multi-millionaire.

❧❦

As Jack sat at home contemplating his meeting with Elliot Lawson, he was certain of one thing: Walter Hayes had to be checked. And at the same moment, across Anchorage in a high-rise apartment, Marcus Coble understood precisely the same thing. The deteriorating circumstances of Walter Hayes demanded immediate action. Equally pressing on Marcus were his personal issues: his growing involvement with BOC and his infatuation with Rachel, both of which he found increasingly hard to control. His exposure to criminal liability also was pressing, since no matter how much he had distanced himself from Walter's activities over the years, nothing he accomplished was ever perfectly clean.

After canceling his two appointments that day and arranging for a P.I. to follow Walter, Marcus left his apartment for a walk along Anchorage's coastal trail. He rarely exercised, but he enjoyed the dense winter air and the orange tinted sky to the southeast that hinted of a sunrise. For the first time in his life Marcus stressed about his uncertain future. He knew better than anyone how fast the house of cards could tumble. The sudden indictments of two prominent legislators brought into sharp focus the unpredictability of the justice system. A long walk was exactly what he needed to sort it out, he thought to himself, as he reached into his pocket and silenced his cell phone.

Marcus was not the brooding type. He was all action, a tobacco-chewing, Red-Bull-fueled high-wire act. And yet he was cautious and meticulous by nature. His mind was always working on the details that he knew from experience made a difference. He liked to remind his detractors that a Rembrandt consists of thousands of detailed brush strokes and palettes, none of which are distinguishable from twenty feet away. While it is at a distance that the painting is viewed and appreciated as a masterpiece, it would not exist but for the minute detail.

At that moment, however, it was neither the larger canvas nor the finer brush strokes that consumed Marcus' mind; he was pondering whether or not to pick up the brush. Whatever action Marcus pursued, or elected not to pursue, would have lasting consequences. His actions would influence the future of Alaska and the fate of important people.

One serious option he now considered was the option of doing nothing, of retiring from BOC and from his law practice completely. With his respectable savings and his stock options in BOC, Marcus was assured of a comfortable life free of personal jeopardy. Almost unconsciously, he started to mouth the words of an old Alaskan Iditarod song: *When you're born to run, it's so hard to sit at home, so don't be surprised to see me back in the race to Nome.* Marcus was not about to retire.

The simple truth was that Marcus' business with Beaufort was so convoluted that something needed to change. Shortly after Beaufort Oil Co. was formed, the opportunity for Marcus to act as a corporate officer was viewed as a calculated investment by Brady & Coble to build the firm as well as an interim step to qualify BOC to bid on oil leases. But now the relationship was clouded, the conflicts of interest more acute. Bill Brady, Marcus' senior law partner, seemed more distant and distrustful of late, and he needled Marcus daily about the increasingly hostile media coverage.

There was also the matter concerning Rachel, his boss' wife. The frequent meetings and social engagements between Marcus and Rachel fueled mild speculation about an affair, and Bill had warned Marcus more than once about the consequences of such a relationship. To Marcus, Bill's indignation was simple jealousy over his success with BOC and his growing independence from the firm. What was becoming clearer to Marcus each day was that he could resolve these conflicts and improve his status by leaving the law firm to work full time for BOC. Convincing Jack to guarantee his future with BOC would be easy, he reasoned, and so he resolved to break the news to his law partner as soon as he returned from his walk.

As Marcus steeled his nerve, he quickened his pace along the trail. He was Jack Randolph's obvious successor, the only other person with the experience to operate the privately held company. An entire life of preparation converged with this opportunity in a manner that was more than serendipitous. He would not hesitate. As he turned the corner on his two-mile loop, he powered up his Blackberry and phoned Jack.

"Marcus here. Got a minute?"

"Sure, go!"

"I've got a trail on Walter, and I called a San Francisco trial attorney, Byron Sanders. Turns out he knows quite a bit already. He'll talk to Walter as soon as I can arrange it. He has some interesting legal strategies. If we stress an attorney-client privilege with Walter, we can protect BOC by preventing incriminating documents from seeing the light of day. It may also help solve the issue of legal fees."

"Let's hope it holds up," said Jack. "When I called Elliot, we decided on a face-to-face meeting at the Goldmark Hotel this afternoon at 4:00 P.M. I'm on a commercial flight to Juneau leaving within the hour."

"About my meeting with Walter, are you sure it's a good idea?" asked Marcus.

"Absolutely, but be careful! We can't leave anything to chance. I'm sure Walter factors heavily in Elliot's case, but I don't know all the angles yet. Elliot sounded anxious to meet with me."

The prospect of meeting with Walter made Marcus nervous. The underbelly of politics was that everyone was expendable. Friendships were expedients, mere conduits to gain advantage and wealth. The truth was that Marcus had little to gain from a face-to-face meeting, besides hearing directly the litany of questionable tactics sanctioned by himself and BOC: political polls paid on behalf of candidates with "undeclared" contributions; direct cash payments disguised as loans to legislators; the more visible scheme, investigated by the Alaska Public Offices Commission in 2004, to funnel political contributions from supposedly voluntary (most would argue coerced) employee payroll deductions. APOC declared the ploy to be legal, which confirmed what an already cynical Alaska electorate knew: Corruption and influence-peddling were sanctioned in Alaska.

Suddenly, a bore tide of incriminating evidence was flooding Alaska's field of dreams. What only months ago was considered to be politics as usual was now labeled a brazen raid on the public trust. One recent editorial pointed out that 70 percent of Walter's $900,000 in APOC-reported income came from BOC. A blogger wrote:

> Even a blind man can see that Walter Hayes is a shill for BOC and for all intents and purposes its officers and employees too. BOC should be held accountable for Hayes' actions, and Hayes' actions should be regarded as those of BOC.

The fact that Marcus Coble trusted Walter Hayes as much as anyone meant nothing under the circumstances. The paranoia that gripped the capital played into the hand of the Justice Department very well. Everyone was a target, running for cover and willing to step on the back of an associate if it helped him to climb out of the cauldron. Marcus was very conscious of the potential pitfalls of meeting Walter, not the least of which was that he could be set up. As he prepared for his upcoming reunion, the idea that weighed most heavily on Marcus' mind was the realization that any misfortune would likely be his.

## Chapter III
*Friday, January 18, 12:10 P.M.*

**THE DRAB, LOW OVERCAST SKY** clung to the Anchorage skyline like unwanted hair on the walls of a bathtub. The high winds out of the mountains to the east and the driving drizzle announced the incoming low-pressure system and the deteriorating road conditions to the south.

Marcus' Bootlegger's Cove home was a shapeless shoebox and faced west over Cook Inlet where the deadened sky yielded no evidence of the waning sun. The old-town oceanfront subdivision is an odd mixture of expensive homes, nondescript apartments, 1940s era ranches, and flat-roofed bungalows owned by old-timers who never had the urge to upgrade. As Marcus looked out the huge picture window of his living room, the silt-encrusted ice flows moved in unison up the inlet like decapitated cars on a gridlocked freeway. The graceful shape of Mount Susitna ("Sleeping Beauty" in Athabaskan) appeared flattened and lifeless against the grayness. Marcus had just tossed a towrope and flares in the back of his Lexus LX10 when he received a call from the private investigator.

"Marcus, I have an update for you," said the P.I. "Walter left Anchorage just before 11:00 A.M., made a fuel stop, and then drove straight to the Van Gilder Hotel in Seward. He carried an overnight bag inside, so I suspect he's camping here. I can't tell if he's meeting with anyone, but the weather here stinks. What do you want me to do?"

"Keep a close watch on him until I arrive, which won't be for a few hours. If he leaves the hotel, follow him. I want to know his every move. Leave me a message if you can't reach me."

When Marcus hung up, he realized that the business that he was conducting on behalf of BOC was precisely the conduct his law partner Bill Brady would not condone. There was no more postponing the inevitable. Marcus pinched a wad of chew from his Skoal container and packed it in his jaw. When he felt the jolt of nicotine leeching through his gums, he picked up the phone and placed the dreaded call to his law partner.

"Bill, this is Marcus. I have to make this quick, but I suggest we set some time aside early next week for a follow up. Jack has me working on this Walter Hayes ordeal, and I won't be in the office for a few days. But Hayes is typical of the business Jack is asking me to perform for BOC, much of which you would not approve. I've given this a lot of thought, and I think it's time to dissolve the firm and go our separate ways. I'm sure it doesn't come as much of a surprise to you."

There was silence on the other end.

"We've talked about the conflicts with Beaufort for years and neither of us is comfortable with the present situation. I have no idea where things are going, but I could quickly become a liability to you."

More silence, which Marcus interpreted as feigned disappointment and a practiced tactic whenever a negotiation was imminent.

"Look, Bill, the line between my actions as an attorney for Brady & Coble and my actions as vice president of BOC is razor thin. It's unmanageable. Jack is asking me to do things that fall outside our firm's contract with BOC and beyond your comfort zone, things I can't always disclose. I can no longer distinguish between my duties to Jack and my responsibilities to you and the firm."

"One can't expect to hang around a damn pig pen and not attract flies," said Bill in an uncharacteristic reprimand. "I don't want any unpleasant smells to foul the air in this office."

"I agree, Bill, it's for the best."

"I assume this is of some urgency or you wouldn't be calling me on a Friday. Is there anything affecting the firm I need to know about?"

After a moment's pause, Marcus admitted to a few hot spots they both needed to be alert to. "Nothing I can't handle, " concluded Marcus confidently.

"This deserves our full attention, without any distractions. When can we meet?" asked Bill.

"Early next week, Tuesday, the usual place."

"Fine. I understand the complexity of the situation. Governor Thompson called me to express his concern about the repercussions to the Alaska Gas Line Inducement Act if Jack is dragged into this mess. He's obviously looking out for himself and for Elliot, but he asked me what we're doing about Walter Hayes and whether you were the right person to handle it. So this is timely."

"I hope we have time. I'm not sure if I am the right person to deal with Walter, especially as an attorney for Brady & Coble."

"Has Jack offered you a package?"

"Not yet, but I intend to approach him soon. I wanted to clear it with you first."

"I'm sure Jack will ask what our intent will be regarding our existing contract with BOC. What will you tell him?"

"If our firm ceases to exist, the contract with BOC will terminate, which I'm sure is a disappointment to you. We can discuss it, although you haven't been involved with the account for years, and frankly a little distance might not be a bad strategy at the moment. Think about it over the weekend."

"See you Tuesday," said Bill coldly.

The revenues to Brady & Coble from BOC were more than $1 million annually, supporting a staff of six lawyers and class-A office space in Anchorage, Juneau, and Washington, D.C. Even if the firm dissolved, BOC would still require independent legal counsel, and it was a bitter slight to Bill that Marcus did not even hint at the possibility of retaining his services during a transition.

After he hung up, Marcus scanned his missed-call index on his Blackberry. Rachel had called during his walk. Marcus hit speed dial.

"Thanks for calling me back," said Rachel. "Please tell me what's going on. Why is Jack flying all the way to Juneau to meet with Elliot Lawson, who we all know is in deep trouble? He left in a hurry and was real short with me, so I know something's up. Is Jack in trouble? I heard him say something about following someone."

Marcus felt compromised in such conversations with Rachel, which were becoming more frequent. His interest in her had always been more than professional. And it was true their friendship had on one occasion crossed the imaginary line of professional discretion. But what to Marcus were signs of sexual temptation from Rachel were to her nothing more than calculated risks designed to keep his fire burning. She knew, for example, that Marcus was interested in succeeding Jack as CEO, and if nothing else Rachel intended to protect her investment. She was equally aware of Jack's jealousy toward Marcus, but to Rachel a certain amount of that was healthy in a relationship.

"Rachel, this is not a personal matter that concerns you, and Jack is not in any trouble. Please trust me on that. His visit with Elliot is all business. We're investigating ways we can help our friends and protect ourselves from our enemies. We hired a P.I. to follow Walter just in case we need to meet with him. The less you know about that the better. Please trust me. No one is in any danger."

"Jack's business is my business, Marcus. You and I have talked about this, and we trust each other. We've agreed that we wouldn't keep secrets from each other. I want to know what's going on. I hate secrets, especially between people who love each other."

Marcus smiled to himself, confident that she was referring to the two of them. In truth, her reference was intentionally vague, a patterned tease designed to elicit complete disclosure from Marcus. Marcus weighed the risks of confiding more fully in Rachel; she was always discreet, and he knew he could trust her with sensitive information. He therefore shared what he knew about Jack's negotiations.

"Do you feel better now, Rachel?"

"I do, Marcus, thank you."

"I know Jack told you he'd be back tomorrow but we may have some business in Seward. Don't be surprised if he isn't back until Sunday."

"And what about you? What are you doing tonight, Marcus?"

Once again Marcus' fantasies indulged the idea that

Rachel's question was a veiled invitation. For Rachel, it was the one question she knew would provoke an honest response.

"Actually, I'm driving to Seward to meet with Walter as soon as we hang up."

"I don't understand. Why are you having anything more to do with that man? Isn't he under arrest or in prison? And why Seward of all places?"

"He's not in prison yet. Really, the less you know the better. I doubt you want to be called as a witness in Walter Hayes' trial."

"Fine, but I doubt you do either. Why is everything happening so fast?"

"We're worried he might be turning himself in under the Federal Witness Protection Program. Jack wants me to explore other options. Look, Rachel, you know everything that I know, and I really need to go. I'll call you later, OK?"

"I don't like it, Marcus. Be careful!"

After loading his car, Marcus dialed Jack to brief him on Walter's whereabouts and to confirm the outline of his intended negotiation. Poor cell reception en route meant this would be his last opportunity to discuss the matter with Jack before he reached Seward. There was no answer, so Marcus left a voicemail stating that he would meet Walter at 10:00 P.M. Setting up a specific time directly with Walter, however, would risk alerting the feds or tipping off anyone inclined toward chicanery, so Marcus resolved to make that call once he arrived in Seward.

At her Anchorage hillside home, Rachel anguished over the day's developments in solitude. For the first time in her six-year marriage to Jack, she was genuinely worried about his safety. She sensed a looming disaster, and yet there would be no use explaining her premonitions to others. She could not identify the exact source of her anxiety, or to whom it extended. But the fact that her husband, whom she often accused of being too trusting of others, was holding impromptu meetings with Elliot Lawson was enough to cause her deep despair. Her curiosity led to increasingly dark premonitions about the upcoming weekend. Rachel could not stand by and wait for events to unfold; she had to follow Marcus to Seward. Her own safety would be in doubt, she reasoned, so she picked up the phone and called the one person she felt could be trusted with her confidential disclosure—Bill Brady.

# Chapter IV
*Friday, January 18, 7:15 P.M.*

**ELLEN WINDEMUTH** was a sprightly and vivacious woman of twenty-six. With the exception of her diamond nose stud and excessive makeup, she looked just like her mother. As Ellen entered Christo's Palace, she made directly for the bar without hesitation.

"I don't know about you, Mother, but I need a beer," she shot back over her shoulder.

A single woman in a red robe and large silver loop earrings was the only other patron in the restaurant. She seemed oddly out of place with her brightly colored Rastafarian headpiece. Her arms and neck were thickly layered with cheap jewelry and her hands were clasped in front of her, back rigid and eyes closed in silent meditation.

"I wonder what her story is," Ellen wondered.

"I hope she's praying for better weather," said Inga.

The two women sat themselves at the bar, a beautifully restored dark mahogany showpiece recently rebuilt to its original 1922 splendor.

"Two Alaskan Ambers, please!" Ellen shouted down the bar.

"Well, my dear," said Inga, "we're here for adventure, so let's celebrate being in Alaska. We have no place to go and nothing to do. We can't get to Alyeska any time soon, so let's enjoy the moment."

Inga had arranged a mother-daughter foray of sorts, with an indefinite itinerary. She had recently suffered a politically motivated "re-organization" within Russia's British Embassy, where she had worked for only a short time. Rather than suffer the indignity of working under an "arrogant bimbo" (which is how Inga referred to her replacement), Inga resigned. Ellen was equally in need of companionship and escape, having just divorced her husband of only two years. Alaska, they mutually agreed, was as far away from their troubled lives as they could venture.

It helped their celebration that Inga's travel budget included a large bonus from her former employer, which was all Inga would volunteer on the subject. Ellen knew better than to ask questions about the money, but she suspected, on reasonable grounds, that Inga's replacement wasn't appropriately screened for the job. Ellen knew the money her mother was spending so freely was not performance related, but she wouldn't dare broach the subject with her.

When the bartender returned with the drinks, Ellen asked him for an update on the weather and the roads, and he was quick to oblige.

"DOT cleared the small slide at Kenai Lake, but they still have the one at the cutoff. It'll be a few more hours before they open up the road, assuming the weather lets up. It's supposed to warm up and turn to rain sometime tonight."

"Well I guess that settles it, eh, Mother? We're not traveling anywhere tonight!"

"Where are you two lovely ladies staying?"

"The Van Gilder," Ellen responded.

"Very nice!"

The bartender's endorsement sounded genuine.

"What can you tell us about it?" begged Ellen.

"It's a cool place, full of history. I believe it's the oldest remaining hotel in Alaska. I know the new owners have spent a lot of time and money restoring it. Actually, I hear wonderful things about it."

"When we checked in, we were told about a murder that took place there years ago. What do you know about it?"

The Van Gilder was well known for its ghost, enthusiastically embraced by some and rejected as poppycock by others, but the bartender knew it was a controversial subject just as likely to stir resentment as favor among bar patrons. The ghost was certainly not the most flattering attribute of the beautifully restored hotel and was generally a subject to avoid.

"I've read their little story about it. Some people can't resist the idea that something that old has to be haunted."

"I don't get that," replied Ellen. "Why are only certain buildings haunted?"

"All I know is what I overhear, which is that spirits occupy spaces that have no soul, places that lack any sense of permanency or investment of passion. If you think about it, buildings hosted by transients and temporary owners who care only of profit—it represents abandonment, a kind of spiritual void. The vacuum invites a spirit to dwell there and to fill the space with a greater purpose. I've heard some suggest that it is the same for humans: If there is a void, a lost soul, spirits will then occupy and seek to redeem the emptiness."

"It's all silliness if you ask me—a marketing gimmick, I'm sure," said Inga in a clear attempt to distinguish herself from such people.

"We don't believe in ghosts and have to wonder about those

who do. But, as fate would have it, we're staying in Fannie's Suite," said Ellen.

The ladies clanked their glasses in cheerful agreement that residing with ghosts was all part of the adventure.

"Tell me ,,, uh ... ," Ellen hesitated as she struggled to recall the handsome bartender's name.

"Jon, name's Jon," the bartender interceded. "And no, I haven't met Fannie. I personally don't buy into it, the paranormal activity or whatever. But I've met people here who tell me straight up that they've encountered spirits—CEOs, doctors, even a retired judge. Hey, if ghosts are real to these people, who's to say they don't exist? I mean, just because I haven't met one yet doesn't mean I never will."

Ellen looked skeptically at the young bartender.

"Most people don't volunteer their stories. It's not like they boast about it," said Jon in defense of his point. "But they insist visitations are common; it's only our inability to recall or discuss the experiences that make them appear unusual."

"So what else do people do in Seward besides chase ghosts?" asked Ellen, anxious to change the subject.

Ellen's bleach-blonde hair, thin but buxom build and penetrating blue eyes were perfectly suited for engaging the opposite sex. Her natural curiosity and penchant for gossip made her a perfect traveling companion for her mother. The two were virtual twins, thirty years apart. They shared a slightly cynical view of the world but were fun and engaging conversationalists. Between Inga's repertoire of dirty jokes and Ellen's wry one-liners, they kept each other entertained. They each loved beer and men—in volume and "without the head," as Ellen loved to say. Traveling and barhopping, they were fast discovering, was a shared genetic predisposition.

After her third beer and an hour of listening to Jon, Ellen summoned the courage to ask about the Jamaican-garbed woman who had since left the bar.

"She's from Homer. Her name is Juliet Castellani. You're going to think the entire town is crazy when I tell you this. Are you ready?"

The two women looked at each other with approving grins. "As long as you don't insist she was an apparition!" chided Ellen.

"I'm ready!" said Inga.

"She's caused quite a stir in Seward the last few weeks."

"How? Tell us!"

The two women shuttled their bar stools closer and locked arms in a display of giddy anticipation.

"We love gossip," said Ellen.

"This is not gossip, Ladies! It's front page, headline news. I don't think you're ready."

Ellen glared at Jon and drew her arm back in a mock punching motion.

"Alright," Jon said as he drew his face in close to theirs and narrowed his already tight eyes. "She's a healer!" He let his revelation sink in before he turned to busy himself with the few remaining glasses at the bar.

"What the hell does *that* mean?" asked Inga.

"It's what a Golden Retriever does, Mother. It heels at your side before retrieving a duck, isn't that right, Jon?" offered Ellen.

"Seriously, Ladies., she cures terminal illness." He waited for the slightest sign of affirmation, which was not forthcoming. "Jane Parmely has lived in Seward for seventy years, former city council woman, Chamber president, and all that. She owns the liquor store up the road. She was diagnosed with cancer a year ago and went through chemotherapy. Last April, she was in Hospice home care with two weeks to live, on morphine and in a ton of pain. Mrs. Parmely had the nurse call Juliet, who at that time was a total stranger, a hitchhiker Parmely had picked up a few weeks before. According to the nurse, Juliet worked on Mrs. Parmely for fifty hours without rest, using only a copper spoon, herbal wraps, and candles. The burns over Mrs. Parmely's body were so bad after the second day that the nurse was forced to call the police, who arrested Juliet. Three weeks later Mrs. Parmely walked out of the hospital cancer-free."

"Miracles happen," said Ellen dismissively.

"I can tell you're not convinced, so fast forward to three weeks ago. The Sea Life Center was ready to euthanize a baby killer whale that was so diseased it couldn't swim the length of the pool. The whale refused to eat, had lost eighty pounds, and was anemic. It had boils the size of my fist on her skin."

Jon grabbed a copy of the *Seward Sun* off the bar counter and thrust the paper in front of Ellen to corroborate his story. "Diseased Whale to Be Euthanized," read the headline.

"Mrs. Parmely has been on the Sea Life Center's board forever," Jon continued. "She stood up in front of the entire board, with Juliet at her side, and begged them to let Juliet save the whale. Well, who the hell was going to say 'no' to that? Of course, no one thought there was chance in hell anything would change. The one board member who opposed the idea did so only on the grounds that there was no need to go public with their rescue effort because there was no chance of success. Everyone else agreed to keep the matter from being formalized in a resolution and to spin it as an internal gesture to honor Mrs. Parmely. That was three weeks ago. Yesterday, the center released a perfectly healthy whale into Resurrection Bay on

Juliet's bidding and tracked it forty miles out to Johnstone Bay before they lost contact."

"A publicity stunt, no doubt!" snapped Ellen.

"Definitely an amazing coincidence. Don't tell me you actually believe Juliet did those things, Jon," said Inga.

"Of course, the center refused to credit her for the whale's recovery. Since no one expected a miracle, they never addressed how the center would explain one. I can't see our senior U.S. Senator blessing this press release: "Center Uses Mystic to Rehabilitate Whale Nearly Killed by Sea Life Center!" Their board met tonight and confirmed that their original intent was to accommodate a board member but to avoid controversy, regardless of the outcome. Juliet was pretty upset when she came in, but she calmed down eventually."

"I don't know what to think," said Ellen. "Could Mrs. Parmely and Juliet be working together to draw attention to themselves?"

"Unlikely," said Jon. "It's not the lack of credit that bothers Juliet, it's the lost opportunity. The center was more worried about losing their grant funding than saving the whale, apparently."

Ellen emptied the colored foam in the bottom of her glass in silent protest and motioned Jon to hold off on the refill.

"And you'll be happy to hear Juliet is staying at the Van Gilder Hotel," Jon continued. "You should introduce yourself, get a little local color! She's a bit nutty but very smart. I think you'll like her."

Ellen turned to her mother. "Looks like we're surrounded by kooks, Mother. We'd better get back to the hotel. James wants us to attend that meeting at 9:00 P.M., and it's close to that now."

"Thanks for the company, Jon," Ellen whispered across the bar.

She drew her wide smile into a blown kiss and winked, leaving Jon in a mild state of fantasy.

❧❦

James was moving chairs into the lobby when the Windemuths returned from Christo's Palace. Ellen was full of both food and alcohol as she pulled herself up the red-carpeted steps one step at a time as though her legs were in a full-length cast. James was busy updating his guest folios after his final check-ins when Ellen poked her nose past the gate at the doorway.

"Good evening, Sir James!" she boomed, still amused by his themed attire. "Thank you for the recommendation. The Mama Mia was great!"

"Shhhhh," gestured James in his friendliest voice, pointing at room 102 across from the lobby. "We've got a full house!"

Inga started for the stairs but paused just before the stairwell and turned.

"You were not kidding about that ghost, Dr. Watson," Inga whispered loudly. "It seems the whole town knows of it. Are you sure we're safe?"

"I thought you did not believe in ghosts, Ma'am," replied James sarcastically.

"Ghosts, hah!" she shot back thrusting her stern face out from behind the partition. "I have survived holocausts and horrors you cannot imagine. Do not talk to me of such things! Do you imagine that anyone who suffers from real human deprivation believes in ghosts? No! It is the nightmare of evil deeds committed among the living that haunt them! If these so-called healers communicated with the living half as well as they do with the dead, the world would be a better place!"

As Inga turned abruptly, the stairs creaked and then there was silence. James sat quietly and listened intently for the Windemuths to enter Fannie's Suite, just above the library. He half-prayed the lights would all function properly.

"I told her. It was our last room," muttered James in his defense to anyone who might be listening.

## Chapter V
*Friday, January 18, 8:55 P.M.*

**JAMES HAD ADVISED** all his guests at check-in that he would host a brief meeting in the Van Gilder lobby at 9:00 P.M. to update everyone on the deteriorating weather conditions. Electrical spasms throughout the day and the clickitty-clack of equipment repowering itself were recurring reminders that a prolonged outage was likely. To prepare his guests for the inconvenience, James had set up a communications center, which was just a flip chart with emergency contact numbers and a recently posted DOT advisory stating "The Seward Highway will remain closed as of 6:00 P.M. until further notice when safe travel can be re-established."

The hotel's small library was too small to hold the twenty-three guests who were wandering about and overflowing into the corridor. The library's oak table was oversized for the space, and the ornately carved arms of the high-back chairs were too high to tuck under its wide rim. Above the table, framing Adams Street, was a large picture window whose original wood mullions and chicken-wire reinforced glass were visible remnants of the 1916-era construction. The burgundy velvet curtains, stained-glass chandelier, and bookshelves stacked with Alaskan classics were tasteful but more modern touches that added richness to the space. Tightly framed between the cabinet uppers, however, was a shoulder mount of a Kodiak black-tailed deer that jutted out from the wall above the television. Were it not for the brass-framed plaque memorializing the legendary kill, the dead animal would have appeared incongruous and out of character with the surroundings. In a tribute to Mike "the chief" Callahan, the plaque read:

> From a distance of 400 yards, using iron sights, this 226 pound buck was shot on the run by Mike Callahan on Kodiak Island 11/2/94. Witnessed by Spike Kristopherson.

    Mike Callahan's penchant for storytelling was well known throughout Alaska. Seward's chief of police for sixteen years, he had made a name for himself as the police academy's golden-glove boxing champion and was highly regarded as a marksman and ballistics expert. When it came to hunting and fishing, however, he was known as a great storyteller—or more accurately, a master bullshitter—but therein was the chief's gift. With his innate skills as an outdoorsman, combined with a delivery honed from a lifetime of detective work, the chief could take you hook, line, and sinker. Anyone who knew the chief was aware that virtually any tale he spun could just as easily be true as not, and there was no shortage of witnesses willing to vouch for him. This was all part of the fun that had over time contributed to the making of his legend.

    With few exceptions, the guests who were milling around the lobby appeared relaxed and accepting of their circumstances. The man asleep in the wingback corner chair, however, was an enigma. His tan Carhardt jacket hosted a Chugach Electric logo, and the black fedora he wore was pulled tightly down over a bearded face and a thick mass of black hair that was partially dyed metallic red. When the middle-aged man arrived a half hour earlier, he had casually helped himself to coffee and guided himself through the historic panels lining the corridor. It was common for the public to come and go in this manner, as the hotel was of historic interest to people. The gentleman was there to warm himself, thought James at the time, and would soon be on his way. Now that the meeting was starting, however, James decided to approach the man.

"Excuse me sir," said James as he gently patted his arm. "If you're not a registered guest, I'll need you to go. I'm preparing for a private meeting here."

"No worries," said the slightly raspy voice as he snapped to attention. "I'm just killing a little time. I'm on-call with Chugach Electric. They sent me here to troubleshoot some cabling equipment, and they have me on standby."

"I'll tell you what, you can hang out for another thirty minutes. Heck, we might need you if the power goes out."

"Sounds like a deal. Am I OK right here?"

"It's going to get crowded in here. If you don't mind, I need you to move to the library."

"Not a problem."

James moved to the opposite corner of the lobby where a beautiful walnut and stained-glass antique player piano served as the focal point of the historic décor. To capture everyone's attention, James hit "play" and Scott Joplin's "Pineapple Rag" boomed into the far corners of the compact hotel.

The sudden jolt of music enlivened the guests as they herded into the lobby. Over the near-deafening volume, which could not be controlled, James pointed to his improvised bar at the front desk and shouted, "Emergency rations are available. First round is on the house!" Derby in hand, James bowed, drawing applause from the tightening crowd.

"It's amazing what booze can do to lift spirits," James

whispered to himself as he made his way to the bar.

"Now that I have your undivided attention, I have a few announcements to make," shouted James. "I'll be your host, your housekeeper, front-desk clerk, bartender, maintenance man, whatever you need me to be. The first round is on the house; after that drinks are four dollars. Please do not leave the hotel with alcohol, or I'll be arrested. Board games, puzzles and DVDs are in the bottom drawer of the TV cabinet. Our voice-mail system is not working so all messages will be posted there," James said pointing to the flip chart." He paused and looked around. "Are there any doctors in the house? The hospital called and wanted to know in case of an emergency. The usual rotation of weekend doctors from Anchorage couldn't make it in."

An elderly woman raised her hand.

"Be sure to tell them long retired," she said to everyone's amusement.

"Dr. Strayer, thank you. May I have your full name and type of practice?" asked James.

"Dr. Elizabeth Strayer," she responded. "Physician of general practice. My son William is one of the visiting doctors who couldn't make it down today."

"An esteemed author of several Alaskan biographies and short histories, the most recent of which is *Over the Back Fence*. She's also a shareholder of the hotel," said James. "Welcome, Dr. Strayer."

"Any others?" James inquired.

A voice from the hallway yelled, "Over here!" prompting James to scan the back, where the man was pointing. A large hand barely extended above the heads of the crowd.

"Juliet, thank you for volunteering," said James with a forced sincerity.

Inga turned to Ellen and whispered, "Be sure to tell them 'faith healer.' That should inspire everyone's confidence."

"Juliet, the hospital may ask for your credentials, so please see me later," James added tactfully.

"I heal every life form," said Juliet loudly.

More than several heads turned in awkward unison to see who was speaking. Ellen was certain everyone in the room shared the same thought: *God forbid if one of us needs to call on her for medical attention.*

"Anyone else?" James inquired to no response.

"On to the next item of business then," said James.

At that instant, the lights flickered and the entire room went dark. A quick succession of power surges caused spasms of light to partially illuminate the worried expressions of the guests. The hotel's emergency lights cast just enough light to illuminate the passageways, but outside the hotel was pitch black. The high-pitched whine of the hotel's alarm system told James the battery backup supply for the phone system was operational.

James had been standing on a chair to elevate his 5'5" frame above his audience when the lights went out. As he reached down from his high perch to turn on his flashlight, beams of light reflected off the metallic-gold ceiling tiles with a strobe-light effect, mesmerizing the crowd. James propped the flashlight between his feet and pointed it straight up, flooding his frame in an eerie outline of black and white, the dramatic effect of which was not lost on his audience.

It was generally known that the Van Gilder Hotel hosted a ghost, the form of which was sometimes described as an elderly man in a classic derby and bow tie. Originally performed as an act of humor, James' impromptu skit had two unintended consequences: Half the guests appeared to be uncomfortable while the other half shouted for more.

"We want to hear a ghost story," chimed a young man in the front. "Tell us about Fannie."

Several in attendance found little humor in the request, but James elected to act out the part. He raised his arms over his head in a mock spell-casting position and fluttered his derby in an act of showmanship.

"Just call me Jasper, the friendly ghost!" he deadpanned.

At that instant, the lights came back on, prompting widespread applause.

"Thank you, thank you. Timing is everything," shouted James.

"Encore! Did you rehearse that? Encore! Encore!" shouted a man in the back.

The mixture of cheer and muted laughs revealed a restive uneasiness among the guests, and James was grateful that the outage lasted only a minute. As he stepped back onto his chair, James noticed the man in the Carhardt jacket at the lobby entrance fumbling with an earphone adapter to his Blackberry.

"I'll call you back" is all James heard, but he took note of the sleek, hi-tech device.

"Are you getting reception?" James shouted across the hallway, to which there was no acknowledgment.

James turned back to his audience. "On a more serious note, we need to conserve heat in the building in case we lose power. Keep windows and doors shut to conserve heat. The emergency lights last four-to-five hours, so we could go totally dark. Only use the candles in an emergency and only where they can be constantly monitored. This is an historic hotel, and we have no sprinkler system. The lobby and entry doors lock at eleven, but I will be on site. You can reach me by dialing "0" from your room phones or the lobby phone just outside the gate. The main number is call forwarded after 11:00 P.M. to my cell in case you find yourself locked out. However, the phone battery backup lasts about two hours, so an extended outage could interrupt phone service. No one should be out that late in this weather anyway."

"Will cell phone coverage be affected?" asked the man in the Carhardt jacket. "I'm on call with the power company."

"I have no idea," responded James. "On a final note, the official report from DOT is that the road is closed, but they expect it to be open around midnight. If there are no more questions, the bar is open."

A man's hand shot up in the back.

"What about internet and fax service?"

"Phone, fax, and internet are working but could be lost anytime," responded James.

"What do we do for breakfast?" said an anonymous voice from the floor.

"There will be donuts, coffee, and fruit available in the lobby at 8:00 A.M.," said James. "And Bloody Marys in honor of Fannie unless ya'll run me out of booze."

With that, a long line began to form at the bar. James adjusted his garter, pulled up his starched sleeves, and went to work doing what he did best: slingin' drinks.

James was a master bartender and his jovial, fast-talking personality instantly melted any tension among the guests. His blue eyes were tight and deep set into a meaty, round face. His polished, bald head was set atop a thick neck and weightlifter's build. In his official dress, he looked like a blackjack dealer.

"What can I get you, Dr. Strayer?" James asked. His manner

was friendly but respectful, and he poured with an efficiency that confounded everyone.

"Two chardonnays, please," said Dr. Strayer, and before she had time to put her reading glasses away, the drinks were in front of her.

"You're fast," she offered. "James, I'd like you to meet my friend, Professor Doyle. She's from Oregon, here working with me on my next book."

"Welcome, Professor, of history, I assume," James said recalling Dr. Strayer's biographies of Alaskan pioneers.

"Political science, actually," responded Professor Doyle. "And please, call me 'Marie.' I'm not one for titles, especially when I'm on vacation."

Dr. Strayer moved to the side, allowing James to continue serving.

"Can you reveal the topic of your next work, Dr. Strayer?" asked James.

"Certainly, it's the most ambitious project I've undertaken, actually. I'm tracing the political history of the state, the development of the party system in Alaska, and its major political figures, beginning with our territorial governors. Marie is helping me with research. We're interviewing Governor Thompson tomorrow."

Dr. Strayer was seventy-five years old and compensated for her slight loss of hearing with a strong, commanding voice. Her last comment caught the attention of the next in line at the bar. Dr. Strayer recognized him instantly as the disgraced lobbyist, Walter Hayes.

In a straightforward but personal manner, honed from years of tending to patients, Dr. Strayer was able to initiate conversation quickly. She possessed a sharp intellect and gentle manner that was instantly endearing. Combining these attributes with a blunt but equally informed curiosity, Dr. Strayer was an exceptionally astute interviewer. While she was eager to meet Walter Hayes, she harbored nothing but disdain for his self-dealing ethics.

"Mr. Hayes, what brings you to Seward?" was all she could muster for an introduction.

"Quite incidental, actually. I am here on a weekend getaway of sorts. These last few weeks have been stressful, as you probably can guess, and I needed a little time alone to reflect on things."

Dr. Strayer was skeptical that Seward provided the welcome retreat in January that Walter claimed, but she kept her doubts to herself.

"Are you here alone?" she asked.

"Actually, no. To be honest, I'm here visiting friends. I left Anchorage without a particular destination in mind but landed here. How about you, young ladies, what brings you here?"

The sharp-witted doctor noted the minor inconsistency in Walter's story but responded quickly to avoid any hint of suspicion.

"We're here on business; we're actually doing research on a new book," said Dr. Strayer matter-of-factly. Above all, she was anxious to keep the interview alive and was confident her statement would stimulate Walter's curiosity. From there the conversation would flow naturally into a topic of vital interest to her.

"And the subject, if I may inquire?" asked Walter.

"Certainly; it's a history of statehood really, and the rise of political parties in Alaska."

Dr. Strayer was an adept conversationalist with a memory

for names and events that confounded everyone around her. Her age and frailty cast an innocence over her questioning and delivery of facts that was as compelling as it was disarming. After an awkward pause, she said: "And you are certainly one of the more informed on the subject. Would you be available to talk with me at some point?"

"It's how I've made a living the last thirty years. I'll have to pass on the interview for now, but thank you for asking."

"Perhaps in the future when things are less hectic for you. From what I've read, you've acted very honorably since your indictment, but I have to ask you: Where is this going to end? How deep will these scandals go?"

"Very deep, I'm afraid. It is all as unbelievable to me as it is to you. There is a lot I'm not at liberty to discuss, but let's put it this way: Your suspicions are well grounded."

Walter's admission did not surprise the two women. Ever since FBI agents raided the offices of several legislators a year earlier, there was rampant speculation about who would fall and how far. It was then that the nation learned the FBI had engaged in a two-year undercover investigation designed to expose corruption in Alaska, a wide-ranging political dragnet involving wiretaps and taped confessions that would culminate in the conviction of the U.S. Senate's longest serving Senator from Alaska. It was widely known how vital Walter's testimony would be to the prosecution in several upcoming corruption trials.

Dr. Strayer was sensitive to the fact that she was talking to a powerful man whose reputation as Alaska's top lobbyist was ruined forever. She knew, for example, that during a recent special session, Alaska's legislature passed a law restricting anyone under federal indictment from registering as a lobbyist—

a statute singularly directed at Walter. But her reference to Walter's honorable fall was sincere because his rumored cooperation with the feds was regarded less as an admission of a weak case than as genuine remorse and a desire to repair the damage he had caused.

How wide the scandals would reach was a matter of daily speculation. The governor himself, it was rumored, could be implicated and it was an election year. The "old guard" Republican Party, which had ruled Alaska since statehood was experiencing a virtual meltdown, and a rising Republican star from Wasilla was challenging "the good ol' boys club" by declaring her candidacy for governor on a platform of transparency and open government.

At the core of this sordid business were charges, now seemingly corroborated, that Alaska's oil industry had openly engaged in buying votes. Through an effective network of lobbyists, phony subcontracts and "consulting fees," the oil companies secured the loyalty of key legislators who managed to quash legislation that would raise taxes on North Slope oil production, saving the oil companies billions. Walter Hayes, it was widely acknowledged, was one of the masterminds behind it all.

"Forgive me for asking, Mr. Hayes, but how does one go about buying off an entire legislature?" inquired Professor Doyle politely.

"I forgive you, but understand that it's not my favorite subject to discuss. Last year's legislature was under intense pressure to revise the tax structure on oil production. Oil companies were experiencing windfall profits from record high oil prices, when just three years earlier Alaska was running budget deficits of over one billion dollars a year. There was talk of imposing a state income tax. The so-called PPT tax was eventually passed by the thinnest of margins but at a rate that was 2 percent lower than what the majority of legislators favored, saving the oil companies a projected $30 billion over twenty years. Criticism of back-room deals and political payoffs are always present, but no one at the time knew how extensive it was. Coincidentally, the U.S. Justice Department's initial probe was not focused on legislative corruption but on the oil company's influence over national energy security and the proposed trans-Canada gas pipeline."

Dr. Strayer could not resist the opportunity and pressed on.

"Interesting. You're saying the FBI initially came to Alaska to investigate the possibility that the oil companies were trying to undermine the Alaska Gas Line Initiative?"

"That is correct. Their focus on Alaska actually began when the pipeline was forced to shut down due to a leak caused by corrosion and improper maintenance. From there, it didn't take long for the FBI to uncover the ease with which a few influential people had completely stymied regulatory oversight by the legislature."

"How much actual influence did these alleged payoffs have on the passage of the PPT tax last session?"

"Let me put it this way: The bill was altered by voice amendment about four minutes before adjournment. Debate was cut off by the chair and no public hearings took place on the amended bill. One oil company disclosed that the 2 percent reduction in royalty tax saved their company $6 billion over fifteen years."

"I read that two legislators were bought for under $10,000; quite a return on their investment I'd say!" injected Professor Doyle.

The professor's sudden realization that it was likely Marcus who had arranged the deal hung in the air like a poorly delivered punch line.

"Under normal circumstances I would say 'thank you,' " he said with forced smile.

"I applaud you for coming clean with the public, Mr. Hayes. So what will you do from here, if I may ask?" inquired Dr. Strayer.

Walter turned suddenly morose. Whatever cleansing he felt in discussing the sordid details of the past year ended abruptly.

"My practice is ended. My family will never recover. My wife is hospitalized in California, and I rather suspect if she recovers she'll be filing for divorce. She knew nothing of my work, and yet she is made to suffer fully for it. My only friends are being pressured to testify against me—and I against them. I'm hoping my cooperation will find me some peace, and maybe a break down the road."

"Your willingness to cooperate seems to have won you praise in the media, and with the people," offered Professor Doyle. "No doubt it has earned you enemies too. Are you at all fearful of how all this will end for you?"

"Honestly, no. This is the right thing to do, and it's a nest of my making. All I have to look forward to at this point in my life is forgiveness."

"So does this mean you won't be waging a defense?"

"I don't know. To set the record straight may require a trial, Dr. Strayer."

Just as Walter raised his glass and signaled a silent retreat, an attractive woman in her mid-thirties wormed her way through the crowd to Walter and leaned in to speak.

"Can I talk to you alone?" she mumbled with a sense of urgency on her face.

"Good luck with your history, Dr. Strayer. Treat me kindly, will you?" said Walter as he excused himself.

By now, the chatter in the lobby was amplified as the third round of cocktails was taking effect. The middle-aged man in the Carhardt jacket boisterously edged his heavy frame up to the bar. Before he could order, James already had his drink poured.

"Jack on the rocks, last call. That'll be four dollars."

James knew from his earlier introduction that the man was quiet and humorless, so he confined his conversation to business.

"So you work for the power company?" James prodded as he handed the man his change.

"I do," said the man stiffly.

"If you're on call, are you sure you should be drinking?"

The man grinned at James and walked away without responding.

"Something doesn't seem right with that guy," James whispered to himself.

At that instant Walter returned looking mildly agitated.

"Mr. Van Oss, I'm expecting a call shortly. Could I ask you to deliver any messages to me personally, rather than post them? I'm going up to my room, but I want to know if anyone is trying to reach me, even if you have to wake me."

"You got it," said James.

"Well then, I'll see you bright and early. I hope the road will be cleared by then."

"I take it you're not sticking around for the ghost stories, then?" inquired James.

"No, I'm afraid I have enough of those in my life already!" With that cryptic closing, Walter turned and disappeared up the narrow stairs.

# Chapter VI
*Friday, January 18, 9:20 P.M.*

**IT WAS 9:20 P.M. WHEN JAMES SHOUTED,** "Last Call!"

"It's been a long day, and I have the graveyard shift," joked James.

"How about that ghost story?" asked a young man standing at the doorway.

"I second that!" echoed Juliet.

"Go for it!" shouted a man seated at the player piano.

James turned to Dr. Strayer.

"You might be better at this than I," he whispered.

At that very instant the lights flickered.

"I didn't do that," said James.

"I think we just received Fannie's approval for a reading," said Juliet.

"Dr. Strayer, I guess you're up!" said James.

James broke down the bar as the guests seated themselves in the rows of chairs. Dr. Strayer typically shunned the spotlight, more so on this occasion given her conviction that all paranormal activity was nonsense. She was too tactful to say so here, but she believed ghosts were fabricated by those with deep insecurities or a perverse need for self-promotion. At the same time she loved the Van Gilder and its unique history; as a shareholder, she shared a desire to please any guest who favored storytelling over retiring to an empty room. In a soft, broken voice somewhat raspy with age, Dr. Strayer began telling the story of Fannie the Ghost.

"By way of introduction, I need to say that I'm hardly an authority on ghosts and actually do not believe they exist. Nevertheless, Fannie Guthry-Baehm was murdered in the room above the library in 1950."

As though on cue, the lights flickered off and on again, followed by a brief second spasm of light, and then expired completely.

Without hesitation, James reached for his flashlight and leveled the beam at Dr. Strayer. The din and reorganization passed quickly as the streaking light reassured the audience. Quickly assuming the role of artistic director, James summoned his most authoritative voice and exhorted Dr. Strayer to continue her story without lights.

The repositioning of chairs and bodies ended abruptly as the room quieted. The unfolding drama had the rapt attention of everyone seated in the tiny makeshift theater.

At the instant of silent anticipation, as when the stage curtain rises up before the opening scene, a man stumbled in the back of the room. As he careened forward, his arms and hands came crashing down onto the keys of the player piano. The shattered silence sent a shock to the collected nervous systems and a direct injection of adrenaline into the hearts of the patrons. Darting, strobe-like beams of light magnified the terror on everyone's face.

"Holy shit, *that* was a buzz killer!" said a voice out of the darkness.

"I'm starting to feel like a long-tailed cat in a room full of rockin' chairs. I plum near messed my pants," said another.

James quickly determined the man had simply stumbled in

the dark; he was neither intoxicated nor injured and was all-too-anxious to resume his anonymity in the back row. The theater-like atmosphere was restored quickly as an imaginary curtain lifted and the broad beamy stage lights refocused on the narrator.

Dr. Strayer in her quaky but measured voice called to the back room:

"This time I'd like Pachelbel's Canon in D Major, Sir. Can you slow the tempo this time?"

The strained laughter had the effect of drawing attention to itself.

A veiled woman carrying a candelabra suddenly entered stage right. Juliet seemed to float over the carpeted floor as she glided barefoot into the room, her heavily adorned head and neck shimmering but motionless. The sheer gown streamed behind her like a trail of vapor, curling and groping at her body. Her Mona Lisa smile and flowing hair created a near-perfect image of a ghost, an illusion so flawless in its effect that the audience was now convinced this was a well rehearsed play.

Juliet's appearance was the ideal prompt for Dr. Strayer, who played along without delay.

"The Van Gilder Hotel is now, and has been for decades, home to a ghost by the name of Fannie. She is here now among us, just as she was sixty years ago the night she was murdered in room 202.

It is reported that the ghost of Fannie is witnessed in two forms, that of Mr. Willard and that of Fannie Guthry-Baehm herself. She plies the attic and empty spaces of the Van Gilder and is reputed to visit only those with evil intentions in their heart. It is theorized that she does not engage the evils of the past but rather those yet to be committed. She does not intimidate the guilty with the redundant thud of a telltale heart, for their crime shall become their punishment. Rather she flickers and fades in the minds of evil intent so as to deter the passion and to give pause to those who might reflect on their schemes—and thus to reform them before the curse is cast. It is said that she will leave a seashell for those of conflicted conscience, as though to remind them of their fragile frames, and how fickle is the moment's truce. But I am getting ahead of myself," said Dr. Strayer apologetically.

"The real story begins on a clear spring evening in April 1950." Dr. Strayer picked up the short biography written by a Seward eighth-grader, Ashley Levenworth, as part of a school research project

> Seward was full of activity and cars were parked along the curb. People were walking along the wooden boardwalks laughing and talking about their day at work. Stores were closing and mothers with children were waiting anxiously for their fathers to come home.
>
> Joe's Bakery & Diner was very busy that evening. There were plates and silverware clanking and the scent of fresh coffee and fresh-baked wheat bread wafted down Second Avenue.
>
> Fannie Guthry-Baehm worked there as a waitress. It had been a long day of customers ordering her around and she was tired. Patiently she watched the clock as it slowly ticked closer to closing time. As she packed her belongings to return to her room at the Van Gilder, she heard a friendly shout from behind her.
>
> "Hey, Fannie. I need ya ter come over here and taste this wheat bread that just came out of the oven. You know you want to," Joe joked.

Joe Guthry and Fannie were married when Fannie was sixteen and started a family one year later. They divorced after several more years, but they elected to remain friends because of their two children.

Joe popped his head out from behind the ovens.

"Please! P-p-p-p-p-please!" he begged.

Fannie smiled. "All right. You win, Joe."

After she thanked Joe and said goodbye, she crossed the hard gravel street and headed for the Van Gilder. Why she detoured to the beach to join a group of girls searching for seashells, we'll never know, but we do know she stuffed her pockets with beautiful seashells that afternoon.

Fannie walked slowly back to the hotel as she thought about how she would react when she saw her husband. She had married Joe Baehm, her second husband, a few years before and, unlike her first marriage, their relationship had been rocky from the start. Joe Baehm was constantly drinking and picking fights with her. Tired of the arguments, Fannie decided to leave him. She took her girls and moved back to Seward to be closer to the girls' father.

Fannie had been in Seward for about two years by this time and had been living in the Van Gilder hotel for three weeks. Her two girls had been living with their father and his new wife, but they often stayed a few days at a time with her. The young girls could come and go between their two homes, and Fannie was grateful that she maintained a friendly relationship with Joe.

As the hotel loomed in sight, dread began to fill her body at the thought of seeing her husband. She knew she had to meet him because he was the only person who could sign the form needed for her surgery, which she needed badly.

Fannie said hello to her neighbor, who was standing on the stairs in front of the hotel, and then walked inside. As she closed the door of the hotel, she could hear poker chips being thrown on the table. The men were talking and laughing in the library. Heavy smoke filled the air from the men's cigars. She heard the bell going "ding! ding!" to her left as a customer summoned the desk clerk. Bob Lewis was in the background talking into the dispatch radio, telling a cab driver about a pick up at the Brown & Hawkins store. Bob was the brother of Burt Lewis who was the owner of the hotel.

As she walked up the stairs to her room, Fannie felt tired but relieved that her paycheck would come the next day. Having enough money was always a problem, but she hoped someday to buy a little house for her and the children. Fannie reached the door to her room, #12, on the second floor. She unlocked it and went inside. It was a very bright and comfortable room, although it was tiny. She had added decorations and pictures to make it feel more like home.

She looked in her mirror and picked up her sterling silver brush and hair comb. She changed out of her work clothes into a comfortable dressing gown.

As she was reading a book she heard a shot outside the front of the hotel. She ran to the window but didn't see anything. All of a sudden, Fannie heard stomping up the stairs, and fear flowed through her veins. Instinctively, she knew it was her husband. The door swung open and there was Joe Baehm standing there with a .22 caliber pistol in one hand and an almost empty whiskey bottle in the other. He stood there glaring at her and then pushed his way in and slammed the door. An argument soon erupted. It was the same thing she had dealt with every time Joe started drinking.

"You still love Joe, don't you? Your place is with me; I'm your man!"

All of a sudden Joe started wildly waving the gun around the room and then carelessly spinned and pointed it at Fannie. For a moment, everything went quiet. The piercing silence was more deafening than the gunshot itself.

And with that, Joseph Baehm shot her once in the heart. The force of the shot and the shock itself knocked her backwards, landing across the bed. She looked at Joe in astonishment that he actually shot her. The last thing she saw was the smoke curling from the gun barrel and the last thing she felt was the warm oozing blood staining her fIngertips. As she lay there, her lifeblood flowing out of her, all she could think about was, Why?

Fannie died almost instantly at twenty-three years old after being shot in the left ventricle of her heart. Joe Baehm was found holding his dead wife in his arms crying out "You can't be dead. It was an accident." He kept telling people he didn't mean to shoot her, just scare her. During his trial, it was found that he shot the pistol into a toilet through the lid to make sure it worked. He was sentenced to twenty-five years in prison for murdering his wife Fannie Guthry-Baehm in her room at the Van Gilder Hotel. He got out of jail several years ago after serving his sentence.

Dr. Strayer signaled the end to the creative biography by folding the paper and placing it on her lap.

"So what do you know about Fannie the Ghost?" inquired a voice out of the darkness.

Dr. Strayer was familiar with several renditions of alleged encounters, one of which was in the form of a letter from a former guest, Dr. Karl Hunschild, a professor of psychology at the University of Alaska. As she motioned to James to produce the letter, she did her best to summarize the sightings in a form true to their authors.

"The ghost of Fannie has been sighted by relatively few people, which prompts people to ask why she reveals herself to some but not to others. Are only those who are guilty of premeditated sin visited by Fannie? We know this not to be true, especially since it would have the effect of stifling such storied reports as surely as a would-be criminal would shy from confession. On the other hand, if Fannie were known by reputation to visit only those of virtue and a pure past, would she not inspire false testimony by those who wish to proclaim their righteousness?"

Dr. Strayer grabbed the envelope from James and raised it in the air, clearly enjoying the moment.

"Dr. Hunschild is a university professor with a Ph.D. He was a guest in July 2009 and wrote the following account, which was featured during a live interview on the evening news last Halloween eve."

> We had not been in bed long and the Liberty Theater, which has a door just below our window, ended its 7:30 show and people left the building. It was about 10:00 P.M.
>
> At about 12:30, just after midnight early in the morning of the 13th of July, the room was beginning to get dark, as it was summer in Alaska. As I rolled over, out of the corner of my eye, I saw what I perceived as a woman in a dressing gown with long light colored hair. I could not tell if it was blond or gray, but my sense was the woman was not old and gray. She appeared tired as she moved from the corner of the bed "through" the dresser and to the door. She paused and went "through" the door and out of the room. My wife was sound asleep beside me. It appeared that I had seen a ghost.
>
> In the morning I asked the manager if the Van Gilder was

haunted and he said no, not really, but some folks say it is. He related a story of a woman who was killed on the second floor. He then proceeded to pull out of his filing cabinet a written account from 1950. As I began to read, he also reported that one of the housekeepers would not go up to the third floor as she was too uncomfortable up there.

As I read the account, the hair went up on my neck and arms. A young blond woman in her dressing gown had been killed in 1950 while coming out of the door of her second floor room.. What I had seen and its location were so close to this account that I became convinced that I had seen a ghost. The similarity from what I had seen and this previously unbeknownst story is haunting.

I would say that room 202 of the Van Gilder hotel in Seward Alaska does house the ghost of Fannie Guthry-Baehm who was shot to death by a jealous husband.

Dr. Strayer eagerly circulated the letter as a means of authenticating her account.

"In a way, Fannie is an enigma. If she reveals herself to only those with dark designs, she would deprive the virtuous of the opportunity to meet her. The ghost of Fannie, while fantasy to some, has among her acquaintances people of genuine reputation, like Dr. Hunschild. Do not think, therefore, that only kooks or the careless of tongue bear witness to her—which causes the curious among you to re-phrase the question: Why would Fannie communicate only with those who believe in her? To which I think Fannie would reply: 'It is those of guilty conscience who are haunted by my mission, but those of faithful following who find favor as my friend.'"

"How does Fannie contact her friends?" shouted Juliet from the back row of chairs.

"At her death, among the seashells found in her pockets, Fannie had a poem by an unknown author entitled 'Reflections.' The first line to the poem tells us something about her I think; it reads:

> On a pane of glass a reflection drew, a picture only the worthy will see through.

The spell cast over the assembled guests was broken by a sudden flood of light that penetrated the curtained windows from outside. In spite of the filter of stained glass from the lobby window, the streetlights had a blinding effect on the group as they were transported back into real time. Groans of protest transformed into expressions of relief as everyone realized that power had been restored to the downtown grid.

As James peered out the lobby window across Adams Street, the glowing amber street lamps of the historic district illuminated an otherwise darkened business district. The strong resurgence of outdoor power was in contrast to the weak, pulsating flickers experienced earlier, and James was confident that full power would be restored to the Van Gilder soon.

As guests exited the lobby, James heard small talk about "amazing coincidences" and "eerie effects." James heard one woman lament that the group had awakened a ghost and another admit that she was not sure she wanted to overnight there.

One person remained motionless in the back corner as though in a deep sleep. The awakened movements had no effect on Juliet Castellani. Her eyes were closed, her head was tilted slightly back, her palms faced up. Her lips moved in a silent mutter:

... as on a pane of glass a reflection drew, pictures only the worthy see through. Receive me, Fannie, cleanse my soul of evil thoughts and fill it with Peace. Perform your will upon me ... and ...

"Show's over, folks," shouted James in an attempt to clear the lobby of stragglers. "It's time to wake up so we can all go to bed! Make sure you have your flashlights and keys. Juliet, it's time to wrap it up!"

Juliet straightened from her meditation. She had an expression of bewilderment on her face that bordered on concern.

"Are you all right, Juliet? Pardon the pun, but you look like you've seen a ghost."

"I have. I mean I just did," slurred Juliet. "Fannie said she would wait. She's busy now, but she needs me. She said ... that ... something bad is about to happen."

James looked over his shoulder to make sure no one else overheard the prediction. He shuddered and felt a flush of adrenaline rush to his heart.

"Sounds like Fannie and I work the same hours, Juliet. Here, let me help you up."

Juliet's 200-pound frame went limp in James' arms as she collapsed to the floor. She was breathing heavily and beads of sweat dampened her hair.

"This is all I need right now," muttered James.

"Juliet. Wake up! I need you to put in a good word for me! Hey, Juliet! Tell Fannie I really need some sleep!"

As James bent over to scoop Juliet's arm, a piercing scream echoed from seemingly every corner of the poorly soundproofed hotel, but James instinctively knew it was from Room 201 directly above his head.

"My god, what could be next?" came a loud exclamation from the library.

"No doubt someone's idea of a bad joke," replied a second voice.

James rushed to the hallway and up the stairwell. He ran headlong into a panic-stricken young woman careening down the stairs with a terrified look on her face. It was Ellen.

"Oh my God, help! I think there's a dead person in room 201," she shouted.

## Chapter VII
*Friday, January 18, 10:07 P.M.*

**THE BARELY DISBURSED CROWD** of ghost revelers froze momentarily in disbelief, then pursued James up the stairs. Thundering feet and nervous chatter reverberated off the walls, shaking any who had retreated to their rooms from early retirement. As James approached room 201, he could see that the door was barely open.

"Is this how you found him, Ellen?" asked James.

James peeked into the one-inch gap and could barely see the outline of a body on the floor. Only a faint glow of light from the street filtered in through the windows. James turned in frustration and noticed with some curiosity that the hallway was completely dark; even the emergency lights on the second level were out, leaving only the floodlight from the stairwell to illuminate the corridor. There was a flashlight on the floor, which James picked up and pointed into the room.

"Yes, exactly like this," said Ellen. "Can you see him?"

"Barely."

"I came out of my room, and I saw his door was open, so I knocked. Oh my God, I'm so freaking out. Is he really dead? Shit, I can't be here!"

James pushed gently against the door, and it hit hard against the steel safety bar on the inside of the door jamb.

"Mr. Hayes! Can you hear me? Is there anyone in there?"

The one-inch slit afforded by the safety latch was barely enough for James to see inside, let alone identify the body, but the protruding legs were bare of clothing and white.

"Someone call 911 now!" James yelled down the hall. "Ellen, get me a stick or something to prod him, and a metal hanger. I may be able to flip the lock."

Ellen dashed into her room across the hall and quickly produced a telescoping walking stick her mother always carried with her. James poked the body through the one-inch crack, but there was no movement. He quickly fashioned a hook out of a metal hangar and narrowed the opening in an effort to flip the bar open from the outside. James knew from prior experience this was possible but usually a matter of luck or considerable time.

By now, every guest in the hotel was crammed into the narrow second-floor landing. Their squirming bodies pushed up against an imaginary border of yellow caution tape drawn taught by the grim air of death and a natural revulsion to unknown threats. A well-dressed man in a suit coat, whom James did not recognize, had wedged his way to the front.

"I'd be careful not to disturb too much, Sir," the man said. "You should wait for the police to arrive."

The Van Gilder Hotel is one block from the fire station, where weather contingencies had the full force of firefighters and EMTs on full alert. In what James later calculated was less than three minutes from the time of the call, a team of paramedics arrived at the second floor landing. Just moments before, the lights to the hotel had snapped on, creating the sensation that the simultaneous events were linked.

After a brief exchange on their radios, a third EMT and two

police officers arrived with fire axes. One EMT wedged the sharp end of one ax against the inside latch in a chisel-like fashion while the other used his as a striker. With one heavy blow of the ax butt-to-butt the latch flew off the door.

The paramedic leaned his full weight into the door, which was pressed fully against the prostrate body inside, and wedged his wide frame through the opening. Only then was James able to confirm his worst fear: the half-naked body was that of Walter Hayes. James clamped his hands around his bald head and recoiled in disbelief.

"Oh my God! This can't be happening."

From James' reaction, the officers could tell instantly that he knew the deceased man and that the circumstances confronting them were unusually troubling.

As the paramedics readied their equipment and checked vitals, a perfunctory exercise by all indications, a man in a long green Helly Hanson raincoat and Seattle Mariners ball cap approached James.

"I'm Sergeant Graham, Seward Police," he said as he thrust out his hand. "Who are you?"

"I'm James Van Oss, the general manager."

"Do you recognize this man?"

"I do. He's Walter Hayes. I checked him in to this room around 3 P.M."

"Is he the only person registered to the room?"

"Yes. As far as I know, he is here alone."

"Any idea what might have happened here?"

"I last saw him in the lobby about an hour ago. He was sharing a drink and conversation with guests in the lobby, and then he left to go to his room. He seemed fine at the time."

"What time was that?"

"I'd say around nine-thirty," replied James.

"Did he have any visitors, say anything unusual, complain about not feeling well—anything that might shed some light on this?"

"No, he was actually in good spirits. But I did notice a woman come in and interrupt his conversation with Dr. Strayer. He left with her for no more than a couple minutes. When he returned, he seemed a little edgy and impatient and then went up to his room."

"Can you describe the woman? Is she a guest?"

"Not a guest. She had short, reddish-brown hair, maybe five-foot-five, 115 pounds, mid-thirties, pretty cute."

"Any idea what this woman might have wanted with him?"

"He said he was expecting a call and asked me to hand deliver any messages in person. He said he didn't want anything posted on our board."

Sergeant Graham turned to the onlookers, who were growing more curious and bold with the arrival of the police, and motioned them to move back.

"Folks, I'm Sergeant Graham, Seward Police. Is there anyone here who knows this man, or knows what might have happened here? Anyone who heard or saw anything?"

Ellen stepped forward and stated that she occupied the room across the hall and had discovered the body but that she didn't see or hear anything unusual. "I was leaving my room to check on the power, and I noticed that the door was cracked open. I didn't think it was open on purpose, so I knocked. I saw his body, and that's when I screamed and ran for help."

A tall man in a blue sport jacket and gray khaki pants raised his hand.

"I know Walter, how can I help?"

One of the EMTs overheard the declaration and quickly interjected.

"Could you please come forward, Sir? I'm Jim Crick, EMT. How well do you know this man?"

"I have no idea who's in there, but I overheard someone mention Walter Hayes' name. I know him well."

"Step inside the room, Sir; what is your name?"

"Marcus Coble."

"Mr. Coble, can you identify this person quickly."

The EMTs were crouched over the body preparing to use the automatic defibrillator. Marcus looked with keen interest at the body and then quickly scanned the room.

"It's Walter Hayes."

"Come here, Mr. Coble," said the EMT pointing to a connecting room—201B. "Do you know Mr. Hayes' medical history? Is he diabetic? Does he have any history of seizures, or heart trouble?"

"As far as I know, he is not diabetic. He has no history of seizures, but I'm pretty sure he suffered from some form of heart disease—V-fib, I think."

"Apparently he has a pacemaker. Do you know who his heart specialist is?"

"No, I don't. I didn't even know he had a pacemaker."

"Any other medical history you're aware of that might help us?"

"No, I'm sorry I'm not much help, but I can make a phone call. His wife is hospitalized in California and may not be reachable."

"We don't have much time. He's not showing any vitals at the moment. We'll see if he responds to the A.D., but make the calls. I'll check back in a few minutes."

As Marcus scrolled his speed dial, he heard a muffled sound like an air rifle blast and a slap against bare skin as the defibrillator released its energy. Sergeant Graham was on the corridor side of the wall that separated him from Marcus; his brief instructions to the guests to return to their rooms and remain there were easily audible. Officers were now posted at every hotel exit, he explained, and all movement in or out of the hotel was restricted. It occurred to Marcus that room 201 was being treated as a crime scene. As he reflected on his circumstances, he felt compromised. His presence in the hotel would raise questions since he was not a registered guest. He looked at his Blackberry: 10:26 P.M. His last outgoing call was to the P.I. who, if questioned, would confirm that he met Marcus at the Van Gilder Hotel at 7:30 P.M. that night.

Within a few minutes, it was known throughout the hotel that the dead person was Walter Hayes. Just as rampant was the speculation that his death could not have been an accident. A flurry of phone calls and instant text messages created a frenzy of reporting that surpassed any definition of gossip. Twitter spread the information to the world in a matter of seconds. Suddenly and uncontrollably, the breaking news gripped Alaska's attention like a 5:00 A.M. revelry. The stakes in the FBI's ongoing corruption investigation in Alaska had just been raised.

It took Sergeant Graham all of five minutes to realize the gravity and sensitivity of the crisis. He wasted no time contacting the chief of police, in spite of the late hour and the likelihood that his boss was drunk.

"Chief Callahan, Sergeant Graham. I hate to disturb you, Sir. I'm at the Van Gilder Hotel, room 201 responding to a 911. You need to know about this situation."

Sergeant Graham summarized the details of the scene to the chief: no vitals; likely dead for about an hour; no obvious signs of struggle or foul play; in fact, the body had been discovered behind a latched door.

"Identity confirmed with two sources, Chief. Request direction on how to proceed," said Sergeant Graham.

Chief Callahan's twenty years on the force had prepared him well for such a crisis. This was about to become the highest profile investigation of his career, and he knew it.

"I'll need a few minutes to tidy up, Graham. The place will be swarming with media any minute, so move fast! Set up a mobile command post on Adams with level-two security. Treat it as a homicide for now. I don't want to miss anything. No one comes or goes from the hotel, understood? Keep the EMTs there. I want the room sealed, nothing disturbed. What else? Have the GM print out his guest list. Make sure everyone is accounted for and begin the interviews. Has power been restored there yet, Sergeant?"

"As of ten minutes ago. I understand I am to seal the room and the exits; verify occupants against guest ledger and begin interviews. Level-two security. That it, Sir?"

"Roger. Tell everyone to expect the feds. They'll be all over this. We need to be on our best behavior, Graham."

Sergeant Graham signaled the other officers in the corridor to approach.

"Callahan's on his way. Wicks, get the command post here. Close off Adams Street to all traffic, level two security. Dye, assemble the team you need to secure the room and close off all hotel exits. Expect the feds, Gentlemen."

Within minutes the chief's action plan was fully implemented. The Windemuths were relocated to the lobby;

their adjacent room was subject to a routine sweep for evidence while other guests were directed to return to their rooms. The lockdown served to confirm what everyone already suspected—that this was a high profile murder investigation.

When the paramedics finally emerged from room 201, they made a formal pronouncement of death to Sergeant Graham. The apparent cause: cardiac arrest. The sound of heavy lumbering footsteps suggested a man of considerable size was approaching just as the medics completed their briefing.

"Chief, over here!"

"Tell me what you got fast, Graham, and skip the bullshit."

"Victim is Walter Hayes, male, mid-fifties, cause of death likely cardiac arrest. Based on core temperature and other factors, he died thirty to forty-five minutes ago. Last reported seen in the lobby by the GM, James Van Oss, around 9:25 P.M.—ten minutes before power was lost. The GM confirmed Mr. Hayes went to his room just before the ghost story started."

"The what? Did I hear that right?"

"Yes, Sir, you heard right. Just before the lights went out, a woman started reading a ghost story."

"That's just great, Sergeant. I can see the headlines already. Skip the ghost story, Graham. What else do we know?"

"Two people came in looking for Mr. Hayes shortly before he was found dead, a middle-aged man and a young brunette. The woman broke into Hayes' conversation at the bar and pulled him away with some sense of urgency—that was around 9:25 P.M. When he returned, he acted distracted, told the GM he was expecting a call and then went to his room. She was the last known person to speak with Mr. Hayes. The GM described her as mid-thirties, five-five, 115 pounds. So far no leads on her ID or what her business was with Hayes."

"Get a sketch and complete profile circulating with an APB. I want every desk clerk in every hotel and B & B to see that sketch within the hour. She's not leaving Seward we know that! What about the guy?"

"Mid-fifties, balding, six-two, 190 pounds. He came into the lobby about fifteen minutes after the story and started looking for Hayes. He told James Van Oss, the GM, he had an appointment with Walter Hayes and asked for his room number, which the GM swears he didn't give out; apparently it's against hotel policy. But he did ring Hayes' room, and there was no answer; he figures that was around 9:50. When the GM couldn't reach Hayes, the mystery man hung around a few minutes and then left."

"Did the GM go up to Hayes' room?" asked the chief.

"He claims he went up, knocked, and when there was no answer, he came back to the desk."

"Interesting, what do you make of it, Sergeant?"

"It's clear Hayes was expecting someone. I suspect the woman stopped in to deliver a message. Hayes told James he was expecting someone and then went directly to his room—or possibly someone else's room. The meeting was important enough that he asked the GM to wake him if necessary, but he didn't want any messages posted. The GM said Hayes didn't appear to be hiding anything. He was enjoying himself, talking openly with the guests. It looks to me like a good old-fashioned heart attack."

Sergeant Graham flipped through a small notepad while the chief digested the information.

"There was a clear intent to meet someone, but who?" asked the chief. "And we're not sure he went directly to his room. There is a closed door and no answer at 9:50 P.M. and a bolted but open door with a dead body behind it a few minutes later. What else do we know about this male visitor, this mystery man?"

"Sorry, sir, I've got a few notes here," said Graham as he fumbled with several loose papers. "The GM asked the man if he wanted to leave a message, but he declined, said he would try back later. He lingered a few minutes, but the GM can't recall seeing him leave the hotel. He thinks he might still be here. We have a detailed description of him. What else? He's not a registered guest."

"When was the last time the GM saw this mystery man?"

"He's pretty sure he passed the guy in the hall on the way down here a few minutes ago. We sealed the hotel within a few minutes of our arrival. If mystery man is still here, there's a good chance he's been here the entire time."

"Anything else, Sergeant?" asked the chief.

Graham scanned his notes.

"Room 201 is directly above the lobby. The GM was in the lobby the entire time after Mr. Hayes left the party," said Graham pointing directly down. "He recalls hearing a loud thud above his head sometime during the ghost story, but he can't be sure of the exact time."

"So we have a potential felon and protected witness wandering around in the darkness during a ghost story. We have a suspect who claims to have a meeting with Hayes wandering around the hotel at the same time. Go on, Sergeant."

"I've recreated the scene just as the medics found it when they arrived. As you can see, the victim is in his underwear, wedged between the bed and the door. I figure he was in bed, experienced a heart attack, and got up to exit the room, or maybe something caused him to come to the door. The safety latch was fully deployed when we arrived."

"But the button lock was released and the door cracked open. If he was experiencing heart trouble, why would he not pick up the phone? It's right there! Or why would he not flip the latch before opening the door? The GM reported that the door was closed when he came up fifteen minutes earlier, correct? And what is Hayes doing undressed if he's expecting a visitor?"

"Good questions, Sir, but the power went out just after he reached his room, around 9:30 P.M. It was dark, and he's in an unfamiliar setting. It's possible the phone wasn't operational, or he couldn't find it in the dark. Maybe that explains why he got up and went to the door. Maybe he was expecting someone, but when the power went out he gave up on the appointment and went to bed. Maybe he was meeting a lady visitor, a prostitute."

"The lady visitor doesn't fit, but I agree he might have been experiencing a medical emergency, or was surprised."

"But check this out," said Graham pointing to the emergency lights in hallway, which were unplugged from their ceiling receptacles. "The GM reported the corridor was pitch-black when he arrived, and he's certain none of his staff touched the lights."

"Interesting; someone didn't want to be seen. Let's assume he had a surprise visitor for now. What do we know about the cause of death?"

"We know he had a heart condition, look here." Graham pointed to a two-inch scar over Walter's right atrium, which the medics confirmed was likely from an implanted pacemaker.

"There was no sign of a struggle, nothing out of place," added Graham.

"You're thinking natural causes?"

"That's what it looks like to me."

"Get Crick in here. I want to know more about the body."

The chief stepped over the body toward the window as Graham radioed the chief's request to the EMTs.

When Graham finished, he turned back to the chief. "I overheard them talking about how tight Hayes' jaw was when they found him. They had different opinions about it—whether rigor mortis was the cause or something else. I guess they really had to pry his mouth open."

"What the hell does that mean?" growled the chief as he peered out the west-facing window.

"Maybe nothing, but it is unusual. Usually it's associated with seizures or electric shock, not heart failure."

"Let's get the lab in here right away," said the chief as he scanned the floor.

As he knelt down to inspect under the bed, a small piece of paper partly obscured by the bed ruffle caught his eye. He picked it up and observed the number 202 neatly written out, followed by some random letters. The chief handed the paper to Graham.

"Bag that, Graham. What do you make of that code?"

"It's a website address. I'll check it out."

The chief didn't know a URL from a UFO, but he knew that the paper could be important. He moved back to the window and casually pulled back the curtains to inspect the view, which consisted of nothing but darkness and the solid concrete façade of the Liberty Theater. The wind was driving wet snow against the window from every direction, rattling the loosely fit and slightly warped window. It was quite obvious to the chief that no one could enter into the room from any direction. As he studied the perimeter, something fluttered off to his right, and he pressed his cheek against the window for a better look.

"Sergeant, get me a team on the roof ASAP. Something is hanging off the roof. I'm not sure what it is, but it doesn't belong there."

Chief Callahan tested the window, which was latched from the inside. On closer observation, he noticed that a thick bead of white caulk sealed the window completely. No one had come through the windows, he thought to himself.

"Sergeant, get one of your men to measure the gap from a door with an identical latch. I want to know how much space there is, whether a hand can fit through. Another guest discovered the body through the cracked door in total darkness, is that correct?"

"That's what was reported, Sir," said Graham with a grin.

"What's on your mind, Graham?"

"Nothing important, Chief."

"Get it out, Sergeant."

"Everyone thinks the Van Gilder is haunted. When people find out Hayes died during a ghost story, in the room adjacent to Fannie's Suite, we'll be looking for a ghost, that's all."

"I don't find that too amusing, but I tell you what. I'll refer all questions about the ghost to you, Graham!" said the chief with a chuckle.

There was a slight pause as the chief reflected more seriously on the matter. The subject would come up, no doubt, and a more decisive policy statement was called for.

"Don't count me among the believers, Sergeant. In fact I don't want anyone on my team saying a word about any damn ghost, understood? After I talk to the EMTs, I want to meet the woman who discovered the body."

Chief Callahan was one of the most respected police chiefs in Alaska and the small town politics of Seward suited him well. He had devoted himself for more than twenty-five years to keeping the criminals out of Seward and equally to the task of not making criminals out of its residents. He was known for being reasonable, in some cases even soft, but a tougher, more honest cop did not exist.

The chief was a full-blooded Choctaw Indian, a handsome man with a thin mustache and a striking resemblance to Rhett Butler in *Gone With The Wind*. His hands were massive and thick, but proportionate to his large head and his 6'-3", 260-lb. frame. His deep-lined ruddy complexion and watery eyes gave him a stern and wise look, but they bespoke of deep tragedy and a few too many indulgences with the bottle. It was well known that when he lost his son to a snowmobile accident, he lost a part of himself. His otherwise Santa-Claus twinkle and penchant for magic tricks was not entirely lost, but something that made Mike Callahan larger than life was gone. There was a dark and brooding side to his character that was hidden from everyone but his closest friends.

Mike spent his early years in Ukiah, California, logging and picking fruit. He experienced poverty and racial discrimination and learned early how to defend himself, how to work hard and to keep his mouth shut, which he found hard to do. He loathed bullies and fakes, perhaps the reason he perfected the skills and intuition necessary to identify them.

Above all, he didn't mince words with anyone when it came to police work, especially politicians. He had a few critics, mostly the "hippie" types who would notify the media when he was spotted in a public place with a few too many in his ample stomach. But everyone on the force was willing to put their life on the line for the man, and no one was more trusted to do honest police work. So when the FBI arrived at the Van Gilder, they were met by a man with a sterling reputation, a man not threatened by jurisdiction or protocol, a man trusted to get the job done. Above all, there was unanimity that if a crime was involved, Chief Callahan would solve it.

Jim Crick met the chief at the door to 201 with a big smile on his face.

"Here's the fiver I owe you, Chief, but that's the craziest damn magic trick I've ever seen. So simple. I can't believe I didn't see it. What can I do for you?"

"Tell me everything you know about this."

"Cause of death symptomatic of sudden cardiac arrest. No signal from his pacemaker, so there may be a contributing cause there. No signs of struggle or external wounds. No bruising, contusions, broken bones, or blockages in his airway. We'll request a full autopsy. Is there anything special you want me to look for now?"

"I guess not. I'll be interested in a diagnostic on the pacemaker. Can we do that?"

"I'm sure the lab can. How much more time you need with the body?"

"Forensics will be here any minute. I'll want a complete screen so maybe thirty minutes."

When Sergeant Graham left to locate Ellen Windemuth, Chief Callahan continued to inspect the room. He had never been inside a suite at the Van Gilder, and he marveled at the elegant furnishings. As he glanced around the room, the chief noticed a small suitcase pushed far under a dresser, an odd and inconvenient location given the ample floor space.

The chief pulled the daybag out and opened it up. Among

the change of clothes and winter gear were a few legal documents, some beef jerky, and a bottle of Captain Morgan's Spiced Rum. As he ruffled through the belongings, he felt a bulky object stuffed inside a sock. As he folded the sock back to observe its contents, the chief heard a muffled voice coming from behind a door to his left. Unconsciously, the chief thrust the sock into his front pocket and moved slowly across the room. The chief's relaxed disposition turned wary as he cocked his head toward room 201B, a side door he hadn't noticed until now.

"What's in there?" he whispered to Jim Crick, pointing to the door. "I hear something!"

The chief carefully turned the knob as he reached for his arm holster and pushed open the door. Before Crick could react, a loud "Freeze!" shattered the quiet tension. The chief had his .38 Smith and Wesson leveled at the head of Marcus Coble, who dropped his cell phone and raised his arms in panic.

"Don't shoot!" yelled Jim Crick as he jumped to his feet. "He's OK!"

The chief lowered his weapon but kept both hands in a tightly gripped ready position pointed into the floor. He knew instantly that the man in front of him met the description of the mystery visitor given by the GM.

"Shit, Chief, I'm really sorry," said Jim. "I asked him in to help ID the body. He knows the victim and was trying to help me with some medical background. I sent him in there to make a call, and I got distracted."

The chief's deep scowl registered the severity of this senseless breach of protocol; he holstered his weapon and turned to Marcus.

"Come on out, Sir. I'll need to search you," said the chief.

Marcus pointed to his cell phone on the floor as he bent down to pick it up. He put the phone to his ear as he stepped out of the side room.

"Jack, I can't talk now, I need to go."

"What the hell was that all about, Marcus?" said a voice through the phone.

"A misunderstanding with the police is all. I have to go. I'll call you back."

Chief Callahan had completed his pat down and was offering a conciliatory handshake when his own cell phone rang. The chief guided Marcus to a corner by the window and turned to shield the conversation. Officer Cange explained to Mike that he was in the entry when he heard a command to "freeze!" He described several findings concerning a man named Jack Randolph, whom he was holding for questioning over several unexplained articles in his vehicle.

"Escort him to the command trailer and hold him there. I want a full statement including whereabouts over the last hour. Check the engine and tail pipe temperature. Seal the vehicle and get the lab on it. I'll be there in ten minutes."

The chief turned back to Marcus and tried to smile. "When I heard a voice through the door, I had no idea what was going on. Chief Mike Callahan," he said extending a trembling hand.

"I'm Marcus Coble, pleased to meet you. I might need a few minutes to recover from that one! That was close."

"So you know this man?" asked the chief.

"I do."

"Are you a guest in the hotel, Mr. Coble?"

"No, I'm not."

The chief said nothing in reply, pausing for Marcus to explain his presence more fully.

"I'm staying at the Orca Inn," said Marcus.

"Well, as you can see, Mr. Hayes didn't pull out of it. No determination yet on cause of death. Do you know anything that might shed some light on the situation?"

"Absolutely nothing. I'm as shocked as you are. I arrived at the hotel just as a young woman came screaming down the stairs."

"And what time would that have been?"

"I don't know, it must have been close to ten."

"You're certain you were not in the hotel any time prior to that?"

"Yes, Sir, why?"

"Well, according to the general manager here, you came into the hotel around 9:45 P.M., looking for Mr. Hayes, a little over a half hour ago."

At that instant, Sergeant Graham stuck his head in the door.

"Chief, I have Ellen Windemuth here. Are you ready for her?"

Marcus would not wait to register his protest. "That's impossible. I have never met the manager here. I have no idea who he is or what he looks like. As I said, I arrived just as this all happened, around 10:00 P.M."

Chief Callahan turned to Graham.

"Have her wait downstairs, Sergeant. I'll be a few more minutes. I want the GM up here right away."

The chief turned back to Marcus and calmly said, "I'll get him up here to clear this up. While we're waiting, can you tell me who that was on the phone?"

"Jack Randolph. He's in Juneau."

"In Juneau, you're sure of that?"

"Absolutely!"

"Could I have his number, please?"

Marcus thought momentarily about invoking his attorney-client privilege but quickly reconsidered and volunteered the number.

The chief quickly called Sergeant Graham back to the room and handed him the number.

"Could you call Mr. Randolph at this number, Sergeant? I want to confirm his whereabouts and what these two gentlemen were discussing a few minutes ago."

A moment of anxiety overtook Marcus. He looked squarely at the chief, who detected his sudden discomfort.

"Why are you here at the Van Gilder, Mr. Coble?"

"I came to see Walter."

"At ten o'clock at night?"

"I had a meeting with him," Marcus said quickly, satisfied that the phone call to Jack would corroborate his story.

Chief Callahan had a rare gift envied by every detective the world over. He provoked a combination of trust and fear at the same time. Not the kind of fear that stems from a physical threat but a psychological insecurity that befalls a person who reveals less than the whole truth—a gnawing anxiety that invites confession.

The chief's jovial, deep-set brown eyes evoked sympathy, and his rugged complexion, set against a square meaty jaw and large frame, commanded immediate respect. He inspired comparisons to great Indian chiefs, such as Sitting Bull and Red Cloud, due in part to his heritage but equally owing to the mysterious powers of influence he held over people. Regardless of the source, everyone agreed that "Chief" was an appropriate title for Mike Callahan.

It was, therefore, for good reason that Marcus felt intimidated by the situation he found himself in. If Marcus was lying, the chief knew that the mere anticipation of the general manager's arrival would exert mounting pressure on him, an opportunity the chief would probe and press to every advantage. The fact that Sergeant Graham was phoning Jack Randolph for a statement played perfectly into his plan to test Marcus' veracity.

"What time were you to meet Mr. Hayes?"

"Ten."

Marcus checked himself, shuffled and turned his eyes. He thought quickly about clarifying his response. In fact, he had never confirmed the time with Walter for several reasons, not the least of which was the danger of walking into a trap. But how could anybody confirm this now that Walter was dead? Besides, Marcus reasoned quickly, he told Jack the meeting was at 10:00 P.M., and he would confirm as much.

"Well, maybe you can answer this. What the hell was Walter Hayes doing half naked and in bed if he was expecting to meet you?"

Marcus went cold. What he thought was an innocent truth was now an exercise in backpedaling. His hesitation was obvious, and he had one clear choice: come clean.

"I am a lawyer. Walter Hayes and Jack Randolph are clients of mine. The truth is that I kept the precise time of my arrival hidden from Walter because of the sensitive nature of our business. I did plan the meeting for 10:00 P.M., and that is what I told Jack."

"I see, let me get this straight. You had an appointment with Mr. Hayes at 10:00 P.M. that you never confirmed. You planned to surprise him."

"Correct, but he had requested a meeting with me."

Marcus straightened himself, showing signs of obvious stress. Sensing his vulnerability, the chief pressed his attack.

"So Mr. Hayes requested the meeting, and yet you never bothered to tell him you were coming, or when?"

"I was trying to be discreet."

"And that is why you elected to surprise him at 10:00 P.M. on a Friday night? It strikes me as particularly indiscreet, given the man is in bed. Why not wait until tomorrow?"

"I suppose I could have; in fact, I would have when I discovered he was in bed. But I'm not one to waste time."

"When is the last time you talked to Mr. Hayes?"

"This morning around 9:30 A.M."

"How about Jack Randolph? When was the last time you were with him?"

"Yesterday for lunch. We've talked on the phone several times today. Chief, I have to ask: why all the curiosity if Walter died of natural causes?"

"Did I say he died of natural causes?"

"Well, no. But I couldn't help but overhear the briefing you received."

"Until I receive an official cause of death from the coroner, this is all routine. I have a few more questions before I talk to your client. I assume you have no objections to that?"

"No, please go ahead."

"Why was Mr. Hayes in Seward? You said you talked to him this morning. Did he tell you he was coming here?"

Marcus admitted to himself his story was sounding more unlikely by the minute.

"I don't know why he came to Seward other than to get away. He did not tell me he was coming here."

"Then how did you know where to meet him?"

"I had him followed," said Marcus sheepishly.

"Ahhh. I thought you said Mr. Hayes requested the meeting. Why was it necessary to have him followed?"

Marcus could hardly fathom how far and fast his standing had deteriorated. He was usually the one in command of the subject, but now he seemed to be spiraling out of control.

"Walter was not answering his phone. He left Anchorage in distress, but I knew from a prior conversation he wanted to meet."

"Who else knew you were here in Seward and planning to meet Walter at 10:00 P.M.?"

Marcus was silent, stalling for time, contemplating his answer.

"I want you to think hard about it," said the chief sternly. "Was there anyone else who might have known about your plans to meet Mr. Hayes here tonight?"

"Chief, I sure credit you with being thorough. Jack was the only other person I can think of immediately, but it's been a long day. You'll have to ask him if he told anyone else. I doubt he did."

"Is there anything else you think I should know?"

Sergeant Graham entered the room and indicated that James Van Oss was waiting outside.

"Would you like me to bring him in, Chief?"

"One minute, Graham."

The chief turned and drew himself to within a few inches of Marcus, his eyes fixed in a mesmerizing glare.

"One more thing I want to clear up before we bring the general manager in. He's positive that he met you in the lobby around 9:50 P.M. and that you were looking for Mr. Hayes. Can you think of any reason why he would lie about that?"

"No."

"You mentioned you were trying to avoid public attention. Can anyone corroborate your arrival time at the hotel?"

"It was a little chaotic when I arrived; likely not."

"Was there anyone you were trying to avoid, anyone who you regarded as a threat to you or to Mr. Randolph?"

"Certainly nothing life-threatening, no."

"And what were you doing for the thirty minutes before you arrived at the Van Gilder, which you said was about 9:45 P.M., correct?"

"No, I said 10:00 P.M., or just after. I was driving here from Anchorage."

The chief turned to an FBI agent standing by and indicated that he wanted that point recorded. The chief was certain the Seward Highway had been closed for hours prior to 10:00 P.M., and he was increasingly skeptical of the answers he was getting. He asked Marcus where he was parked.

"Agent Johnson, I want detailed photos of every car within a two block radius of the hotel right away. Would you mind? Confirm ownership of the vehicles and find out the last time each one moved. Look at snow accumulation, tracks, everything."

Johnson nodded in the affirmative as he wrote in his notebook. At that moment, Sergeant Graham approached the chief with a serious look and summoned him out into the hall. After the brief interruption, the chief returned to continue his interrogation of Marcus.

"Sergeant Graham just called Mr. Randolph. Turns out your client is nowhere near Juneau. Do you care to comment?"

"The last I knew, Jack was on an 11:30 A.M. commercial flight to Juneau."

"Sergeant, are you getting all this?" asked the chief with a glance over his shoulder.

"I find it hard to believe that you talked to Mr. Randolph ten minutes ago, and he failed to mention that he's right downstairs. Seems to me you two are hiding a few things from each other, or from me. My question is why?"

Marcus was dumbfounded by the revelation. His mind froze. Suddenly, he was unsure of anything, particularly why Jack was in Seward. His expression was guilt-ridden, full of awareness that his story sounded like one lie after another. The rush of adrenaline that flushed his veins felt cold, and yet he felt his body start to sweat all over. His torso shook in mini-spasms in a telltale sign that Marcus was cracking.

"Sergeant, show Mr. Van Oss in, please," said the chief.

When James stepped forward, the chief introduced the two men and asked James if he could identify Marcus as the man he saw in the Lobby at 9:50 P.M.

"No, Sir, it was dark, but this is not Mr. Coble—or at least the man who identified himself as Mr. Coble."

The chief was not surprised. If Walter's death was caused by anything but natural causes, it was well planned. The person who killed him did not walk in and announce himself to the manager, unless such a bold move was the work of a very brave killer.

"Could I see your identification, Mr. Coble?"

Marcus produced his driver's license.

"That will be all, Mr. Van Oss. Thank you."

"Wait one minute!" interjected Marcus. "Describe the man you saw!"

"That'll be all, Mr. Van Oss," said the chief peremptorily. "Thank you!"

"It appears likely someone used your name, Mr. Coble, but who and why would someone do that? Mr. Randolph was the only person who knew you were planning to be here, and apparently he didn't want you to know he was coming here too."

"He's the only person I told."

"We'll make sure we introduce him to Mr. Van Oss soon," said the chief with notable sarcasm.

Marcus remembered his brief conversations with Rachel and the P.I. who trailed Walter to Seward. He was sufficiently nervous at this point that full disclosure was more than a passing temptation, but he checked himself at the opportunity to end the interview with the chief.

"A few more quick questions, Mr. Coble, and you can go. Did you ever see Mr. Hayes, or approach room 201 at any time prior to 10:00 P.M., before the body was discovered by Ellen Windemuth?"

"No."

"How much time elapsed after Ms. Windemuth came running down before you went upstairs?"

"I admit I hesitated to get involved. I had no idea it was Walter at the time. I guess it was a few minutes, just after the paramedics arrived."

"And when you came upstairs for the first time, were the hotel lights on or off?"

"I'm sure they were on, why?"

"Just trying to get my timing straight is all. I want you to keep everything you've heard and witnessed in this room to yourself and to refrain from all outside communication. Remain on site and surrender your cell phone to Sergeant Graham," added the chief as a test of Marcus' resolve.

"Absolutely not. My cell phone poses no danger to anyone. And I demand to know who used my name!"

The forensic team was approaching, offering the chief the

opportunity to break off the conversation with Marcus abruptly. The chief ignored Marcus completely and motioned Graham to take him away. His silence left Marcus feeling vindicated but certain he had squandered any remaining credibility he had with the chief.

"I want a nasty man," said the chief to the forensic team, which in cop jargon meant to check every crack and hole. "Pay close attention to the pacemaker."

As the chief turned to leave, two local officers approached in heavy winter layers, looking as though they had just been plucked from a snow bank.

"We have a report from the roof, Sir."

"Let me have it quick."

"There were two different sets of prints up and down the fire escape. One set ends at the second-level landing. There's a steel ladder from the second floor to the roof. One set of prints is heavily drifted coming and going from the ladder to southwest corner. We found a rope secured to a vent, hanging over the west side. No signs of climbing or hauling activity over the side of the building. Unlikely the person knew much about rigging, and the knots weren't tight, indicating that no weight was applied. We photographed everything as best we could."

"Good work, boys. Check the west side for signs of a rappel just in case. Get the rope to the lab for fiber analysis and have them look at the ladder rungs; there's bound to be some glove fibers on 'em. If you're done making snowmen, I want to know what kind of alarm or security systems exist here. I asked Agent Fell to pull together the FBI team for a full briefing in twenty minutes, and I'll want you both there."

When the chief completed his directives, he went straight to the hotel's library to meet Inga and Ellen Windemuth. As the chief descended the crimson-carpeted stairs, he reached into his front pocket to retrieve his note pad. As he fingered the soft object in his pocket, he recalled the stuffed sock he had removed from Walter's day bag. He unfolded the sock to reveal the hidden contents. The chief halted abruptly and scanned the vicinity as he unrolled 50 crisp $100 bills. He shoved the contents back into his pocket as he turned down the first floor corridor toward the library.

## Chapter VIII
*Friday, January 18, 3:10 P.M.*

**JACK RANDOLPH'S** Alaska Airlines flight arrived in Juneau at 3:10 P.M. Friday afternoon. The cloudless sky and lushly forested slopes surrounding the state capital were a welcome contrast to the sludge of Anchorage. The slightly sulfuric smell of saltwater flats mixed with jet fuel whipped around Jack as he stepped onto the tarmac. The long drive down the narrow channel from Douglas to Juneau, past the warehouses, converted canneries, and the freshly painted homes perched on piling seemed unusually deserted for that time of year, a week before the legislative session. The irony of the moment was not lost on Jack, who smiled at the thought that everyone in Juneau was hiding.

When Jack walked into the Goldmark Hotel, Elliot Lawson was there to greet him. After their familiar club-member greeting, the men parted company, following protocol and separate paths to their twelfth-floor suite. The historic hotel was a second home to Jack. The elegant, black-veined white marble floor tile matched that of the Capitol. The copper and crystal chandelier was a handcrafted masterpiece of bowhead whales and the eighteenth-century schooners that hunted them. The yellow cedar totem poles and bright-colored Tlinkit ceremonial blankets added a vibrancy and richness to the lobby.

Beaufort Oil's twelfth-floor luxury apartment, with its full-height surround of glass overlooking Gastineau Channel, was a popular after-hours hangout for lobbyists and politicians, located only four blocks from the Capitol.

Exactly five minutes after their initial lobby greeting, in the privacy of Juneau's only four-star hotel, Jack poured Elliot his usual drink of Jack Daniels "neat" and came directly to the point.

"We've all got a lot on the line with this Hayes business, Elliot. Let me get to the point. Marcus tracked Walter to the Van Gilder Hotel in Seward this afternoon. We think he's there to strike a deal with the feds, possibly as early as tomorrow."

"You know the FBI is basing their operation in Seward, don't you?" Elliot interjected.

"I had heard that. It only confirms my suspicions. We've got one shot at stopping Walter before the shit hits, Elliot."

"What do you mean stop him?"

"Cut him a deal before the feds do. If I offer to help with his defense and some hope once he's out of prison, I think we can come to an understanding, maybe contain the damage here."

"Why are you telling *me* this?"

"From what I hear, you're in as deep as he is," Jack said. "You can't afford to have his testimony see the light of day."

"May be true, but I have no idea what he's already told 'em. Besides, I'm in no position to negotiate."

"But I am. Marcus is in Seward as we speak. We figure we have at most a day or two, maybe only hours to get to him. It's no coincidence that Walter is in Seward. That much should be clear."

"The governor is there you know," Elliot said. "Morrie's holding a press conference tomorrow, after he meets with the Asst. U.S. Attorney General."

"You're goddam shitting me!"

"I'm dead serious. The meeting and the press conference are both about me. I'm under a lot of pressure to resign, and Morrie wants to hear their case against me in person before he makes a final decision. I don't know what's on your mind, but it couldn't have come at a worse time."

"Or a better time! Hear me out. But first, tell me this: Why are you on the sidelines when your ass is on the line? Why aren't you in Seward with Morrie?"

"No one invited me. Besides, he's putting a little distance between us. The last thing he wants is the perception that he's using his influence to save my ass—especially now that the media is asking him what he knew and when."

"Jesus Christ, Elliot! I can't believe this is the first I've heard of it."

"This entire investigation is out of control," said Elliot despondently. "It's cascading like a waterfall. The entire inquiry only started a month ago, and now I guess they have enough on me for a grand-jury indictment."

"What exactly do they have?"

"I was too aggressive horse-trading on the governor's agenda. That and my fundraising activities for his re-election. We looked at the Alaska statutes but not federal ethics laws, which are broad enough to nail me. At best, I'll go broke fighting them; at worst, spend some time in the slammer. I guess everyone is talking."

"How much does Walter factor into your case?"

"Quite a bit, I'm sure, but I don't want anyone to know that. Walter was instrumental in helping line up the votes we needed on the royalty tax, and I was working with him on some key legislators. You know how it works. I probably trusted him more than I should have."

"The ways these federal guys work, it ain't a matter of breaking trust. I'm sure they made it real simple: talk or you're somebody's bitch in prison."

"Maybe so."

"So you've submitted your resignation, and tomorrow there's a press conference to announce it?"

"I'm hoping for the best, planning for the worst. The governor and I have an understanding; if he feels he needs my resignation, he has it. Actually, that's what I thought this meeting was all about, a gentle letdown, a job offer of some kind."

"There's still time, Elliot, but we need to act fast."

"Fine, but I still don't see where you're going."

"Look, we've known each other a long time, helped each other out of jams countless times. It's no different here, only the stakes are higher and the heat's turned up."

"OK."

"I'll make Walter an offer he can't refuse," said Jack. "What I need in exchange is a favor from the governor.

"I'm listening."

"The state is threatening to take back my Endicott leases, as you know. We were required to drill by 2005, and our exploratory wells indicate it would not be profitable with oil prices below $75 a barrel, so it hasn't been feasible until now. Oil prices shot up so fast that we didn't have time to react. At current prices, we're committed to move forward, but we need that lease extension."

"Where do I come in? That's a legislative matter that I can't influence."

"I have an approach that bypasses the legislature, a simple addendum to the lease. I've checked with the AG, and it can be done by executive order. I have ample backup for the director of DNR, who will write the recommendation to the governor. That way, Morrie won't be out in front; he just needs to accept the recommendation and sign the addendum."

"Assuming I can get his attention, what's your offer?"

"I'll get Walter a lawyer, put up a strong defense, and shoot for a deal involving low time and no testimony."

"Sounds a little thin on Walter's side of the ledger. There's always the risk that the feds will reject a plea bargain."

"Leave that to me. If he balks, we structure something that hinges on your acquittal. Listen, he doesn't have any options. He'll take the deal."

"I don't know, it sounds like obstruction, Jack!"

"Give me a damn break. We've been running interference like this for years. If anyone's guilty of obstruction, it's the feds. Besides, the lease amendment is good for everyone."

"I'm not sure. We're *all* under the microscope, Jack."

"There's no trail back to you or Morrie. You have my word; this stays right here. Walter won't know anything about the lease extension. As far as he knows, I'm simply protecting BOC from damaging testimony. And as far as Morrie is concerned, he's following the advice of his cabinet and acting in the best interest of Alaska. I can get the senate leadership to back it if necessary, but I want to keep the legislature out of it."

"I'm not sure I can get to Morrie until Monday. When do you need an answer?"

"Now!" It's a long shot, but we should fly to Seward tonight."

Elliot was shocked.

"Why the *hell* would we want to do that? The place is swarming with FBI and media. Morrie specifically directed me not to go, and there's a goddam storm that's closed the airport. Brilliant idea, Jack!"

"Morrie will understand. Hell, he doesn't even need to know we're there. I've got the jet on standby. No media, no expense reports. Just a weekend walkabout."

Elliot stood up and stared blankly out the window into the dark skyline. He knew one thing from his political life: he was either on the inside making things happen or on the outside looking in. If he wanted control of his future, he needed to be in the game, not a spectator. Seward was the place, and now was the time. Jack was watching Elliot closely and was determined to close the deal.

"What's the downside, Elliot? Think about it, what's the worst that can happen? Whatever it is, the risk is greater with you sitting on your ass!"

The idea of doing nothing was almost demeaning to Elliot.

"Are you thinking I would clear this with Morrie or just show up unannounced?"

"I'd make the phone call, but don't tell him about any meetings with Walter. Ignorance of evil makes an angel. But remember, saving your job as chief of staff is a worthy goal, but staying out of prison is the prize."

"You sure you know what you're doing? I trust you, Jack, but I'm not sure I trust Marcus."

"You need to be around for this business, Elliot. It ain't the kind of negotiation we can bring you in on long-distance, you know what I'm saying?"

"I guess."

Elliot poured himself a quick shot and slammed it down to calm his nerves.

"Then we have a deal?"

"We're close, Jack. I've got a couple conditions. First, the deal with Walter has to be tight enough to convince Morrie to keep me on. Two, you're dealing with the AG and DNR directly. If they don't buy in, that's your fault, not mine. Three, I want Victor Yushenko off my ass. He's insisting the governor revoke every joint exploration and technology exchange agreement we have with the Russians. Alaska benefits hugely from these joint ventures. If nothing else, it'll help me get Morrie's attention."

"What's Victor using to squeeze you so hard?" Jack wanted to know. "Just tell him to go to hell."

"I tried that, trust me. He's tight with the U.S. State Department and CIA. He's a damn god to them. They're using Victor to get to me, I know it. The greedy bastards! Everyone wants the Russian nationalization plan to fail, and I'm gettin' the squeeze."

"And no doubt he's telling you he has some influence with the Justice Department over your indictment."

"How did you guess?"

"You should have come to me earlier, and I could have saved you some grief. Look, in spite of everything you read, the Russian president is saying one thing and doing another."

"Big damn deal; I make a career of that."

"President Martov says he's kicking foreign oil out of Russia, but the truth is, he's paying them off. I know this because BOC is one of the companies being bought out."

"You're kidding me."

"No I'm not. It's all about Russian pride in the motherland—Bolshevik strength and victory over foreign capitalists. Yushenko's job is to provide cover to both sides of the deal. That way, Martov is a hero to the Russians, investors are whole, and the oil markets stay restless long enough for Martov to pay for it all."

"Jesus Christ, I hate this job! Let me get this straight. Neither side gives a shit what Alaska does with our Russian joint-venture agreements?"

"You got it. Russia could care less. We simply need to keep up the image of a fight. If Alaska threatens trade retaliation, it makes the battle real and Martov a national hero."

"So Victor's threats are a goddam ruse? I can't believe what I'm hearing."

"We have a deal then?" asked Jack in a final effort to close.

"Alright, we have a deal. Only two people know about this suicide mission, you and Morrie!"

The two men shook hands, clanked glasses, and exchanged a smile that bespoke of mutual confidence born from a hundred such deals.

After a few seconds, Elliot asked, "What the *hell* makes you think you can get into Seward, Jack? As of three hours ago, the entire town was shut down."

"Not sure I can; let me make a few calls."

Jack Randolph had connections, and he knew how to use them. When he picked up the phone to set up his flight plan, he knew precisely who to call to arrange for special clearances—and anonymity.

"We're on, Elliot! 5:20 P.M. departure. Expect a few bumps, but the pilot tells me the front will pass within the hour. If we can't land, we'll continue to Anchorage."

With that confirmation, the two agreed to meet at the hangar at 5:15 sharp. Jack picked up his cell phone to dial Marcus, but quickly reconsidered. He could always call him later, he thought to himself, and besides, he had a ready excuse for showing up in Seward unannounced. After all, it was Marcus who wanted the BOC jet on standby over the weekend, and Jack was simply the delivery boy.

# Chapter IX
*Friday, January 18, 10:55 P.M.*

"**ARE YOU THE WINDEMUTHS IN ROOM 202?**" inquired the chief of the two women in the library. "Pleasure to meet you both. I'm Mike Callahan, Chief of Police."

The two women were sitting at an oval table, on which sat an open laptop and a fully consumed bottle of Opus cabernet. The chief's introduction prompted Inga to rise, but her eyes hesitated and glanced back at the TV, which was airing the finale of *American Idol*. Ellen didn't even acknowledge the chief.

"Nice to meet you, sir. Ellen, this is Mr. Callahan," said Inga.

"Hello," responded Ellen. "Mother, we have to see this last song. She's incredible."

"You'll have to excuse my daughter, she's addicted to the show." After a slight pause, Inga added: "I recognize your name from somewhere." Another pause. "That's your deer up there; is the story true?"

"The deer is mine, but the credit is definitely not mine," said the chief. "I actually won that in a poker game."

Ellen's laugh sounded more like a tire screech, which contrasted with Inga's fixed scowl all the more sharply because Ellen never looked up from the TV.

"That's a riot," she said without a hint of recognition as to her intended reference.

As soon as the Idol contestant bowed, the chief motioned to the door and asked the two women to follow him outside.

"Be sure to bring your computer," said the chief. "We may be a while."

As the three ventured into the night blizzard, the chief soon discovered that Inga's formal command of English did little to compensate for her accent, which rendered her conversation almost unintelligible. His continual pleas to Inga to repeat herself, which he blamed on his poor hearing, made for an awkward introduction. When they entered the trailer, the chief apologized for the makeshift accommodations and motioned to the cheap plastic chairs.

"Sorry to bring you out into the cold; I thought it would be more private here. Coffee?" asked the chief as he turned to pour.

"No, thank you," they said in unison.

"I understand you're both in room 202, and Ellen you were the first to discover Walter Hayes' body."

Ellen nodded tensely. Her squinting eyes were unadjusted to the bright florescent lighting, causing her face to contort and turn away. It was obvious to the chief that Ellen had been drinking heavily, and she was nervous.

"Ellen, I want you to walk me through everything from the time you left the party to the moment you discovered the body."

Ellen immediately corrected the chief.

"We were never at the party or whatever it was. We came back from Christo's, and Mother went straight to the room. I hung out for a few minutes. The power went off just after I got to the room, which freaked me out, but we lit a candle and just hung out and talked."

The chief looked at Ellen expectantly. When she didn't take the hint, the chief prompted her to continue.

"So then what?"

"What do you mean? We just stayed in our room."

"What made you leave the room, Ellen?"

"Oh, after maybe thirty minutes, Mother asked me to go check with James to find out how long the power would be out. So that's what I did. But when I left the room, I noticed that man's door was open, so I went over to close it and that's when I saw him. That's about everything really."

The chief was unable to determine if Ellen was nervous or intentionally evasive, so he continued to probe.

"Before you left the room, did you hear anything, or see anything, anything unusual at all?"

"Such as? I mean, this is not exactly a quiet place, even with the lights out. We even commented to each other about it. We heard lots of stuff the whole time: doors slamming, people coming and going. We heard a piano crash at some point. I guess you'll have to be more specific."

"Did you hear any visitors to room 201? Any unusual noise from the hallway? Maybe a fight, a struggle, anything like that?"

"No, just a lot of general activity," said Ellen with a slight slur.

The chief pondered whether it would be better to postpone the interview, given Ellen's inebriety. But he was content to get what he could and to follow up later on anything of critical interest.

"OK, take me from there. You left the room to check on when power would be restored. What time was that?"

"Oh, man, I have no idea."

"OK, then what? As you're leaving your room, you notice the door to room 201 is open?"

"Right. I walked over and knocked on the door, which had

the lock-thingy flipped over, and so I called "hello" through the crack. That's when I noticed his body on the floor."

"Was it dark in the hallway?"

"Yah, I guess. I remember some lights being on, but it was pretty dark."

"It's important that you think hard about this, Ellen. Was there any light in the hallway?"

"It was pretty dark, except for the stairs, I think. I can't remember exactly. We were in our room, and we noticed the streetlights come on outside, and that's why Mother asked me to go check on the power."

"The general manager, Mr. Van Oss, stated that when he first arrived at the scene the hallway was so dark he could barely see anything. We think the emergency lights in the hallway may have been unplugged."

"I wouldn't know about that, but I can remember thinking to myself that the electricity must have just come on or something because I could suddenly see everyone when I came down the stairs."

"So if the hall was dark and the room was dark, how could you see that the door was open?"

"I don't know, I just did, OK?" said Ellen defiantly.

"Look, Ellen, I'm not accusing you of anything. I'm just asking for your help to re-create the scene so I can try to understand what happened."

"From what I've heard, it sounds like he died of a simple heart attack," said Inga. "What is there to understand?"

The chief ignored the question and focused on Ellen, who had stood up and was now pacing nervously back and forth.

"It's just that I've had a little too much to drink, so I'm not exactly thinking straight, OK?"

"Try not to over-think things, just tell me what you remember. How could you see this body on the floor when the room was pitch black inside? Mr. Van Oss indicated he could barely make out anything."

Ellen shot a glance at her mother as though seeking approval—and an alibi. Her discomfort was visible, and her voice quickened almost to a panic. Unlike her mother, Ellen's English was perfectly clear.

"Look, shit, I'm freaking out here, OK! I really don't want to be here right now. I don't want to have anything to do with this. We're supposed to be on vacation! Can we maybe do this later?"

The chief studied Ellen carefully. His stern but sympathetic glare was a vice-like grip that few could escape without revealing something about themselves.

"I don't know, OK?" Ellen continued. "I really don't. You're looking at me like I know something. I don't know anything more that what I've told you. I saw an open door and thought it would be a good idea to make sure that's what … that he didn't want it closed."

"Relax, Ellen. You're not in any trouble. But I need your help. Think hard, how could you see?"

"Now that I think of it, there was a flashlight on the end table right by the door. The flashlight was on and pointing up to the ceiling, and I grabbed it and pointed it inside the room."

"I'm glad you said that because the manager reported that he found a flashlight on the floor. Do you have any idea how it might have got there?"

"No, but I can remember grabbing it."

"Seems a little awkward, doesn't it, pointing a flashlight into a stranger's room when it's locked from the inside."

"Yah, I guess, but I had knocked a couple times. I just sensed something was wrong, OK?"

Ellen's growing irritation was bordering on hostile, so the chief decided not to push too hard. He let her continue.

"As soon as I saw his white legs sticking out in the dark, I freaked. That's all I can tell you."

"Ellen, according to Mr. Van Oss's statement, when you met him at the bottom of the stairs, you yelled that you had discovered a dead body."

"I did?"

"Yes, you did. What made you assume Mr. Hayes was dead if all you saw were his legs through a one-inch crack?"

"I don't know, he wasn't moving! I told you I freaked out."

"I need you to think really hard about this next question. As you ran down to seek help, did you see anyone in the corridor?"

"I don't remember. Wait, maybe. I think I passed a woman going down the stairs. And I remember seeing someone else going into their room, but it was dark."

"Which room?"

"I just recall it was close to the stairs on the left, but I really can't be more specific."

"That's fine for now. If you remember anything more, please let me know. Do you remember when the lights came back on?"

"Sometime after I came back up the stairs with James. The lights were on when the police arrived, I remember that."

"Did you know who was registered to room 201 prior to this point?" asked the chief casually.

Ellen looked at her mother and then shook her head unconvincingly in the negative.

"Neither of you had ever met or seen Mr. Hayes before?"

"Nope!"

After an awkward silence, Ellen added, "On second thought, I could use some of that coffee."

The chief handed both women coffee, using the opportunity to change the subject. Inga had been quiet up to this point, her hands politely folded and legs crossed in a practiced manner.

"Inga Windemuth, have I been getting that right?"

"The W is pronounced like a V, but otherwise perfect."

"Are you two visiting from out of state?"

"I'm from London, my daughter lives in Vermont. We're here on a ski vacation, trying to get back to Alyeska. Seward was supposed to be a day trip."

"You're timing is good. Alyeska has thirty inches of new snow, and the roads should be open by morning."

"What do you do in London, Ms. Windemuth?" asked the chief, more out of genuine interest than investigative routine.

"Please, call me Inga. I'm retired, but formerly East German and Russian Intelligence."

Chief Callahan's eyes lit up and a broad smile revealed a handsomeness Inga had not observed to this point. Among the chief's talents was storytelling, and he launched into one of his favorites about Victor Yushenko, a Russian MIG pilot who defected to the U.S. via Alaska in 1979. By quirk of geography, Chief Callahan had been involved in the original intelligence debriefing. Victor loved to hunt and fish, and the two men had become good friends over the years. Surely, the chief insisted, Inga must know of Victor.

"I'm acquainted with the man. He caused quite a scandal at the time, and an embarrassment for my department. But that was long ago. What is Victor doing now?"

The chief struggled to decipher Inga's heavy accent.

"Quite an interesting man. He jets around in his F-4 Phantom, delivering lectures and brokering deals between U.S. and Russian businesses. He still has some very high level contacts in Russia."

"Seems he's done well for himself. He was a top priority of ours for years, but no one could locate him. I hear his name mentioned everywhere now."

The chief began to reflect on the topic more seriously.

"After Russia nationalized its oil industry and oil prices soared to over $125 a barrel, Venezuelan President Hugo Chavez offered free oil to low-income Alaskans. I remember Victor advocating for an embargo against Venezuelan oil to the Alaska legislature. Now that I think of it, he was teamed up with our friend Walter Hayes for a bit."

"We dropped him years ago, but I know he was a thorn in Russia's ass for a while."

Inga was all German. Her bright blue eyes, high cheekbones, and short-cropped blond hair bespoke of a youthful beauty that had long passed. Her puffy cheeks and thick neck dropped into an overweight frame. But one could easily picture her as a young, sophisticated operative, recruited to work undercover and trained in the art of seduction. The chief was intrigued by Inga's lively elegance, but there was something about her he did not trust. Her over-applied makeup and sharp wit reminded the chief of Marlene Dietrich, the classic film star who mastered the role of a *femme fatale*.

"I didn't mean to get us off the subject," said the chief. "We were talking about Mr. Hayes."

"Just make sure you're not chasing ghosts, Chief," said Inga with a wag of her finger. "I admit Mr. Hayes' circumstances appear suspicious, but the hotel was full of people. If there was foul play, there will be evidence. You can count on it. There's only so many ways to kill someone through a locked door. Did anything unusual show up on the body?"

The chief knew better than to share information of this nature, but he was an expert at recruiting help while at the same time intimidating a suspect.

"Nothing yet. The autopsy report will nail it down. But tell me what you know about non-traceable poisons."

"Plutonium isotopes, but they need to be ingested. Hard to manufacture and acquire, and very unstable. Not likely the culprit here. Anthrax, of course. I'll get you a list of others to look into."

Inga stared back at the chief for any hint of suspicion. With her background, she realized, the chief could assume that she was an expert in such matters. The chief was a smart man, she thought to herself, and he was testing more than just her credentials.

"I appreciate any help you can offer. I'll need all the help I can get," said the chief.

"Speaking of which, I overheard that nutcase Juliet insisting that she can help. One of your officers was taking her statement, and she was adamant that the officer find James and confirm her story. She had a premonition or something about a murder and apparently told James about it minutes before Ellen found the body. Now that strikes me as suspicious."

"You mean she might have killed Mr. Hayes just so she could draw attention to herself?" clarified the chief.

"It's very possible. More likely than a visitation from a ghost, wouldn't you say? I wouldn't go chasing those."

"I don't intend to. If she did in fact predict Mr. Hayes' death, she's either very lucky or has some explaining to do."

"I met her in the library fifteen minutes ago, and the woman is obsessed with public validation. I think she's mentally unstable and has enough bitterness built up inside that she might just do something crazy."

"I'll look into that, but I have one more question for the two of you if you have a few more minutes."

Inga and Ellen exchanged a quizzical glance.

"Sure, whatever," said Ellen.

The chief stood to refill his coffee cup, deciding to pose the question while watching their reaction carefully from behind.

"Do either of you know what Mr. Hayes might have been doing with your room number?"

Each woman turned to face the other. Blank looks passed between them. Was it a trick question? Ellen was sure she had stated she never met Mr. Hayes. Neither woman feigned a response.

"Seems odd is all; I found it at his bedside," said the chief as he tossed Inga a Ziplock baggie with a light blue Post-it note in it.

Seconds of awkward silence passed.

"He checked in before we did, maybe the desk wrote down room 202 as an available room," said Inga quickly.

"Well, that's the curious thing; on this same piece of paper is a website address, which turns out to be Ellen's. Now how, or why, would Mr. Hayes have your room number and web address if you two had never met and you checked in after Walter? Just something curious I need to clear up."

"Goddam this shit!" shouted Ellen as she stormed out of the trailer.

A full minute passed before Inga summoned the nerve to respond. "I apologize for my daughter, Chief. She doesn't handle stress well. But I have to confess that your tactics are somewhat aggressive to a twenty-one-year-old girl."

"And how do they appear to a veteran field agent?"

"Maybe a bit hard if I may say so. You said yourself we're not suspects."

The chief stood up and walked over to the fax machine. He pulled the artist rendering from the tray and thrust it in front of Inga's face.

"Do you recognize this woman?" he asked gruffly.

"She was the last known person to see and talk with the victim. She came into the hotel moments before he left for his room. I thought you might have seen her."

"No, I don't," said Inga.

"Why do I get the impression you're not telling me everything you know, Inga?"

Inga looked sternly into the chief's watery eyes. Her face hardened and her accent thinned.

"It's pretty clear that you're holding things back yourself," Inga responded calmly.

"Have it your way. I'll need your passport, Inga."

"I assure you, the note means nothing. Maybe he wanted to document Fannie's room number so he could avoid a ghost. Your guess is as good as mine."

"And the web address?"

"You'll have to show it to me. Ellen's blog is very popular. It's like TMZ—the gossip column on the rich and famous. Are you sure it's Mr. Hayes' handwriting?"

"Not yet. Tell me this: You're here on a ski vacation, and yet the day it dumps snow you decide to navigate a treacherous pass with clear avalanche hazards and to drive to Seward of all places. Why?"

"I admit we were not paying attention to the weather. I'm on a mother-daughter bonding mission, not on a schedule."

"I see. I checked on your rental car and hotel registration. You're paying cash for everything, why?"

"I'm a foreigner; the exchange rate surcharge on all credit card transactions is 11 percent. I'm retired and guilty of trying to pinch pennies. I think they pay cops better here in the states than they do in Russia."

The chief mustered a laugh to ease the mounting tension. "No doubt they do."

After a brief pause the chief lowered his voice to a soft pitch and pulled his chair close to Inga.

"I'll tell you what's bothering me the most. It was pitch-black in that corridor. As your daughter left your room, she paused long enough to spot a one-inch opening from a dark hallway against the backdrop of a darkened room. Then she knocked on the door, and when there was no answer, she grabbed a flashlight to peek inside. It all sounds a bit implausible, especially for a young girl who seems to frighten easily."

"You don't know my daughter at all. She's considerate and inquisitive. And she's afraid of nothing."

"The best explanation your daughter could offer was that she was concerned. It doesn't strike me as unusual or worthy of investigation that someone leaves their door cracked open during a power outage, especially if the only light source is from the corridor. Certainly not enough to justify probing around a stranger's room with a flashlight anyway."

"I'm sure we could both use some rest, Chief," said Inga politely. "Ellen's tired and she's had quite a bit to drink."

The two stood up and exchanged a forced smile.

"I'm going to insist that you remain in Seward for the time being. I hope you understand."

"I do, and I'll have my passport for you in the morning. Good night."

As Inga stepped outside, the snow had finally turned into a steady rain, a sudden but common transition during the Gulf storms that pound Seward in the winter.

# Chapter X
*Friday, January 18, 7:24 P.M.*

**JACK AND ELLIOT'S FLIGHT** from Juneau on the Leer 210 lasted almost two hours. With the exception of the white-knuckle descent into Seward, their trip had been surprisingly uneventful. Predictions of high winds aloft and icing conditions did not materialize until they were well west of Prince William Sound. The violent wind shear and turbulence on final descent into Resurrection Bay had shaken the men, but they were optimistic that their gambit was about to pay off.

If Seward was the blue-collar equivalent of Homer, then Dale Minert was its union boss. It was Dale who arranged for the grader to plow the runway and made sure the airport's navigational aids were operational. When Jack Randolph had called a couple hours earlier, Dale understood perfectly the meaning of his request for a "midnight special," a term coined thirty years before on the Grayling Platform in Cook Inlet where the two men worked together as roughnecks. No outsider would suspect the diminutive, soft-spoken gentleman with a Texas twang of holding court over Seward politics, but few people knew that Dale Minert was Jack Randolph's best friend. When Elliot and Jack ducked into the heated car Dale had waiting for them on touchdown, their smug grins of satisfaction—that unmistakable arrogance of invincibility—had returned to their faces. As they drove away, their silence communicated everything.

Off the runway, the fourteen inches of slush Jack had to navigate in the borrowed Malibu Classic proved to be a considerable challenge. As they drove past the cruise ship dock, even the elevated coal conveyor, which normally stood out like a giant praying mantis, was obscured by the blinding snow. The blinking hazard lights that identified its profile against the black sky were invisible.

"How the hell did we land in this shit?" said Elliot, pressing his nose against the tinted glass.

Since landing in Seward, Jack had tried several times to reach Marcus. His phone must be off or his battery dead, Jack concluded, because his own cell reception was fine. Jack had intentionally delayed alerting Marcus to his flight plan until his touchdown in Seward, which at the time of departure from Juneau was anything but certain. There was also Elliot's presence and confidentiality to protect. But if Jack were truthful with himself, his primary reason for stalling was a growing insecurity over his wife's fidelity. Rachel and Marcus were unreachable, and neither had made an effort to contact him. Jack's obsessive fears had him convinced that he would surprise them both and finally expose their relationship for what it was: a well-concealed love affair.

"How about some dinner before we check in, Elliot? My treat."

"Honestly, I prefer to be alone. Just drop me off at the Orca, and let me know when you connect with Marcus."

Jack turned discreetly to observe Elliot in the darkness. He seemed pensive, withdrawn, and his dismissive tone sounded almost resentful.

"You OK?" asked Jack.

"I'm fine, just beat. I'll be ready."

When Jack pulled up to the Orca, Elliot hesitated and pointed to a small group of people just leaving the lobby.

"Just give me a minute here. I want to sit tight until the lobby clears."

A few minutes later, Elliot pulled his high collar coat tight around his head and clutched his L.L. Bean travel bag to his chest.

"See you in an hour. I'll be at the Waterfront if you decide to join me," said Jack.

As he pulled away from the curb, Jack noticed a car approaching in his rearview mirror. The distinctive orange color and front-mounted snowplow identified the truck as a DOT maintenance vehicle, which Jack recognized instantly as the one leaving the airport only minutes before. He resolved to maintain a watchful eye as he turned left onto First Avenue and drove north back to the harbor.

The Waterfront Bar looks like a tattoo parlor with windows. Its flat roof and parrot-blue siding sticks out like a black man at one of Seward's several churches. The cedar shakes that trim the soffit are painted black, and the only decoration is a neon sign that says "BAR." It's the lone survivor of the Harbor Rim "upgrade" that created prefabricated miniature barns designed as part of a theme village. The smell of spilled beer, cigarette smoke, and grilled hamburgers invaded Jack's nostrils as he entered the old town bar.

Jack was comfortable in nightclubs, an ease acquired from many late nights in Juneau with the Corrupt Bastards Club, a brazen and cynical name for that nucleus of big shots who paraded around the Capitol in cocksure defiance of the public process. Tonight, however, Jack was tired, contemplative, and in no mood for conversation. He picked his way to a quiet corner surrounded by fake fica trees and mirrored-glass plaques advertising vodkas. His booth overlooked the small boat harbor, which now looked like a storage yard for dry-docked tour boats covered with puffy white shrink-wrap. The muted orange light from the high-pressure sodium lights reflected off the low clouds with a campfire-like glow.

"What can I getcha, young man?" asked the bartender. "Menu's short tonight. All we have is the prime rib sandwich. Been expectin' the power to go down all day."

"Double Crown, rocks."

Jack flipped his phone open and dialed Rachel. No answer. Then Marcus, same result. He nervously looked at his watch: 8:05 P.M. "Where the hell are you?" he grumbled to himself.

Jack scanned the side room, where two deckhands in hoodies and Xtra-Tufs were playing pool. In the far corner, partially obscured by a partition wall were two men huddled in quiet conversation. Jack fixated on the man in the leather coat and black Stetson hat. His huge frame, bushy eyebrows, and oversized glasses gave away his identity even at that darkened distance.

The man was Rick Fulton, the self-appointed president and founder of the Corrupt Bastards Club. He was conferring with Stuart Bond, president of the Alaska Senate and the son of Alaska's senior U.S. Senator. Jack's curiosity propelled him forward instinctively, in spite of his introspective mood. Jack was invisible to the two men as he approached, and he slowed his pace to observe their interaction.

"Rick, my friend, Stuart, what a surprise! I haven't been to Seward in twenty years and whadda ya know, I goddam bump into a couple of club members. What the hell brings you guys to this oasis of winter activity?"

Their mild irritation was barely detectable to Jack. All three men were masters of deception and bar-babble. Abrupt interruptions were common in their line of work, and the otherwise suspicious nature of their reunion was lost in the almost rote ritual of introductions.

"We actually just sat down, covering a little business, killing time waiting for the damn road to re-open. Dale over at Petro Marine is buying our Kuskokwim operation, and we're getting ready to close. USX is stealing my company from me, so I'm peeling off a few properties they don't want." After a short pause he added: "I'm buying, care to join us?"

Jack knew the invitation was disingenuous, a means of cutting the interruption short.

"I guess not, Rick. You guys look hard at it, but thanks."

"So what brings you to town on such a lovely evening for the first time in twenty years?" asked Stuart.

"Free drinks. Word all over town is that Rick's hosting," offered Jack, which he followed up with a gesture known only to the Corrupt Bastards Club as "The Bell Ringer." After a shared laugh, Jack sensed he needed better cover.

"Actually, Rachel was meeting me here for a quiet weekend in Seward, but the road closure prevented her from getting here."

Stuart and Rick looked at each other skeptically.

"You keep a close eye on that wife of yours, Jack, you lucky sonofabitch. I wouldn't make a habit of ditchin' that girl!"

Rick Fulton had been the first and hardest to fall, the king in the house of cards now crashing down. There was good reason for it. If Alaska's political elite could be compared to a crime family, then Rick Fulton was the godfather. He reigned supreme in the high-stakes game of Juneau influence peddling.

The expensive gifts he bestowed and the lucrative fundraisers he hosted did not violate Alaska's ethics laws, but they never passed the sniff test. For a decade or more, everyone knew what no one would openly discuss, let alone expose: that Alaska's legislature was corrupt and Rick Fulton was the kingpin. He bought senate votes favorable to his oil industry clients in exchange for jobs for the senator's family members, money, campaign contributions, even important committee assignments, which he brokered like over-the-counter stocks. In turn, he received lucrative contracts from Alaska's Big Three oil companies.

It wasn't clear if the raids on several legislative offices caused Rick Fulton's federal indictments or if his indictment precipitated the raids. It was all kept very secret. But Alaskans knew that Rick Fulton was now cooperating fully with the Department of Justice under a tell-all plea bargain that won immunity for his wife and family. It was the beginning of what was to become the most sinister chapter in Alaska's political history. Before it was over, one of the U.S. Senate's longest standing members would be convicted of ethics violations—almost entirely on the self-serving testimony of Rick Fulton. In an effort to ingratiate himself to the senator, or possibly to blackmail him, Fulton's company made improvements to the senator's rustic home that far exceeded approved scopes—and then drastically under-billed him. This was the backdrop to a corruption trial that ended in the conviction of Alaska's beloved senior U.S. Senator Bond.

Rick Fulton was perceived by most as a smooth talking roughneck, whose brazen tactics would inevitably result in an ignoble end. . He was certainly not someone with whom Jack wished to associate too closely, and yet he was still a man of considerable influence. Jack was not about to pick a fight or say anything to antagonize a man he knew was capable of falsifying testimony to a jury simply to even a score. Rick had cut his deal with the feds and his ties to the Corrupt Bastards Club. He was likely wearing an ankle bracelet, and there was no telling what he was doing with Stuart Bond.

Stuart was another tar ball altogether. Here was a young and successful politician who was in line to succeed his father in the U.S. Senate. His office was among those raided by the FBI a year earlier, but he had yet to be indicted. A description emerged from Rick's grand jury testimony of an anonymous "Senator S," which everyone acknowledged could only be Stuart Bond. Over the past year, investigative reporters had uncovered several undisclosed "consulting contracts," which Stuart could not produce work product for, amounting to hundreds of thousands of dollars. He had been waiting a year for the ax to fall.

"So I'm curious, guys," said Jack. "I overheard the bartender say something about big shots in town; he must have been referring to you guys, eh?"

"When you find the action, let us know, would ya? This town is dead," said Stuart. "I'm trying to get outta here just as soon as that damn road opens."

Feeling more relaxed, Jack took a more direct tack.

"Look, Rick, I may not get the opportunity to say this again, but I'm personally devastated by this whole ordeal. I wish there was something I could do. You've done a lot for Alaska and for our industry. I just want to say thanks. I can't imagine what you're going through."

"Well. Jack, I appreciate that, and since you brought it up, there is something you can do. We were just talking about it, but …"

Rick hesitated and glanced over at Stuart.

"Mind you, this is a chance meeting. There's no conspiracy here, OK? All we need are more surprises, right? Nobody's wired," said Rick.

Rick stared hard at Jack and continued.

"You can call off the dog!"

"Who the heck ..."

"Marcus! Reign in the sonofabitch! He's going out of his way to kick a few friends, OK? You're probably not aware of it, but his law partner Bill Brady is. Marcus is getting a little big for his boots, and he ain't winning any points with anyone by threatening Walter. I'll leave it at that."

Both men looked sternly at Jack, who suddenly went cold. He felt squeezed by what was likely a fabrication, at best hearsay, and precisely the fear tactics that Rick was famous for—tactics that made him an effective power broker even as he was going down. And yet Jack was as street sharp as they come.

"Rick, I have to say I'm shocked to hear it, but forewarned is forearmed. I appreciate the heads up. I'll look into it. Well listen, gents, I've got a few calls to make. I'm staying at the Orca Inn if you're up for a nightcap later."

"Will do, my friend," said Rick.

Stuart stood up to shake hands.

"Give me a call next week, Jack. I may be able to help you with your Endicott leases. If nothing else, I can share some intel on the EPA's impact study; we expect a favorable recommendation."

"I appreciate that, Stuart, but given everything that's going down, I don't see it getting out of committee," said Jack as he slammed his empty rocks glass down and turned away.

At that instant, the lights flickered and dimmed, then went

dark. Only a sliver of light came from the kitchen as Jack made his way past the bar and into the gripping darkness of the outdoors, an unsettling vacuum of light and life. Almost instinctively, in a defensive fear-reflex that had him momentarily disoriented, Jack turned to reenter the bar. The confined spaces of colored streaks and muffled sounds of voices and shuffling feet reminded Jack of the "Haunted Ship" that the Coast Guard hosted every Halloween in Homer. He glanced down at his quaking legs in disbelief, as if his acknowledgement would control the spasms. He stood there motionless in the darkness, unable to advance or retreat.

The sound of shattering glass sent him reeling backwards. He crouched down and covered his head as a deafening clatter of crashing pots and angry shouts erupted into a violent volley. Curiosity and panic gripped Jack as he listened for the familiar voices of Stuart or Rick.

A gunshot cracked open the dark chaos, followed closely by a second. The sounds were so loud and the flash so bright that it disoriented Jack. He stood up, convinced that he was the intended target of an assassination. As he turned away, a crushing wall of bodies hit him from behind, forcing him headlong into the steel exit door. Jack fell to the floor only half aware of the stampede of hard-soled boots that kicked and trod their way over his limp body. He gasped for air as the growing pig-pile of bodies sapped him of consciousness.

❧

Jack was awakened by the sound of his cell-phone ringing and a flashlight pointing down in his face. As he rolled over onto his back, the cold saturated clothing that pressed against his spine sent a shock wave through his body. He fumbled in the darkness for his Blackberry as he faintly heard a voice tell him not to move and that he had been shot and was lucky to be alive.

"Jack, this is Marcus!"

"Marcus, shit, I'm not sure what just happened. Where the hell are you?"

" I've ... stinkin' road for ... hours ... Reception ... nightmare!"

"Marcus, you're breaking up bad. I can barely hear you. Where are you now?"

"Lucky ... Moose Pass ... closed ... sure now ... Seward."

"Say again. I understand you're in Moose Pass, and the road is closed. When do expect to be here?"

"Can't ... here ... guarantee ... dangerous ... tomorrow."

The connection went dead, leaving Jack struggling to make sense of what he heard. Something didn't fit. Marcus' voice sounded excited, and yet he was stuck in Moose Pass, which could only be regarded as a disappointment—or perhaps a convenient excuse. Jack sat up in the entry and patted his body. His head was bleeding and he was drenched, but except for a few aches and bruises he was fine. He wasn't shot.

"Dude, are you all right? I was sure you were toast. Sit tight, man, I've got an ambulance coming," said the man with the flashlight.

"I'm fine, really. No need for that. Where is everybody?"

"We're it, dude, everyone else bailed. I have no freakin' clue what happened. The lights went out and the place went nuts. I thought for sure you were dead, dude."

"Look, whatever your name is, thanks for sticking around, but I had nothing to do with this. I have some personal business I need to attend to. I gotta go. Tell the cops whatever you want, but I ain't stickin' around, OK? I'll be fine."

"Whatever, man. I won't stop you, but I'm sure I'll be asked a few questions, ya know what I'm sayin'."

"Look, here's fifty bucks. It's dark, and besides, I never came into the bar. You never saw me in the bar."

Jack went straight to his car and redialed Marcus. No answer. He glanced at his watch—8:50 P.M. As he scraped the thick layer of snow off this car, Jack noticed the orange DOT truck parked across Second Avenue. It struck him as curious that no snow had accumulated on the vehicle. When Jack took a half-dozen paces toward the truck, it pulled away from the curb.

Ten minutes later, Jack was peering anxiously through the snowfall at the dimly lit facade of the Van Gilder Hotel. There was a stir of activity at the hotel entry as he watched from his parked car across Adams Street. Beams of red and gold light refracted through the stained glass lobby window, casting variegated tints of light into the dark corners and onto the tightly amassed smokers under the archway. Shadowy figures floated behind the sheer curtains of the library on the opposite side. With all the commotion, Jack wanted to be close enough to recognize a familiar face but far enough away to avoid detection.

After twenty minutes of his amateur stakeout, the sustained lull in activity had Jack curious. Now the hotel seemed almost deserted; no one came or went. The lights had dimmed. There was less risk in conducting a limited surveillance, he reasoned, as he pulled his overcoat collar around his ears and limped across Adams Street. At the least, he thought to himself, he would confirm that Walter Hayes was registered at the Van Gilder.

The driving rain provided the perfect excuse to skip any

acknowledgment of the guests and to keep his head down as he swept through the front door.

Once inside, the scene that met Jack was more mysterious than anything he was prepared for. The dim-lit corridor was in contrast to the other common areas of the hotel, which appeared completely dark save for a few candles. The figures he had detected through the veiled windows from across the street were still, and the hotel was strangely quiet and empty. A muffled voice came from his left as he inched forward to the lobby.

The scene was startling; floodlighted heads appeared to be huddled in prayer. Their glowing eyes were tiny searchlights probing the emptiness. To Jack, everyone seemed to be under a fearful spell, as if assembled in a bomb shelter waiting out an air raid. A woman with a flashlight was conducting a reading, and Jack stopped briefly to listen, his features barely distinguishable in the doorway. James rose to greet him, but Jack recoiled in a startled reaction.

"May I help you?" whispered James, "I'm the manager here."

"Uh … well … I'm not sure. Is Walter Hayes' here? I'm meeting him at ten."

"He is, may I tell him who's calling? I believe he was expecting you."

"Probably best if I join him at his room."

"Well, Sir, our privacy policy here prevents me from giving out room numbers. What I can do is call him and let him know who's here, or you can speak to him directly."

"No thank you. Don't bother him now. I'll be back at ten, but thank you."

"Can I tell him who called?" asked James.

"Marcus Coble. Let him know I'll be back at 10:00 P.M. Just out of curiosity, what's going on here?" asked Jack.

"A ghost story. Great night for it, don't you think?"

"I guess, but I think I'll pass."

Instead of exiting the hotel, Jack turned left and walked past the stairwell and the kitchen. With the light from the emergency floodlights, Jack read the history panels that lined the hall and the modest collection of antiques. This was Jack's first visit to the hotel, and he was impressed. James noticed his circumspect movements around the lower floor, but it raised no real alarms, so James redirected his attention to the ghost story.

Jack Randolph lingered in the corridor for a few minutes and then returned to his car, resolved to maintain a watchful eye on everyone coming and going. The power failure that until recently was confined to the port now enveloped the entire downtown area. Only faint beams of light glowed from within a few structures. The abrupt curtain of darkness and the eerie isolation of the street was unsettling to Jack; his nerves were still frayed from his near-death encounter at the Waterfront Bar. The complete blackout made it impossible for him to identify anyone from his vantage point, but he rejected the idea of moving closer to the hotel.

It occurred to Jack that the power outage was throwing his entire plan into doubt. Sitting alone in darkness, he felt nervous and exposed. The urge to move overcame his curiosity, and his best option was three blocks east to the Orca Inn. Now was an opportune time to check into the hotel, he concluded as he stepped cautiously onto the curb. While he was there, he would consult with Elliot on their revised circumstances.

When Jack arrived at the Orca Inn three minutes later, guests were gathered in the wildlife showroom sipping coffee. Furtively, Jack edged up to the counter and announced himself to the clerk.

"Reservation for Jack Randolph please."

The desk agent consulted his screen and mumbled to himself that he was sure he had double-checked all arrivals. After a minute of clicking computer keys and sorting through a stack of scattered folios, the desk clerk turned to Jack in confusion.

"I'm sorry Mr. Randolph, but I show you as already checked in. Did you reserve two rooms for tonight?"

Jack looked at the clerk blankly.

"No. I called a couple hours ago and reserved one room."

"The computer shows you checked into room 216."

"Well that can't be. I'm standing right here."

The clerk produced a registration card and thrust it in front of Jack, whose signature appeared at the bottom.

"Could that be your wife, maybe? It looks like she might have signed as Mrs. Jack Randolph."

Jack went cold. The suggestion numbed him and left him speechless. He gathered his nerve and decided to act forgetful.

"It sounds like Rachel, ever efficient and full of surprises. All I need is a key, and I'll be on my way."

"The computer shows we've issued two keys, which is all I am authorized to give out. Check in with your wife. If she doesn't have a key for you, I'll get my manager to authorize another key."

"Fine, room 216 you said?"

"Yes, Sir"

Jack's curiosity swept him forward impulsively. He halted half way up the dimly lit stairs and turned around. Panic overcame him as he thought about a surprise encounter. What if Rachel was not alone? How would he confront her? Impatience turned to anger. He turned and sprinted up the two flights of stairs.

As he approached room 216, Jack slowed his step and cocked his ear to listen. He knocked softly on the door, but there was no answer. He pressed his ear to the door and knocked a second time with more force. Not a stir. Jack paced the hallway in confusion. He grabbed his cell phone and dialed Rachel. His erupting curiosity demanded an answer. As Jack lifted the phone to his ear, a distinctive ring sounded in his other ear. This couldn't be happening, he thought, but it was Rachel's phone he heard coming from inside room 216. Jack snapped his phone shut, and the ringing stopped. He redialed. A cloud of despair swept over Jack as he heard the familiar ring of Rachel's phone through the door. He stood motionless for a minute agonizing over the implication that Rachel was definitely in Seward and that she was hiding her whereabouts from him.

As Jack paced the hall, he consulted an earlier text message from Elliot and rushed down one flight of stairs to Elliot's room. There was no answer, a surprise that added considerably to Jack's mounting anguish. Elliot had assured him that he would remain in his room until Jack called on him. Jack stood motionless in the hall, wondering what to do. Requesting a third key from the front desk would draw attention to his presence, an unwise move if he expected to surprise Rachel.

Jack looked at his watch. It was 10:00 P.M. He sensed that the growing mystery surrounding everyone's whereabouts had to be linked to Walter Hayes. When he located Walter, he speculated, he would locate the missing persons. He left the Orca Inn and hurried through the slushy snow to the Van Gilder Hotel, intent on locating Walter Hayes regardless of the circumstances.

## Chapter XI
*Friday, January 18, 10:02 P.M.*

**THE DARK SLOG UP THIRD AVENUE** to Adams Street made Jack uncomfortable. He quick-stepped with his head twitching, nervously scanning the alleys for strangers or the orange DOT truck that he was sure was following him. The entire downtown area was dark, except for a faint glow emanating from the Van Gilder.

As he crossed Third Avenue, Jack stopped in his tracks and stared at the soft light that shimmered and danced across the concrete parapet. He shivered at the ghostly images that confronted him. Strange, he thought to himself, how the surrounding area is so dark and lifeless and yet the hotel is so alive, like a spotlighted actor on a darkened stage. Instead of its typical cold stare, tonight the Van Gilder was warm, even welcoming. The apparitions that greeted Jack were not ominous but instead seemed to beckon him inside.

As Jack approached his vehicle, he was jolted from his spell by the restoration of power to the overhead streetlights. Several minutes later the exterior floodlights of the hotel snapped on, followed by the illumination of the Liberty Theater. Soon the entire downtown was bathed in the amber glow of high-pressure sodium light. The sudden transition was both relieving and unnerving to Jack as he stood there in front of the hotel exposed.

Just as Jack reached to open the door to his vehicle, an

ambulance and two police cars pulled up in front of the hotel without lights or sirens. He observed their movements closely and quickly decided to conceal himself in his car. Two more squad cars angled their vehicles across Adams Street, closing off traffic from the west. Jack could see that in a matter of minutes, he would be surrounded by a barricade of police cars, and he decided to attempt an early escape. His departing vehicle was detected by an arriving officer, who sprinted over on foot and motioned Jack to stop. The tiny police force descending on the Van Gilder implied something threatening was in progress, and if the speed and efficiency with which they worked was an indication of the threat level, it was significant.

The officer motioned Jack to roll down his window.

"Good evening, Sir, my name is Officer Cange. Were you in a hurry to leave?"

"Just moving out of your way, Officer."

"If you don't mind, I need you to back up and step out of your vehicle."

Jack turned off the car and reluctantly stepped out. "It's a tad nasty out, Officer. What's the problem?"

"Just a routine check. May I have your name, Sir?"

"Jack Randolph"

"How long you've been parked here?"

"Close to an hour now, I'd say."

"That's a long time to be sitting in weather like this. What are you doing here?"

"I've been trying to reach an associate of mine who was going to meet me here."

"And who would that be?"

"Really, unless this is of some urgency, I'd prefer to keep my business confidential".

"Mr. Randolph, it's of considerable urgency. Who were you meeting here?"

"Marcus Coble," said Jack reluctantly.

As the officer turned toward the unmarked car pulling up to the far curb, Jack could see the letters "FBI" on the back of another man's jacket. The realization that whatever was going on involved the FBI filled Jack with apprehension.

"And what is your business with him here, Mr. Randolph?"

"Officer, that's a matter of some privacy. I need to ask what's going on."

"Well, Sir, this is mostly routine at this point. We're investigating an accident at the hotel. Have you observed anything suspicious?"

"No, Sir. It's been dark and stormy, but otherwise nothing unusual."

"Have you been in your car the entire time?"

"Actually, no. I stepped into the Van Gilder for a few minutes. There was some kind of meeting going on in the lobby, so I left after a few minutes and came right back to the car."

"Did you see or speak to anyone while you were inside?"

"I met the manager, a short bald guy. I found the scene a little unusual for my taste though, so I left."

"How do you mean, Sir?"

"Costumes, candles, ghost stories. Can you tell me what this is all about? It appears a bit more than routine."

"What time would that have been, Sir, that you left?"

"Maybe thirty minutes ago, so around 9:40 P.M."

"Mr. Randolph, I've been asked to interview every person near the hotel. We're investigating a possible fatality, which is all I can tell you. We did receive a report of unusual activity outside the hotel. Do you mind if I search your car?"

"Be my guest!"

Officer Cange opened the passenger side front door and scanned the front seat with his flashlight. He leaned in to inspect the glove box, sorted through some personal clothing left on the seat, and turned to the back. His bright beam immediately revealed what looked like jumper cables laying on the back seat floor and a pair of black cotton glove liners. The officer opened the rear door for a closer inspection. The cables were cut off on one end, leaving the twisted copper leads bare and exposed. Before the officer had time to pose a question, Jack interjected.

"That's strange. I have no idea where those came from. I've never seen them before. They weren't there two hours ago."

"Are you sure about that?"

"Ninety percent sure, but this is not my car. I picked it up from a friend a few hours ago. They're not mine, I'm certain of that."

Officer Cange gingerly lifted up one glove, which was wet.

"How about these? Have you seen these before?

"No, Sir, I haven't."

"They're wet. How long did you say you were away from your vehicle?"

"Maybe fifteen minutes at the most, but that was the first time. Then I walked to the Orca Inn to register, so maybe thirty minutes altogether."

The officer made note of the expanding timelines that seemed to change under questioning. "Did you lock the car when you left?"

"Actually, no; I just realized I left the keys in the ignition. I had planned on being away only a few minutes, and I guess I wasn't too worried about someone driving off in this weather."

"It happens every day, Mr. Randolph. I'll need to see your trunk, please."

Jack was confused. He hadn't had time to reflect on the significance of events: the FBI, a fatality, and now unexplained articles in his car.

"Could I see your license and registration, please? I'll need to secure your vehicle and have you come with me."

Officer Cange quickly jotted down his findings. It was vital to gather as much information as early as possible, he knew, especially when a subject is cooperating or showing signs of restlessness.

"Mr. Randolph, I appreciate your need for privacy, but I'll need to know what your business is with Mr. Coble."

"Well, if you must know, Marcus was coming here to meet with Walter Hayes."

Officer Cange suddenly stopped writing and glanced over to the command trailer pulling into Adams Street. His surprise was visible, but before Jack had time to collect his thoughts, the officer continued: "Just a few more quick questions, and we'll get out of the weather. Was Mr. Hayes expecting you?"

"Yes. The meeting was arranged through my attorney, Mr. Coble, who was supposed to meet me here."

"Where is Mr. Coble now?"

"I have no idea. We talked this morning, but my cell reception here is poor, and I haven't been able to contact him. I thought he said that he was in Moose Pass and stuck behind an avalanche as of an hour ago."

"I see. When was the last time you saw or spoke with Mr. Hayes?"

"I haven't seen or spoken with him in weeks."

"One final question, sir: 10:00 P.M. seems a little late for a meeting. Why were you meeting with Mr. Hayes so late?"

"It was purely a social visit, Officer."

"If you'll follow me, Sir, I'll need you to remain in the command trailer while I get a field team over here to run through your vehicle. Do I have your permission to go ahead with that? You're not being charged with anything, Mr. Randolph, but we have some unexplained events, including some unclaimed personal items in your vehicle, which requires more investigation."

"Certainly, Officer. I'm as baffled as you are."

Jack grabbed his coat and bolted through the driving snow to the hotel entrance, which provided little shelter from the wind. The fact that Officer Cange didn't prevent him from retrieving his briefcase was a welcome sign, but the interruption to his plans was frustrating. The long and stressful day was taking a toll on Jack, and his patience was wearing thin. He was just entering the vestibule of the hotel when his cell phone rang. It was Marcus, who greeted Jack in a low whisper.

"Marcus, is that you?" said Jack. "I can barely hear you! Where the hell are you? I've been trying to reach you?"

"Jack, I'm at the Van Gilder Hotel. Look, I don't have much time. I'm here with the police. There's been an accident. Walter Hayes is dead!"

"Walter dead! Are you goddam kidding me!"

After a moment of silence, Jack added: "That explains what's going on down here. Listen, I could have a problem. Marcus, are you there?"

Nothing but a faint sound of breathing suggested to Jack that he had a connection.

"Marcus?"

Suddenly, Jack heard a commanding "FREEZE!" through the cell phone, so loud it seemed to emanate from the ceiling directly above him. Jack froze as he pressed the cell phone hard to his ear. In the windswept entry, the muted voices sounded tense but unintelligible. Officer Cange stiffened and looked around in an effort to pinpoint the location of the "Freeze" they both heard from overhead.

When Marcus finally came back on the phone, his voice was quaking.

"Jack, I can't talk now, I need to go."

"What the hell was that about, Marcus?"

"A misunderstanding with the police is all. I have to go."

Officer Cange looked at Jack for a fuller explanation of the call, but Jack just shrugged. Unsatisfied, Cange immediately dialed Chief Callahan.

"Chief, this is Officer Cange. Is everything OK? I heard someone yell 'freeze.' "

"Everything's fine. I'm pretty tied up; anything urgent?"

"I may need you down here. I'm holding a Jack Randolph for questioning. He claims he had an appointment with his attorney, Marcus Coble, and a Mr. Walter Hayes at 10:00 P.M. here at the hotel. He's in possession of a borrowed car, which has been parked in front of the hotel for over an hour and contains a couple articles he claims are not his and weren't there a couple hours ago when he picked the car up."

"Escort him to the command trailer and hold him there. I want a full statement including whereabouts over the last hour. Check the engine and tail pipe temperature. Seal the vehicle and get the lab on it. I'll be there in ten minutes."

Officer Cange signaled one of the FBI agents, and the two came to retrieve Jack from the hotel vestibule.

As Jack crossed Adams Street under escort by an armed policeman and an FBI agent, the gravity of the situation suddenly became clear to him. This could get messy, thought Jack, and his interrogation would be more than routine. As the full implications of Walter's death took hold, Jack exhorted himself to remain in control. His circumstances and initial interview with Officer Cange reflected poorly on him, he admitted to himself; and his commitment to confidentiality with Elliot Lawson and his ignorance of Marcus' and Rachel's whereabouts would complicate matters tremendously.

༺༻

Twenty minutes later, Chief Callahan lumbered into the mobile command office.

Jack rose instantly to greet him. "I hear that Walter Hayes was found dead; is it true?"

"Whooa there, oil man! I can see you like to get right to the point. But I'll do the asking for now if you don't mind."

"I'm sorry. I'm Jack Randolph," said Jack excitedly. "Walter was a close friend and client of mine. You can understand my concern."

"Your's and everyone else's, Mr. Randolph. I can't confirm anything for you at the moment, but I understand we have a few unexplained personal effects to talk about."

"We do. Do I need my attorney here?"

The chief did not respond, electing instead to quickly scan the report Officer Cange had just thrust in front of him. Jack Randolph was not being charged with anything, and the last thing the chief wanted was interference from a lawyer with his questioning. For his part, Jack sensed immediately he was not going to control the man or the situation.

"Let's start with when and how you arrived here," said the chief.

Immediately Jack was uncomfortable. This was typical of the questions that had been posed to him by Officer Cange; did "here" mean Seward or the Van Gilder Hotel? Jack resolved to keep his answers short and to get through the interrogation quickly.

"Roughly 9:00 P.M., in a car."

"A borrowed car, I see here."

"Yes, it belongs to Dale Minert."

"Were you alone?"

"Yes," he said as he glanced away.

"I understand you left the car for ten minutes when you went inside the hotel to look for Mr. Hayes."

"Correct, but I was looking for Marcus, not Walter."

"I see, and Mr. Coble had a 10:00 P.M. meeting with Mr. Hayes?"

"Correct."

"And the only person you met or spoke to in the Hotel was James Van Oss, the manager?"

"Correct."

"Did you by chance give Mr. Van Oss a different name than your own?"

"No. I may have mentioned Marcus' name as the person who set up the meeting or who Walter Hayes was expecting at 10:00 P.M."

"I see. Did you ask for Mr. Hayes' room?"

"I did. The manager said he could not give me that information."

"Where did you go after you left the lobby?"

Jack suddenly felt a cold chill run through his body as he contemplated his next answer.

"I hung around a few minutes, looking at the exhibits and then left."

"The general manager never saw you leave the hotel. He was seated at the door monitoring everyone coming and going. He said he saw you disappear down the hall toward the kitchen, but he never saw you return or leave. He figured you were waiting in the hotel for your contact to arrive or for the meeting to begin."

It became apparent to Jack that this was more than a casual interview. He was being treated as a potential suspect in a criminal investigation, and his answers would become his alibi.

"I don't have anything more to add. I left the hotel through the entry door ten minutes after I arrived—must have been close to nine forty-five."

"Were the hotel's interior lights on when you left?"

"I don't recall."

"And you did not lock your car, correct? And no one was with you?"

"Correct."

"You have no idea who the cables or gloves belong to, what they might have been used for, or how they got in your car?"

"No, I don't. I can't help you there. The car was parked outside the Waterfront Bar for an hour before I arrived here. It's possible someone could have placed them in the vehicle then."

"When were you at the Waterfront? Did anything unusual happen while you were there?"

"Pretty quiet actually. I must have left around eight-thirty.

"So you don't recall a fight breaking out, maybe hearing a gunshot while you were there?"

"Nope."

"Was your car locked while you were at the Waterfront?"

"I don't recall, but I don't think so. Chief, if you don't mind my asking, why so much interest in the cables? Are they somehow linked to Walter's death?"

"I have no idea—yet. I'm actually more interested in the gloves, and the fact that apparently someone went to the trouble of placing these things in your car."

At the instant that the chief was ready to release Jack, James Van Oss jumped into the trailer and brushed off a layer of wet snow. He looked at Jack and smiled.

"Hello! We met in the lobby. I guess you're not Mr. Coble after all, the guy with the appointment."

Jack straightened and responded in a decisive tone meant to discredit the account. "I'm the man you met, yes, but I'm Jack Randolph. Mr. Coble works for me. We were both to meet Walter Hayes here at ten. I'm sure you misunderstood me."

James turned to Chief Callahan and shrugged.

"It's possible. I'm sorry if I caused any hard feelings. I admit things have been a little crazy around here today," James offered with a forced smile.

"I'm glad we were able to clear it up," responded the chief.

"Chief, I know you're busy, but I have a guest who insists on seeing you. She claims to have important information that she will only share with you. Her name is Juliet Castellani, in room 106, down the hall on the right. She's a piece of work, I'll warn you. But I figure I had to pass it on."

"Thank you, I'll see her in a few minutes."

When James left, the chief turned to Jack.

"A couple more questions and we can wrap this up and get you on your way. You stated that you were to meet Mr. Coble here at 10:00 P.M. and then the two of you were to meet with Mr. Hayes."

"That's correct."

"That's why I'm puzzled. You see, Mr. Coble had no idea that you would be joining him. In fact, I just spoke to him and he was sure you were in Juneau. So there are a few loose ends to tie up here."

Jack was speechless. That the chief was able to gather this information in such a short time was miraculous. Jack himself was just learning the details of certain events, such as Marcus' whereabouts. There had been little time to sort it all out.

"That's true. I flew in from Juneau to join him. Hell, I didn't even know myself I was coming to Seward until a few hours ago. I knew Marcus was meeting Walter here, but we never had time to coordinate my change of plans."

"I see, so when I asked you how you arrived, a better answer might have been 'by private jet.' "

"I arrived to the hotel in a car, to Seward in a jet, how's that?"

"At what time?"

"Around 7:15 P.M., I think."

"And with the airport closed and a nasty storm brewing out there, this meeting must have been very important trip to you. And yet you described it as a social visit. Am I accurate on that?"

"Yes and no. There was no specific agenda, and I'm not going to hide the fact that Walter needed some urgent advice. But I have other business in Seward."

"Such as?"

"A number of things. I have business with the governor regarding BOC oil leases and with Dale Minert. Do I really need to go into it all now?"

"If your meeting was social, why didn't you simply announce

yourself to Mr. Hayes when you arrived at 9:40 P.M.? Why leave the hotel to wait outside in a cold car?"

"Marcus set the meeting up. We agreed Marcus would handle the appointment. So I was waiting for Marcus, not Walter."

"And you had no reason to surprise Mr. Hayes?"

"No. In fact, I believe Walter initiated the meeting. Marcus wanted to avoid attention for obvious reasons."

"One more question. It would seem that you had plenty of time to contact Mr. Coble between your 7:15 P.M. arrival time and the 10:00 P.M. meeting, and yet you mentioned that you didn't. Explain that to me. You flew all the way from Juneau for a critical meeting that Mr. Coble arranged, and yet he maintains you never tried to contact him. It all seems a little implausible. Or maybe there's something you're not telling me."

"Chief, I'm under no obligation to disclose my entire personal and business life to you. I'm a busy man. I have been busy with one thing or another from the time I landed until now, and I had little reason to confirm an appointment that Marcus discussed with me earlier today."

"Who can confirm your whereabouts between 8:30 P.M. and 10:00 P.M. tonight?"

"I left the Waterfront and came directly here, met the manager, and then walked over to the Orca Inn. I'm sure there is someone there who can confirm that."

"You told Cange you registered at the Orca around ten. There's quite a hole there you'll need to explain at some point."

"I spent most of the time waiting for the meeting alone in my car, unfortunately."

"The report here indicates you've been very cooperative. I

appreciate that Mr. Randolph; I'll let you go. However, I'll need to keep your vehicle for the weekend."

"I understand, although it's not my vehicle, as I said."

"I'll see you tomorrow then," said the chief as he exited the trailer.

# Chapter XI
## Friday, January 18, 11:25 P.M.

**WHEN JULIET OPENED THE DOOR** to room 106, the chief felt uneasy at once. The smell of incense and soft music emanating from the room was enough to stall his progress, but Juliet's sheer nightgown and playful smile introduced an entirely separate set of concerns.

"Good evening, Officer. I'm Juliet Castellani. Please come in."

"Thank you, Ma'am; I just have a minute. A few people are still waiting on me. I understand you may have some information."

"I do ... Officer ..."

"Mike Callahan, Chief of Police."

"Well, Chief, are you a spiritual man?"

"Not particularly, no."

"A man in your line of work should be, I think."

Juliet turned away from the chief and retrieved a perfect sand dollar from her nightstand.

"Do you know what this is?" she asked.

"Sure, it's a sand dollar."

"I found it on the second floor landing just before your team arrived."

"And what does this have to do with tonight's events, Ms. Castellani?"

"Please call me 'Juliet.' I believe it was left behind by a witness to a potential crime."

"You have my attention ... Juliet."

"Before you write me off as a loon, let me ask you something. Do you ever develop a hunch in your detective work, a sixth sense about things?"

"I'm trained to follow the facts, not to invent them. I develop theories on every case, but I check them against the evidence. I don't have the luxury of consulting spirits, if that's where you're going with this."

"You know about the tortoise, which out of steady mind and purpose beats the hare in a footrace. But in the journey of self-discovery, who wins?"

"I'm not following you," said the chief with obvious impatience.

"By his slow pace, the tortoise is able to observe more closely, and he is more likely to understand what he observes."

"If you have information that will help me solve a crime, I need to hear it straight up. Who witnessed what and how did you come into this information?"

"I believe the crime was witnessed by Fannie. Why do I think this? Because I had a visit from her just before everything happened."

The chief looked down, then straight up at the ceiling.

"If you don't believe me, ask James. He'll tell you I warned him. My evidence is that she left this sand dollar behind. As you can see, it's unusual and perfect."

"Who is Fannie?"

"Fannie Guthry-Baehm."

The chief looked blankly at Juliet.

"You're kidding, you've never heard of Fannie? You would call her a ghost, but she's the spirit who resides here at the hotel. Don't pretend you don't know what I'm talking about, please!"

"And you think she left this seashell. What is the significance of it?"

"I'm just getting to know her, but Fannie visits those with evil intentions in their heart. She seeks to deter criminals of conflicted conscience before their act, not to exact punishment or revenge."

"OK, and what about the seashell?"

"She hands the shell to the person she hopes to influence and reform. I believe it represents the simple beauty found within us. Our natural purity, so to speak, is perfect until we become corrupted by our temptations—our choices. I believe Fannie can distinguish between those of genuine remorse and those who are beyond reform simply by how they observe a seashell. If Fannie's subjects reject her, the seashell materializes and is left for us to find."

"I appreciate your help, Juliet. Is there anything else you can tell me?"

"You think I'm crazy, don't you?"

"I didn't say that. I did say that in my line of work I don't have the luxury of consulting spirits."

"And that's why you need me. I want to help you, Chief."

"Let's keep the lines of communication open. I appreciate all the help I can get. If anything else comes up, please call this number."

Juliet recognized a superficial gesture of gratitude. Mike was a nice man she thought, but a skeptic, which was regrettable because everything she had heard about him suggested he would not be quick to judge her. Juliet looked into Mike's eyes and raised her hand to his face.

"Forgive me for getting personal, Mike, but I see something in you that begs for forgiveness. You are an honest man with inner strength, but you are not at peace. Do you ever pray?"

"Juliet, I really need to go. Can we continue this at another time? It's getting late, and I've got lots of folks to see yet."

"Certainly; I'm sorry if I upset you."

The chief had turned rather suddenly and was half way through the door when Juliet called to him.

"You will find what you're looking for on the second-level fire escape."

The door shut behind the chief without any hint of acknowledgment that he had heard her advice.

When the chief entered the library, the animated conversation between Jack and Marcus ended abruptly. Since their morning phone conference, this had been the two men's first opportunity to interact. In spite of what should have been welcome news, Walter's death had both men on edge.

"I understand we're free to go, Chief?" asked Marcus.

"You are. I've got your statements and your contact information. I understand you're both staying at the Orca Inn?"

Marcus looked at Jack for confirmation, which was not forthcoming.

"I haven't checked in yet," said Marcus. "Jack, how about you?"

"I'm all set."

"I've got a few loose ends here, Gentlemen, so I'll have a patrol officer drive you to your hotel. I'll need you both to stick around tomorrow until I can wrap up my investigation."

"No other restrictions?"

"None. You're free to travel within Seward. I'll call you if I have something. Sergeant Graham will meet you out front in ten minutes."

The chief radioed Graham to arrange the escort, but at that moment he needed Graham to meet him at the back fire escape. As he walked away, the chief heard the earlier argument resume between Marcus and Jack. From what little the chief could decipher, Marcus was vigorously defending his rendition of what was said during an earlier phone conversation.

"I don't know where you got that. I said fifty-fifty whether I could meet him tonight or tomorrow. It's a moot point now."

When the subject changed, the chief was far out of earshot.

"I still can't reach Rachel," baited Jack. "Do you have any idea where she could be?"

"I spoke to her briefly this morning, but she had nothing planned. I assume she's home."

"I'm worried about her," said Jack.

"She's fine, I'm sure. Look, we need to focus on this Hayes business. We should get in touch with Elliot Lawson and the governor right away. The way I see it, everything works to our favor, but you seem upset. What's eating you?"

"Nothing, except that I appear to be their prime suspect."

"It'll pass, Jack. But what the hell do you think happened?"

"I have no idea."

"You seem preoccupied with something; what's on your mind?"

"Just a bit distracted by events, but I do need to ask you something. I ran into Rick Fulton. He mentioned something about you pissin' on Walter. It sounded pretty recent and harsh. Any idea what he's talking about?"

"You're kidding me? Fulton's an asshole! You know better than to believe that lying toad, Jack. You know what's going on?

For Christ's sake, we offered to bail the guy. Two weeks ago, Walter came to my law office looking for a hand out, asking what he could expect from BOC in the way of help. I wasn't there, and it sounded urgent to Bill, so he met with Walter.

"Walter basically told my partner that I had created exposure for the firm and for BOC. Bill asked for specifics, and apparently Walter produced an invoice we paid to Representative Van Fleet for flooring work that was never done—and that he now tells me was never expected to be done. It's bullshit."

"It doesn't sound too clean."

"Bill showed me the invoice. It was a scam, Jack. No check copy, no signatures, no nothing! Just a blank invoice that I supposedly paid in cash. I admit I got a little wound up, but the whole thing was fabricated. That's the full story, there's nothing more to it."

"Damn it! Don't you think this was important information for me to have before going into a showdown with Walter?"

"First, you never told me you were coming. Second, if I brought every minor scheme like this to your attention you would fire me. I never expected Walter to bring it up again. It was bullshit, nothing more than a distress call with penny-ante extortion added as leverage."

"I trust you contacted our accounting to confirm nothing was ever paid."

"Trust me, we have no exposure there. That was Rick Fulton's deal; he funded the pre-election poll."

"Are there any other lurking deals like this I need to know about?"

"Look, you can't worry every time you hear someone running on about our potential exposure on these deals."

"The media's going to eat these scandals for breakfast. We'll both be asked lots of questions about our client relationship with Walter Hayes, and I want to be ready."

"We're ready. "I've … we've got nothing to hide," said Marcus.

"It's curious Bill never mentioned anything to me about the Van Fleet invoice," said Jack. "He called last week and asked if I was satisfied that Brady & Coble was handling everything satisfactorily. He sounded concerned, but now it makes sense."

"Bill's been on edge lately. He's not as active as he used to be, and he's nervous about these indictments and the future of the firm. He knows I'm thinking of leaving and probably thinks I'm bailing on him, saddling him with a bunch of problems. He's tight with Rick Fulton, so who knows what the hell that guy told him. I'll get it all out on the table Tuesday when we meet, but don't stress about it."

Before the two could conclude their consultation, two police officers arrived in an unmarked car to escort them to the Orca Inn.

※

On the opposite side of the Van Gilder, to the north, a driving snow rendered the outdoor investigation a very unpleasant task. On schedule, Graham arrived in the parking lot of First National Bank with two FBI agents.

"Chief, meet Agent Raney and Agent Wills. No official word on cause of death yet, but we're moving the body to the lab now, and they assure me they'll have a report for you in the morning."

"Good work, Sergeant."

The chief extended an introductory handshake to the two new team members as he spoke.

"Welcome to paradise, Gentlemen!"

"Graham, tell your escort that I want Randolph and Coble tailed and any movements reported immediately. After they check in, accompany them to their rooms. We don't have warrants or cause, but I want their rooms swept for evidence. I'm interested in their personals and anything out of the ordinary."

"Will do, Chief. If that's it, I'll seal 201 and join the guys at the Orca Inn."

"I'll want the lab report back on Mr. Randolph's car tonight. Before you go, brief these guys on what you discovered on the backside here, particularly the fire escape and roof."

Graham reviewed his earlier findings with the pair of FBI investigators, and then asked for questions. Agent Wills scanned the back of the building, which was dimly lit by one streetlight. He pointed to the Van Gilder's north facing elevation.

"Focus on the lower right corner there," the chief said to the three of them, "and tell me if you notice anything out of place."

The three experienced investigators looked intently at the scene, unable to discover the answer.

"Take a look at the main distribution panel there," said the chief. "Notice anything?"

A second, more focused look elicited the expected response from all three. Every imaginable surface of the hotel, including railings, conduit, even window mullions, had a vertical stack of snow in varying heights rising from their surfaces. The main disconnect on the main distribution panel, a small five-inch wide red-handled bar, was completely bare of snow.

Agent Wills indicated he had known about the electrical failures and investigated the electrical panel as soon as he arrived, about ten minutes before. At that time the footsteps leading to the panel were heavily drifted, but from what he could discern, they matched those coming down from the fire escape.

"Agent Raney, let's get a fix on the exact time power was restored to the hotel," said the chief. "Find out if Chugach Electric had any teams in the vicinity that might have touched that panel. I'll check with the manager. Agent Wills, let's get those cables and gloves from Jack's car to the lab. See if you can get some kind of match from the rope or ladder rungs. Can you guys think of anything we're missing?"

"No surveillance cameras in use. No alarms on the corridor exits, in spite of what's posted."

"OK, let's reconvene in one hour. Graham, don't forget about Mr. Randolph's escort," said the chief as he headed for the fire escape.

Despite his total skepticism of Juliet's reference to a clue on the fire escape, the evidence was leading him in that direction anyway, and he resolved to have a sharp eye.

The moist winter air mass from the Gulf of Alaska had moved through Seward. The temperature was warming and the snowflakes now fell in dime-size clusters of damp cotton. As the chief carefully navigated the narrow fire escape, he cast his floodlight down into the foot thick snow. He didn't know precisely what he was looking for and expected the effort would be futile, but he crouched low and illuminated the shadows cast by wood-framed stairs.

When he reached the second-level landing, a steel grate had allowed most of the accumulated snow to fall through, leaving only an inch of well compacted snow. A small item caught his attention, all but invisible except for the tiny refraction of light that beamed back into his eyes. He bent down and carefully extracted by its edges a plastic magnetically encoded key-card. On the front were small black letters: "Seward Orca Inn." The chief radioed his FBI team to return to the back fire escape and requested an immediate acid print scan.

"Given the conditions, I don't expect you'll find prints. But as soon as the lab is done, I want Agent Fell to get over to the Orca Inn and find out everything he can about that key."

"I'm on it. Give me thirty minutes," said Agent Wills.

The chief walked directly back to room 106 and knocked softly on the door. This time, he thought to himself, he needed more information, and he would rely on different tactics to get it.

"What a surprise," said Juliet as she opened the door. "I expected you but not so soon. You found something of interest, or perhaps you're here for some other reason?"

"I have some police business to discuss, Ms. Castellani. Do you have a few minutes?"

"Please, call me 'Juliet.' So I was I right, you found what you were looking for."

"I can't share certain information with you; you probably know that. But what exactly was I suppose to find?"

"I see how this is going to be, no different than a thousand other dances I've been to."

"Pardon me?"

"Never mind. The answer is I don't know. Not everything I receive is always clear."

"How were you so sure I would find evidence on the back fire escape, unless maybe you placed it there yourself?"

"You know, I hardly know whether to laugh or cry. You people are pathetic. Here I am trying to help you, and you actually accuse me of planting evidence."

"I didn't come here to pick a fight. I'm just asking for a reasonable explanation."

"Let me guess. You want to indulge yourself in fantasy behind the safety of closed doors, where no one can see you and judge you and, God forbid, maybe criticize you?"

"No. I came back because I deserve a straight answer. I'd also like to get to know you better. You saved that baby killer whale, didn't you, in spite of what was in the press release? I'd like to hear more about how you did that—more about your healing powers."

"You're funny, Mike. Powers! You say that like I am superwoman. We all have gifts, an energy field that connects all living things. It is not a power as you perceive it. It is a way of living, a way of perceiving our purpose in this life. It is a way of understanding."

"Well I would like to learn more about …"

"Lead with your heart, not with your head, because your mind will trick you. Our ego demands that we capture things and possess them. We even hide things in order to make them our own. Your investigation is really nothing more than a search for truth, is it not?"

"In a way, yes."

"Do you remember that ancient shell game with the dried pea and walnut shell?"

"I used to be quite good at it, in fact."

"Well, you are in such a game now, seeking a pea of truth hidden from your view. Like the gullible gamblers who bet their money, you watch intently and marvel at the furious shuffle of the walnut half-shells. Your ego demands an ordered response and persuades you to follow the trail of trickery. You snatch up the first shell using reason. But when your head fails to solve the riddle, your passion swells, and you grab at a second shell in desperation. As you move to lift the final shell in a fit of angered resignation, your hand is clamped by the magician, and the confirmation you were seeking eludes you. Does this sound familiar?"

"Sure, although I was never the fooled; I was the man with the magic."

"Then you know what I am trying to say. The gambler admits that he does not know the trick and insists on another round. The profit-minded magician never reveals his secret, but you and I know that the pea was never there to begin with."

"What are you saying? That I'm wasting my time looking for evidence—or looking for it in the wrong place?"

"I mean to say the answers you seek are not hidden from you."

"But they are not visible to me either."

"There are examples everywhere of real objects that are not visible to you. The molecules of air you breathe are theoretical. Just because the dried pea is not under the walnut shell does not make it imaginary."

"But if I abandon my search for facts, then I have no means of convincing others, for example a jury, that someone committed a crime."

"Don't take everything so literally. Each shell is only a metaphor. You are not abandoning your quest for facts. Let me put it this way: I cannot use a vision of mine to persuade a jury. But I can use it to locate a tumor in a human body that might otherwise go undetected. Once I find it, I can extract it, and the healed body should be the only evidence the jury needs."

"You say 'should be'; I wish it were that simple."

"Now you understand what I live through on a daily basis. For every person who believes me, there are a thousand who think I belong in a psychiatric institution."

"I think I understand. It is not the act of searching that leads me away from the answer but my lack of understanding about where to search for it."

"Precisely, or perhaps where not to search for it. If you knew that the pea existed, even if you could not immediately prove it, you would not be inclined to engage so frivolously in proving its existence."

"I still have a nagging technicality called tangible evidence. Convincing a jury is more than a matter of faith."

"Everything starts with faith, Mike, but it does not end there. The system may temporarily control the verdict and the outcome, but it cannot control our minds. There is a connection that binds our heads to our hearts and to our souls in a unity that knows no deception, no transgression of one upon the other. I call it *Teleos*, in honor of the Greek derivative for "perfection," which emphasizes less the substance of perfection than the purpose of it."

"Go on."

"Discovering Teleos is not unlike detective work; it requires training, discipline, a great deal of luck and a lot of error."

Mike stood patiently absorbing her every word. It had been fifty years since his grandfather had spoken to him of the spirits that occupied the living world and that one day would bring destruction upon the White Man. The Choctaw had a deep respect for all living things, for the order and purpose of existence. The shaman who summoned the spirits of the afterlife was the most respected elder of the tribe, and Mike Callahan had never renounced this part of his heritage. However, he could not thrive within the shrinking community of old believers, and he left the reservation for California at an early age. He often regretted that his police work led him away from the spiritual connections of his youth. Juliet was touching an emotional chord that Mike had long forgotten, and his re-awakened curiosity was reassuring to Juliet.

"There is a thin line between faith and knowledge, Mike."

"I'm not sure I agree. In my business, they are distinctly different."

"Ah, but ask me if I have faith in Fannie's existence, and I reply that I know her. Ask a devout man if he has faith in his prophet, and he will reply that he has evidence of his works."

"We operate in different worlds in so many ways."

"How so? Do you believe that juries render decisions based solely on the facts? Or that judges rule consistently on the basis of a fixed system of justice? I'm not that naïve."

"It's the best system we have. I admit it's not perfect."

"Many believe our soul is the separation of our spiritual being from our physical being that occurs upon our death. To say that everyone has a soul is like saying everyone has eyes—it matters how the soul is used, what it reflects from within. Your eyes tell me much about you, Mike. You have a soul, a purpose. But you have deep sadness too. You have yet to discover your purpose."

The chief's cell phone rang, but he quickly silenced it and prodded Juliet to continue.

"Our soul acts like glass. It is transparent, and yet under the right light it will reflect an image like a mirror. The energy that our minds and bodies produce is redirected onto others so that they can see it and feel it, and in rare cases be healed from it. If the energy is harnessed for supreme virtue, then a soul emerges.

If the energy is not harnessed, then light passes through undetected as though nothing is there. The mirror is glass, and the escaping light defies the prism that is our soul. It becomes diffused, undetectable."

"So when you have visions, what do you see?"

"Mostly static to be honest. The forces of light and darkness are always at work within us and require constant tuning. It takes concentration, but the dark matter is filtered by a purity of purpose. What is revealed is a collage of tiny light cells, which is nothing more than a collection of souls. That is one thing I have learned recently. A single soul rarely generates enough light to form a spirit; it must touch another, and another. The more one touches, the more likely it is to form an image. The most powerful images that I experience start as giant smoke rings. It is amazing to behold."

Mike stared at Juliet in a distant way that evoked her trust. He recalled the legend of the boy-eagle, who as a young brave pleaded with his grandfather to join the other warriors in battle. The boy was told "no" but that he could help his older brother by summoning the eagle-spirit, whose sharp eyes would protect the braves from their enemy and lead them to the enemy. That night around the fire, amidst the rising columns of smoke, the boy disappeared before his grandfather's eyes. He was lifted high into the night sky, the spiraling rings of white smoke silhouetted against the new moon, rising higher and higher until the rings dissipated into the form of an eagle. The next day, the warriors followed the eagle over a great distance and surprised the enemy in a great victory.

"The only difference between me and you, Chief, is that I have no need for the protective armor that you require for your job."

"The greatest warriors need none," said the chief.

"We each have unique gifts but few of us learn to master them. You have gifts, Chief; I can see them. But you must … never … forget …"

Juliet's voice trailed off as though she was momentarily distracted.

"I thank you for your help," said the chief. "But I do need to ask you a few more questions."

"Certainly."

"I'll warn you; I'm looking for peas and clues."

"You're hopeless!" said Juliet laughing. "Go ahead!"

"Where were you between 9:00 P.M. and 10:00 P.M. tonight?"

"I was in the lobby indulging in fairy tales. James knows me well and will vouch for me. I never left."

"Did you see any suspicious behavior among any guests in or around the hotel at anytime tonight?"

"Most people I meet are suspicious, either walking con-jobs or afraid of their own shadow."

"Let's say anything out of the ordinary?"

"Then no."

"Did you see anyone tonight on the fire escape—or entering or exiting the hotel through the fire escape doors?"

Juliet hesitated and then spoke in a reluctant drawl.

"I didn't, but Fannie did. The image from Fannie is not clear to me. Someone who I cannot identify used the fire escape."

"I heard you reference the fire escape as I was leaving earlier. What exactly am I looking for?"

"You will know when you find it, Chief."

"Juliet, I'm a cop. I've always been a cop, probably always will be. I find criminals and bring them to justice. I enjoy our talks and respect your special gifts, but I need you to respect what I have to do. Withholding evidence to a potential homicide is a felony. I need you to tell me everything that you know, without the cat-and-mouse."

Mike's matter-of-fact reference to a homicide was intentional, a closely guarded theory at this point that was intended to arouse a reaction from Juliet.

"Mike, if you had not found anything, then you would not be so eager with your question. Secondly, I came to you, remember? I am not withholding anything. I have told you what I know, and it upsets me that you would think I am playing games with you. I don't do that."

"Everything?"

"Yes …well … actually, not everything. Not everything I receive is clear. I have told you what is clear to me. The rest could come over time or may never come. Like anyone, I must be worthy of receiving Teleos. You on the other hand will receive only what evidence there is to see or touch."

"I'm not sure I follow you."

"Fannie Guthry-Baehm. If you do not believe she exists, how or why would she reveal herself to you? If you do not believe me, then what I tell you is subject to a truth test. Do you not see why you will never discover the truth? You want evidence, but what of those things that cannot be touched? Are they not real, or are they just not perceived to be real?"

"What does that have to do with you telling me everything you know?"

"It has everything to do with it. You ask, but you do not receive because you ask wrongly. Even if you pretend to inquire honestly, you do not hear the answer, let alone heed it. So why do you waste my time?"

"Waste your time?"

Mike was becoming frustrated, but he checked himself and decided to take a more sympathetic approach.

"Please understand and appreciate what I'm trying to do here. My job is to protect innocent people. I have to work with many different personalities to do it. My personal beliefs, my religion if you want, cannot …"

"Mike, I am on your side. I am trying to help you."

"Then please, I am asking for your help."

"Do you ever feel as though your endless quest for facts drives you farther away from the truth?"

"I admit that my profession leaves me empty at times, yes, but this is what I do."

"A Little Prince once said that it is only with our hearts that one can see rightly, for what is essential is invisible to the eye."

"Juliet, trust me, I know what you're trying to say, but the evidence I am after is not invisible. It could help us solve a potential murder."

"Let's leave it at this, Mike. I know nothing. From this moment on, I will tell you what Fannie is revealing to me. It is Fannie who will lead you. Then you can—as they say in your business—follow her or get the hell out of the way!"

Mike did not receive this as any sort of provocation but as a signal that Juliet was likely just as she appeared to be—a mentally imbalanced personality who may not be above self-promotion and opportunism. It occurred to the chief that Juliet may well have planted the card key on the fire escape.

"Have you ever stayed at the Orca Inn, Juliet?"

"Three weeks ago, the first night I arrived in town."

"Do you recall what room you were in?"

"Room 316, the cheapest room they had."

Mike's phone rang.

"Juliet, I need to take this call. Thank you, and I'll see you tomorrow."

Agent Fell picked up with the chief quickly.

"Negative on the card prints, clean, no residue of any kind. I'm at the Orca Inn right now checking on who the key was issued to and when."

"When you check in with the desk, locate the room number for Juliet Castellani; she stayed there for one night about three weeks ago."

"Will do, Chief."

## Chapter XII
*Saturday, January 19, 12:15 A.M.*

**WHEN SERGEANT GRAHAM** pulled up to the Orca Inn, Jack and Marcus were just entering the lobby. From Graham's vantage point, it was obvious that the two men were uncomfortable with their armed police escort and were intent on evading them. The quick handshakes he observed were a gentle rebuff, a hint to their escorts that they were no longer welcome company.

Graham exited his vehicle, signaled the agents that he would be replacing them, and fell in line behind Marcus undetected.

"Marcus Coble and Jack Randolph checking in," said Marcus to the desk clerk.

Jack leaned over the counter and quietly corrected Marcus.

"Actually, I'm checked in, but I misplaced my key. I'm in room 216."

"May I see your identification again, Sir?" asked the clerk. "I take it you weren't able to connect with your wife."

Jack produced his driver's license to the clerk, who had a key waiting in exchange.

"What?" asked Marcus turning to Jack. "Rachel is here?"

Jack shot a stern look of disapproval at Marcus.

"We'll see," Jack said dismissively as he turned to leave.

"Excuse me, Mr. Coble could you please sign here?" asked

the clerk, who was oblivious to the growing tension. "Up two flights of stairs and turn left."

"I'm tired, Gentlemen; I'll see you all in the morning," said Jack, tipping an imaginary hat toward his escorts.

"I couldn't help but overhear the conversation at the desk, Mr. Randolph. Your wife is here with you, is that right?" asked Sergeant Graham, ignoring Jack's attempt to depart.

"To be perfectly honest, I have no idea where she is. You might ask Marcus." As soon as Jack uttered the cynical remark, he realized his mistake. "Yes, I am here with my wife, and all I want is a little privacy."

Sergeant Graham detected the sarcasm and the tension, which exposed another surprise.

"She planned to meet you here then?" he said to Jack.

Marcus looked perplexed.

"With due respect, Officer, I have no idea what business that is of yours," said Jack.

"Given today's surprises, anything unexpected is our business."

"Well, I'm sorry to disappoint you, but a surprise visit from my wife is hardly cause for investigation," said Jack in disgust.

"I also heard you say to the clerk that you lost your key. You might be interested to know that Chief Callahan just called, and he's on his way here. He found an Orca Inn key on the fire escape of the Van Gilder. Any chance it's yours?"

"None!" said Jack confidently.

"We'll know soon enough. In the meantime, I've been instructed to inspect your rooms. It would be easiest on everyone if we have your cooperation."

Jack turned sharply to deliver a stern objection, but before he could respond Marcus intervened.

"Jack, it's in everyone's interest to clear this up as quickly as possible. I recommend we let Sergeant Graham do what he needs to do, and then we can all get some rest."

Visibly frustrated but unable to muster a defense, Jack simply motioned the others to the stairs. "After you, Sergeant," he said, cutting in front of Marcus.

As he climbed the stairs, Jack was hopeful that Rachel would still be absent from the room. Worst case, he reasoned, a surprise encounter with his wife might produce a little embarrassment but nothing incriminating. For the moment, his deepest regret was that Marcus and Rachel's likely reunion had managed to escape detection. In reality, the uncertainty of current events had both men in a state of psychological vertigo. Each man felt like an actor dragged forward by an impromptu script. Nothing felt real as they approached room 216.

"May I have your key, Mr. Randolph?" demanded Sergeant Graham as he reached for his weapon. He motioned the two men to stand back. Following protocol, Sergeant Graham straddled the door and knocked heavily.

"Seward Police, open the door!"

Within seconds, a woman cracked the door, with the barrel lock firmly deployed.

"Everything's fine here, Officer, what can I do for you?"

Sergeant Graham presented his badge and commanded the woman to open the door. After an initial pause, Jack stepped forward into Rachel's view.

"It's OK, Rachel. Please do as he says."

"Oh, my God, what ... ?"

Rachel stopped herself, peering through the crack in dismay. She flipped open the barrel lock and stepped back into the room. Her silk robe and towel-wrapped head suggested she had just showered. The fear that registered on Rachel's face betrayed a guilt that Jack had never seen before.

"Jack, I ... I don't know what to say. I was worried about you. I had to come."

Rachel searched Jack's eyes for sympathy, but she could see only anger and resentment. In a gesture of reconciliation, Jack extended his hand to Sergeant Graham and smiled.

"I appreciate your concern, Sergeant, but as you can see, there's nothing sinister going on. My wife arrived unannounced, but this is a really a private matter. Can we be alone?"

With a prompt intended to hasten their joint departure, Jack turned to Marcus and asked him to accommodate the officer's questions fully, but somewhere else.

"I'll meet you outside in a few minutes, Mr. Coble. I need a few minutes alone with the Randolphs," said Sergeant Graham. "I'm going to ask you not to enter your room until I can accompany you."

"Your call Jack. You have the right to have me present for questioning if you choose to," responded Marcus as he grabbed his handbag.

"We'll be fine, Marcus."

Sergeant Graham closed the door and turned to Rachel.

"It will save everyone time if we do this now while we're all together. Do you mind if I ask you both a few questions?"

"Actually, Sergeant Graham, we do mind. My wife and I would like to be alone."

Sergeant Graham was not about to let the opportunity slip away. He sensed confusion among the party, which his twenty-eight years of police investigation had taught him needed to be acted upon immediately. Conducting an interview before a suspect could synchronize his story was essential to discovering the truth, and in this case a joint interview would suit his purposes well.

"I understand your frustration, Mr. Randolph. You've had more than your share of surprises tonight. This will only take a minute."

Sensing a loss of advantage, Jack protested vigorously. "We're under no obligation to answer any questions. Marcus is my attorney, and I would rather you deal with him."

"I can make this easy for you or very difficult. The choice is yours. I recommend that you cooperate with us, given Mr. Hayes death and several unexplained events that concern you directly. I'll be quick and to the point."

"I vehemently object to this intrusion, but go ahead."

Before Graham could begin, Rachel spoke up. Her forceful personality was complemented by a steady nerve. She sensed the need and the opportunity to seize the offensive, which she was able to do with genuine surprise.

"Did you say Walter Hayes is dead? Maybe someone should start by telling me what the hell is going on. What unexplained events? Why is he here, Jack?"

"Mrs. Randolph, I don't believe I've formally introduced myself. I'm Sergeant Graham, and I'm investigating what we think was an accidental death. This is just routine follow-up. When did you arrived in Seward?"

"Just before I checked in, about 6:00 P.M."

"You drove in from Anchorage?"

"I did."

"Did you come alone?"

"Yes."

"You said you came to be with your husband. Is that correct? Did you have any other business here?"

"That's correct, and no, I had no other business."

"Your husband told Chief Callahan that his trip to Seward was unplanned, that it wasn't until 5:00 P.M. tonight that he made the decision to fly here. So I'm curious why you drove to Seward to join your husband when Jack hadn't even made the decision to come to Seward until sometime after you left."

Rachel was quick witted and adept at bending the truth. Her practiced smile was not honed to hide the truth as much as it was to win the friendship and favor of her audience.

"I was worried about my husband, OK? Is there a crime in that?"

"No, but it doesn't answer my question."

"Jack was secretive about his plans, but I knew Marcus was trying to meet Walter in Seward. I assumed, maybe wrongly, that Jack was planning to join him all along. I wasn't sure, but I decided to come anyway."

"Did anyone know you were coming? Did you tell Jack or anyone else?"

"Actually, yes; Bill Brady, under strict confidence, but no one else. I knew if I told Jack, he would disapprove."

"So you checked in at 6:00 P.M.?"

"Yes, to the best of my recollection."

"Do you recall who checked you in?"

Jack intervened. "Sergeant, this getting a little off base, don't you think?"

"I don't recall," continued Rachel, "an older gentleman, gray beard."

"Was anything out of place when you arrived in your room, any evidence that someone had been in here?"

Rachel glanced at Jack, then back at Sergeant. Graham. She suddenly felt squeezed by her dilemma. "Jack's black daypack and those things in the corner were here."

Rachel pointed to the far corner of the hotel room, under the window. A small backpack, black boots, and a small coil of rope lay there in a pile. As Sergeant Graham moved closer to inspect the articles, Rachel looked quizzically at Jack for approval.

"It's OK, Rachel, you did the right thing. There is something going on that I can't explain."

Without handling them, Graham closely inspected each article and determined two things right away. The boots and rope were slightly damp but virtually unused. The boots were the same size and sole composition of the footprints discovered on the roof of the Van Gilder.

"Have you ever seen those items before?" asked Graham pointing to the articles in the corner.

"Aside from the daypack, no, I haven't," said Rachel as Jack echoed her answer with a shake of his head.

"Do either of you know anything at all about them, who they belong to, and how they might have been placed here?"

Both responded in the negative and moved to a far corner of the room to confer in private while Graham called in his discovery to the chief.

"Good work, Graham," responded the chief. "Fell's in the lobby. I'll have him join us in five minutes. I want Mr. Coble's room inspected; get a warrant if you have to. I want 216 sealed, so move Randolph to another room. No one leaves the hotel, understood?"

"Got it, Chief!"

"Keep Mrs. Randolph engaged until I get there, and tell the manager I want the lock to 216 interrogated. I want to know everyone who came and went from that room over the last forty-eight hours. Fell has the key we found on the fire escape; he's confirming who it was issued to right now."

"What are the findings from the lab on prints or fiber work?"

"Negative on the card key prints. We should have something preliminary on the glove fibers within the hour."

Graham called the front desk and arranged a room-move for Jack and an interrogation of the magnetic door lock. The modern key system contains a memory chip that retains a record of whose card was used to access every lock in the hotel and at what time.

When Sergeant Graham turned his attention back to the Randolphs, it was obvious from the tenor and from the few words he overheard that Jack was questioning how Rachel could possibly have known of his whereabouts.

As Graham approached, Rachel made no attempt to muffle herself. "That's not the point. What's important is that you didn't tell me anything; you can't keep secrets from me like this, Jack."

"No, the point is that Marcus' clothes are in your room, and you know darn well I didn't leave my black ... "

A loud knock at the door broke-up the heated exchange. The hotel manager entered the room and busied himself decoding the door lock. Agent Fell motioned Sergeant Graham to join him out in the corridor.

"You won't believe this," said Fell. "The key we found on the fire escape was issued today at 7:24 P.M. to Jack Randolph, room 216."

"This is starting to stink," said Graham. "Let's get a printout of the lock interrogation before we call it in. The chief should be here any minute."

A moment later the Orca Inn manager had what he needed from the card reader.

"I'll take this to the office and have a print out for you in a few minutes," he offered.

"Thank you," replied Graham. "One more thing; I asked the front desk to arrange a room-move for Mr. Randolph."

"In the works," responded the manager as he motioned Jack to follow him downstairs. Agent Fell took advantage of the intervening time to inspect Marcus' room.

A few minutes later, a light knock on the half-open door announced the arrival of Chief Callahan, whose imposing figure instantly brought everyone to full attention. He was accompanied by Jack Randolph and Agent Fell, who had met the chief in the corridor with the news that nothing was unusual or out-of-place in Marcus' room.

"Where is this stash of belongings, Graham?" asked the chief gruffly.

Graham pointed to a far corner of the room.

"The lab can't make it over until morning, Chief, unless you want to call out of Anchorage."

"Unlikely they could make it in this weather anyway, Sergeant. I'll have to wait."

The chief pulled on latex gloves and carefully opened the nylon backpack as everyone watched intently. The contents were few: two carabiners, a figure eight, a climbing harness, and a small radio. The boots were the Sorrel brand with a deep tread and inner wool liner. The rope was stiff and tightly coiled, showing no signs of use. The clothing and other belongings were neatly folded and stacked next to the daypack, causing the chief to conclude that they were likely staged. Agent Fell inched toward the chief and handed him the printout of the lock interrogation that had just arrived.

"Just in. I haven't had a chance to read it," whispered Fell.

The two men eagerly digested the printout together. Within seconds their eyes pulled up in unison, and with a deep, contemplative squint that bespoke of mild satisfaction, they knew instantly the other's thought: the man standing behind them had a lot of explaining to do.

"Get the lab on the phone, Fell. Let's see what they have for us."

Fell's call was short but productive, and he quickly summarized the conversation for the chief.

"There's a ninety percent likely on fibers taken from a ladder rung matching the gloves in Mr. Randolph's car. No glove fibers on the rope, but we have some promising print lifts from the cables. They'll need another hour. I told them we have boots over here that seem to match the impressions on the roof. They'll have a scaled blow-up of the imprint here within twenty minutes."

The chief nodded in satisfaction. His team was assembling evidence quickly and tightening his investigation.

As Marcus scrutinized the clothing piled in the corner from his distant vantage point by the door, a sinking realization overcame him. The blue backpack, boots, and dark jacket looked familiar to him. He owned items exactly like them; in fact, upon closer inspection, he was certain they were his.

Chief Callahan turned to Marcus.

"I'm sure we're both anxious to get this over, Mr. Coble, but I need to discuss some things with you in private. Can you step outside with me for a minute?"

Marcus began weighing the merit of confession; he was sure the chief had discovered something that connected him to the personal items in Rachel's room. His heart raced as he squared up to the chief's towering frame.

"I understand from Graham that you are acting as Mr. Randolph's attorney?" said the chief.

"That's correct."

"We don't have an autopsy on Mr. Hayes yet, so we don't have any reason to suspect a crime has been committed. On the other hand, we can't assume Mr. Hayes died of natural causes. There are some suspicious circumstances that involve your client, as you know. At the least, we need to interview Mr. and Mrs. Randolph separately. Do you represent her as well?"

"Until I'm told otherwise, yes."

"Well in that case, I would like to meet with Rachel first. I also want Jack's shoe size, and to know more about his flight from Juneau this evening: pilot's name, departure time, flight plan, arrival … that sort of thing."

Marcus knew his clients would need time to firm up their stories. "I'm sure Jack and Rachel are very tired, Chief. Can't this wait until tomorrow?"

"No, it can't"

"Well, it may have to."

The chief noted the change in Marcus's demeanor, which he anticipated at some point during the exchange. It was an attempt to gain control of events and to exert a measure of resistance. The chief was prepared.

"Well, Mr. Coble, I don't mean to get between you and your client, but your name has come up more than once today."

"I'm not sure I follow you."

"You should think about the implications of representing someone in a situation where you could be potential suspect yourself. There might be potential conflicts there, I don't know."

Marcus tried to read the chief's intent.

"Mr. Randolph may not consider it in his best interest to be represented by a lawyer who is under suspicion for the same offense that he is. It's something you should consider."

Marcus was no stranger to negotiation. He realized the warning was a stretch but also a clear signal that the chief was not going to allow Marcus to stand in the way of an interview.

"Should we pose the question to the Randolphs?" suggested the chief.

"Not necessary. I'll disclose my situation to Jack and let him decide. I doubt he'll want to meet any further on this subject tonight, however."

"Your call, Mr. Coble. But you might want to let him know I have enough evidence to take him into custody right now. A brief conversation will clear up a few inconsistencies, I'm sure."

"Such as?"

"Evidence that contradicts his testimony about when he checked in and how his room key ended up on the fire escape at the Van Gilder."

Marcus went silent; these were serious accusations that were not to be construed as bluffs. The truth was, Marcus had no idea when Jack arrived in Seward and had been completely surprised by his presence there—and by his apparent desire for secrecy.

"Let me put it this way, Mr. Coble. A little cooperation now could save your client a lot of unnecessary embarrassment."

"I understand. Let me talk to him."

"It's Mrs. Randolph I want to see first; have her meet me in your room right away, please."

When Rachel arrived in room 209 a few minutes later, she had changed her clothes and refreshed her appearance. The chief was instantly consumed by her youthful beauty, her deep green eyes and light complexion. She had a wistful but intelligent air and a natural sophistication that evolved from her confidence but equally from a desire to impress. Her full eyebrows and high cheekbones gave her a firm resolve that many found as disarming as her beauty. She looked at ease in her casual attire. When she entered room 209 to meet the chief, she was accompanied by Marcus, but it was apparent that she would not be deferring to anyone.

"Chief Callahan, Rachel Randolph," Marcus said.

"Thank you for taking the time, Mrs. Randolph. I'll keep this short, as I know you must be tired. Let's start with how you found out your husband would be here in Seward at the Orca Inn".

"Marcus told me … reluctantly. I pressed him about it when I spoke to him early this morning."

Marcus was not about to correct the testimony of his client, but in truth Marcus knew nothing of Jack's unplanned trip to Seward.

"Did Mr. Coble know you were coming?"

"No."

"Did you tell anyone you were coming to Seward?"

"Bill Brady, in confidence, just in case …" Rachel stopped herself.

"Go on," said the chief.

"In case I needed help," she said.

"But you had no reservations, no plans to meet anyone?"

"No. I planned to join my husband when he arrived."

"You mean surprise your husband if he arrived?"

"Correct," said Rachel curtly.

"But Jack was surprised that you had come to Seward and

had checked into the Orca Inn. Why didn't you call him, either once you arrived in Seward, or when you checked in?"

"If we met up, I wanted to explain myself to him in person."

"Do you know why your husband was coming to Seward?"

"Not exactly. Marcus was vague. That's partly why I was so curious and why I thought Jack might need me here. I've learned more since I arrived."

"And what have you learned?"

"That he came to visit Walter to reassure him of our support. I think Walter requested the meeting."

"What time did you arrive in Seward, and what time did you check in here?"

"I'm not exactly sure. The weather was horrendous, and I was exhausted. Isn't there a record at the desk?"

"Yes, but I'm asking you for your recollection."

"I believe I arrived in Seward around 6:00 P.M., maybe 6:30 P.M., and I came here directly to check in."

"When you checked in, what did you tell the clerk?"

"I'm not sure what you mean."

"How did you get a key to this room without registering as a guest?"

"They just gave me a key. I don't know. I guess the clerk forgot."

"Isn't it true that you lied to the clerk? You told him it was your anniversary and that you wanted to surprise your husband who would be arriving later? Isn't it true that you asked him not to register you yet, so there would be no record of your arrival?"

Rachel looked down at the floor as if to acknowledge the ruse.

"I spoke to the clerk," the chief continued, "and that is why he cancelled the reservation Jack made an hour later. He knew you already had a room, and he simply wished to accommodate your request to surprise your husband."

Rachel looked at the chief in stunned silence.

"So either you and Jack were planning a reunion all along and you're hiding it, or your plan for anonymity was foiled by an incredible coincidence."

"The truth is that I left Anchorage in a hurry and forgot my purse. I was embarrassed that I didn't have a credit card or cash to pay for the room. I had to make up the story about surprising Jack in order to convince the desk agent that my husband would be coming later and would pay for the room. You're making this out ... ." Rachel's voice trailed off as she acknowledged her deceit.

"Isn't it true that you wanted your presence in Seward to be completely undocumented so you could hide out, maybe even disavow your arrival in Seward altogether?"

"That's ridiculous and insulting!"

The chief showed Rachel a folio indicating Jack's signature on the bottom.

"I assume you recognize your husband's signature. Is that his?"

"I can't say for sure, but it looks like it, yes."

"When was the first time you saw your husband today?"

"Thirty minutes ago, when your agents arrived."

"I see. So you checked in and went directly to your room; what did you do from then until now?"

"Oh my, I went to Safeway and bought a salad, filled the car with gas, then drove around town for an hour, and then came back here. I've been here for almost an hour."

"And you never saw Jack until just now?"

"Correct"

"And you bought gas and groceries, but yet you had no cash or credit cards."

"I had exactly forty dollars."

"You checked in at 6:14 P.M. according to your guest folio and then went straight to your room; is that your story?"

"Correct."

"You can see from this folio that your husband checked in an hour later. You even stated his handbag was in the room when you arrived. But you still deny ever seeing him?"

"Jack never came to the room, unless it was during my shower."

"We can safely assume that wouldn't have sent him running," said the chief in an attempt at humor. "When you arrived and discovered the personal items in your room that were not yours, why didn't you call the desk and report it?"

"I can't be certain they were there when I first checked into the room. I'm sure I would have noticed them, but then again I didn't check the room thoroughly. I was only in the room for a few minutes before I left. When I returned the electricity was out and everything was dark. As soon as the power came on, I saw them there."

"Where were you between 9:00 P.M. and 10:00 P.M. tonight?"

"Right here in this room, alone."

"One last question, which I hope isn't too personal. Have you and Jack had any recent disagreements?"

"I do regard that as personal. Our relationship is high profile, and we have our share of disagreements. But nothing noteworthy; so no."

"What is your relationship with Mr. Coble?"

"He is a very close personal friend, as well as an employee.

We trust him with our business and with our personal lives. But it is strictly professional."

The chief stared intently at Rachel, then at Marcus, who was standing in the background. He leaned forward and spoke softly but firmly in a voice meant to emphasize the need for complete honesty.

"If everything you have told me is true, and I have no reason to believe otherwise, it should be clear that someone may be trying to implicate your husband in a potential crime. Is there anything you know that we haven't touched on that might shed light on this? Is there anything I should know now that would not reflect well on you or others involved if I were to find out about it later through the course of my investigation?"

Marcus intervened abruptly to preempt a response. "Rachel, I would advise you not to answer that question. Chief Callahan, there is no way she can be held accountable in a ten-minute interview for everything that you might regard in the future as helpful to your investigation. You don't even know if a crime has been committed. We all pledge our continued cooperation, but that doesn't imply an obligation to speculate about people or events."

The chief turned to Rachel. "If I am going to help your husband, the more I know the better. He could be in serious trouble."

"All I can say is that I know my husband; he is not capable of committing a crime. Neither am I. There is nothing that will change that. There are many desperate people out there who will do anything to save their ass, Chief. That much should be clear to you."

"Trust me, Mrs. Randolph, we'll get to the bottom of this. In the meantime, please contact me at this number if you feel like you missed anything," said the chief as he handed Rachel his business card. "Any time day or night."

As Jack entered the room and passed Rachel, his agitation was visible. His heavy, brooding scowl was in stark contrast to his wife's elegant composure.

"Good night, Mrs. Randolph," called out the chief.

The chief turned to Jack, his eyes fixed in an authoritative glare. There was little attempt to appear friendly.

"This should only take a few minutes," was all the chief could muster for an introduction.

"Good, because that's about my limit of patience right now! Go ahead."

"Let me get straight to the point. As things stand now, Walter Hayes died of natural causes. However, if anything emerges from our investigation that changes this, you will find yourself at the center of attention. We have evidence collected from your vehicle and now your room that place you in areas of the Van Gilder that you had no business being near and that appear very suspicious."

"I'm not sure I want to hear this, Chief. Ask me whatever you want, and let me get back to my wife."

"When did you arrange to meet your wife in Seward?"

"We never arranged to meet here. I was as surprised as anyone."

"When was the first time you saw your wife in Seward?"

"Thirty minutes ago with Sergeant Graham."

"What time did you check in here?"

"The truth is that I never checked in. When I first came in to register around 10:00 P.M., that's when I first learned Rachel was here—quite by mistake I might add. The desk agent told me that he had already issued two keys and sent me to locate

Rachel and retrieve my key from her. She was not in the room, so I left and went back to the Van Gilder."

"Seems a little implausible, Jack, since Sergeant Graham overheard you tell the desk clerk thirty minutes ago that you misplaced your key, likely the same key you lost on the fire escape of the Van Gilder Hotel."

"What are you talking about? Obviously, I didn't have a key because I had yet to check in."

The chief showed Jack the registration folio he signed at check in.

"Is that your signature, Mr. Randolph?"

"It can't be if it was produced here. I was never asked to sign anything when I checked in. Sergeant Graham was with me."

"But Sergeant Graham was not there the first time you checked in. This folio was signed by you at 7:25 P.M. A key was issued to you at that time—the same key that was used to access your wife's room 216 at exactly 7:57 P.M.; the same key that was later found at the scene of a potential crime. Your wife had checked in an hour earlier and told the desk clerk you would be arriving soon. It all ties, Jack. This is your key, and I don't need to remind you how bad this looks. Square with me now; what are you hiding?"

The anguish on Jack's face turned suddenly hostile.

"You're baiting me. Get Rachel in here now. This is bullshit."

"I'm not playing games, Mr. Randolph. This is serious business, and you shouldn't need your wife to tell us the truth," said the chief.

"I admit it looks like my signature, OK, but it can't be mine. Marcus, for Christ's sake, there's got to be something …"

"How do you think your wife obtained a key to this room without actually registering under her name?"

Jack concealed his jealousy and real suspicions. "I don't have any idea. I can assure you that I was nowhere close to Seward at six o'clock. I was on a flight plan from Juneau to Seward at that time. You can check it out."

"We did. Juneau departure control has the plane off at 5:36 P.M., but your flight plan was never activated, and of course we have no idea who was on that plane. It could have been the governor for all we know. Of course, Seward's airport was shut down completely. Conveniently, there is no record of your coming or going."

"Bullshit, I took a commercial flight to Juneau."

"You did, but explain this: The desk clerk who checked you in at 7:25 P.M. and witnessed your signature on that folio described you accurately. He claims you identified yourself, paid cash, signed the folio, and asked for directions to the room—after he issued you a key. The same key that we found on the emergency stairwell of the Van Gilder Hotel!"

"That can't be possible."

"According to your wife, she told only one person in confidence that she was coming here. According to you, no one knew you were coming. So who else but you would register as Jack Randolph—and be given a key by trained staff to the same room as your wife? The same staff, by the way, who were told by Mrs. Randolph that you would be arriving soon after she did. Who else would not be surprised by a shared room assignment with your wife!

"I don't have answers, Chief. Look at me! I don't know what the hell is going on here, but someone is going to extremes to frame me for something."

"Precisely my dilemma. Why would someone go to this extreme to frame you unless Mr. Hayes was murdered?"

"Maybe to make it look like a murder when it wasn't, I don't know. But I rather suspect the worst."

"Your wife said she received a key without registration or payment by telling the clerk you would be arriving soon to pay. She made sure the desk clerk could identify you so as not to confuse you with someone else, which evidence suggests is exactly what happened."

Jack's temperament changed, and he suddenly became enraged. He knew no one, not even Rachel, could have known of his plans to fly to Seward since they were formulated well after she left Anchorage. He was increasingly certain that Rachel was covering up an affair, and her likely partner was Marcus Coble. Jack's bewilderment was visible, and the chief was persistent.

"You see my point? Rachel described you to the desk agent, and all indications are that it was you who obtained a key at 7:25 P.M. Who else could it have possibly been?"

"I give up, you tell me."

"Why do you think your wife came to Seward unannounced?"

"She cares about me and the business. She can't sit still when she knows I'm under pressure. I think she was curious and concerned."

"Is it at all possible that she might have come to see someone else?"

This last question was intentionally designed to elicit a reaction from both men. The chief's instincts, based on a lifetime of cracking criminals, suggested that Jack was near a breaking point when useful information would surface. Marcus, the chief concluded, had more than just a professional interest at stake. The chief had little to lose by pressing his point.

"Just what in hell are you insinuating, Chief, that my wife is having an affair ... or worse, might be a murderer? Screw you. I think we're done here!"

Marcus was slow rising to Jack's defense. For the first time, the complete implications of the day's events began to sink in. He realized that the chief sensed enough about his relationship with Rachel to stir the pot. Marcus felt his credibility slipping and remained silent, which left an awkward impression on the other men in the room.

"Marcus, for Christ sake, is there something going on here that I don't know about?"

"Jack, you can't be serious. You're not thinking clearly. It's been a long enough day, don't you think?"

"You set this entire weekend up, Marcus. You shared your plans with my wife, in spite of asking me for total confidentiality. There is no way you or anyone else could have known I was coming to Seward. And yet you arrange to meet her here to check in under my name!"

The chief saw an opportunity to drive the wedge deeper.

"Mr. Randolph, we know that Mr. Hayes was undressed and in bed just before he died. Our team believes he was not expecting company—or planning a meeting of any kind."

Jack glared at Marcus, barely containing his anger.

"What led you to believe Mr. Coble had a meeting planned with Mr. Hayes at ten, Mr. Randolph?"

"Marcus confirmed the time with Walter and then with me. In fact, he left a message on my cell phone, which I still have if you want to hear it."

"No thank you, but I wouldn't erase it," said the chief.

Marcus quickly realized the chief's intent with this line of questioning was to cast doubt on his objectivity and veracity. His command of the situation was slipping, Marcus concluded, and he needed to regain control quickly.

"Jack, you can see what he's trying to do here. I strongly advise you to end this interview. We need time to discuss this in private. Trust me, end this now or you may regret it."

Jack reflected on the unfolding situation. His long association with Marcus demanded a level of confidence and delegation that at times was blind to self-dealing. He was acutely aware of Marcus's ambitions, and of the few occasions his manipulative actions crossed the line between effective legal counsel and deception. Jack was becoming increasingly skeptical of Marcus' motives and his often repeated "legal advice" that Jack needed to distance himself from the more sordid business of BOC.

On the other hand, Marcus was the executor of Jack's will, the trustee of several trusts Jack had created, and was first in line to succeed him as president of BOC in the event of Jack's disability or demise. Hundreds of legal documents had their joint signatures, the full implications of which Jack could not comprehend. He knew instinctively that their business relationship could not be easily unwound. He therefore resolved to be vigilant but to an even greater degree non-confrontational.

At the moment, however, it was Rachel who occupied Jack's mind to an obsessive degree. It was one thing not to trust Marcus but quite another not to trust his wife. He had never experienced the jealousy that now consumed his mind, sparked by Marcus' rejoinder to "just trust me." This familiar refrain burned in his head, fanned by his wife who seemed to invoke the phrase as often as Marcus. Those who are most demanding of my trust, Jack thought to himself, are the least deserving of it. Time alone was what he desired most at the moment; everything else seemed to fade into the darkness that was Seward.

"It is late, Chief, maybe a good night's rest is the best thing. Do you mind?"

The chief had set the stage. It was time to strike.

"I have one more question, Mr. Randolph. Did Mr. Coble come here to negotiate a deal with Mr. Hayes, to offer him money in exchange for favorable testimony—or maybe no testimony that could implicate BOC at trial?"

Marcus stood up in a fit of outrage. His edgy temperament assumed a more physically aggressive posture as he shook his fist at the chief."

"This is outrageous. This is ... Jack, don't answer any more questions. This meeting is over. Let's go!"

"Trust me, Mr. Coble, this is just a warm-up. The FBI will not let you off so easily! I could hold you on suspicion, Mr. Randolph, but I won't. I want an understanding from all three of you that you will remain in your rooms; by tomorrow, maybe you'll have some better answers."

The chief exchanged glances with agent Fell who had been stationed at the door. Fell's look of mild satisfaction confirmed to the chief that he had accomplished his objective. The increased pressure was causing a crack to appear between the two men leaving the room.

The chief turned to agent Fell and issued his final instructions of the night.

"Seal Randolph's room; hold all the Van Gilder guests until the interviews are complete. Team briefing at 8:00 A.M. This case is proceeding backwards: We have evidence and suspects before we have confirmation of a crime. Tomorrow will be a long one, so get some rest."

# Chapter XIII
*Saturday, January 19, 7:35 A.M.*

**"TELL ME EVERYTHING YOU KNOW** about pacemakers, Dr. Strayer," asked the chief as he poured himself his first cup of coffee. The two early risers were the only ones in the library when James came in with an early tray of donuts. "I understand you're a retired physician."

"I am, for fifteen years now."

"And quite a storyteller too, I'm told. Is it true you are a shareholder of the Van Gilder?"

"I am."

"Well, it's a pleasure to meet you. You've done a wonderful job restoring this hotel. I've heard great things about you too, including your biographies of Alaska pioneers and the historic exhibits you created in the hallways. Congratulations on all of it. You strike me as a woman of endless energy."

"You're very kind, Officer."

"Mike Callahan, Chief of Police. Please call me Mike. Now what can you tell me about pacemakers?"

"Well, in the simplest terms, they are small battery operated devises that are implanted into the heart to regulate your heart beat. When arrhythmia—an irregular heartbeat—occurs, the pacemaker sends a mild electric shock to the heart muscles that restores the normal rhythm."

"Who has these devises and why?"

"Usually patients with a history of ventricular fibrillation, which can be fatal. Your heart is a very efficient pump, but the upper and lower chambers, called the atrium and ventricle, must expand and contract in perfectly timed sequences, or the pump fails. The pacemaker maintains the proper timing."

"Very interesting. I am told you were the last person to see or speak with Mr. Hayes before he retired to his room last night. Is that true?"

"I believe so. We talked for maybe fifteen minutes at the bar, and then he excused himself."

"Did he mention anything about a meeting, expected visitors, anything like that?"

"No, I'm quite sure he didn't. I mentioned that we would be reading a ghost story, and I recall him saying something about having enough ghosts in his life."

"Did Mr. Hayes look agitated?"

"No. In fact, after he left, my friend and I both commented on his sense of humor, how calm he was under the circumstances."

"Did he talk about his indictment or his future intentions?"

"As a matter of fact, he did say that he was reconciled to coming clean and to paying for his mistakes. He said he was committed to telling the truth and how that decision had cost him his marriage, his friendships, and whatnot. He sounded genuinely contrite."

"Did you notice anything unusual during this time?"

"You probably know the electricity went out, so everything went dark just after he left. But other than that, no."

"Did anyone follow him upstairs?"

"No, and I was standing by the lobby entrance. I watched him walk to the stairs, so I would have noticed that."

"I'm going to show you five artist renderings, and I want you to tell me if any of them fit the description of the woman who interrupted your conversation last night," said the chief. This was not the first time she had been asked to perform such a task.

Dr. Strayer immediately pointed to the portrait the chief had prepared from James' descriptions.

"That's her, but she has fuller lips and a wider mouth. I think her eyes are brown, not blue."

"Dr. Strayer, thank you very much. We request that if you need to go out for any reason, you leave a contact number for Sergeant Graham."

Chief Callahan was pouring his second cup of coffee in the library when his cell phone rang.

"Agent Fell here, Chief. I have a couple things. The coroner's preliminary finding on the cause of death is cardiac arrest due to V-fib. No other signs of trauma. Apparently, there were minor burns on his left thumb and index finger but nothing else. They're shipping the body to Anchorage this morning. Secondly, Governor Thompson is in Seward. I'm not sure if you knew that. His chief of staff, Elliot Lawson, wants a full briefing at 11:00 A.M. this morning. The media is pressing us for the story, and apparently the governor set a press conference a week ago. Everyone is expecting a statement about Hayes' death. Media speculation is that the press conference was arranged to announce Elliot Lawson's resignation.

"Tell the governor that a briefing is out of the question. We have nothing to report but a cause of death, and even that is premature. We have a highly sensitive investigation, and I don't want anyone out in front of us on this. I'll pull in your boss if I need to."

"Exactly my thoughts, Chief. I'll get back to you."

"One favor, Fell. Have them hold the body a few more hours. I want to have a closer look."

"I'll see what I can do."

The chief quietly shuffled up the corridor, coffee in hand, and knocked softly on the door of 106. No answer. He knocked again and held his ear to the door. It was 8:10 A.M., still early for a visit, but he heard a muffled voice from within that he was sure was Juliet's. He knocked a third time and very quietly announced himself through the door. After a long pause, he slowly cracked the door.

"Juliet, is everything OK?"

There was still no acknowledgment from Juliet, in spite of her clear voice emanating from a side room. Mike realized the awkward nature of his intrusion, an invasion of privacy not sanctioned on any legal grounds. Juliet could be in danger, he reasoned to himself; her claims of clairvoyance were now public, leaving her exposed to any manner of harm.

As he inched forward, Mike saw Juliet bent over the claw-footed bathtub, which was filled with colored water and floating votive candles. A shawl covered her head, and her arms were stretched over the candles, pulling them here and there as though connected by invisible threads. Her canting was rhythmic and prayerful. Mike stared in fascination for several seconds, and then slowly backed up. Now was not a good time to renew his acquaintance, he mused.

As Mike was leaving the Van Gilder, Agent Fell rang him back.

"Good news and bad, Chief. You can view the body before 10:00 A.M. Best I could do. Bad news is the Assistant AG called. You're in the hot spot. He's calling a 3C briefing for 10:30 A.M., and he's not inclined to interfere with the governor's plans for a press conference, which I'm told was set a week ago."

The chief's phone beeped, indicating another incoming call from a local but unfamiliar number. "Damn, Fell, I have another call. Thanks for the help—and the heads up!"

"Chief Callahan here."

"Mike, this is Juliet. That was you in my room, wasn't it? I hope you won't make a habit of spying on me like that."

"I was just making sure you're all right. I'm sorry if I startled you."

"You didn't; I was just coming out of my meditation. How is your investigation going?"

"OK, I guess. And yours?"

"I've lost contact. I have no idea why," said Juliet with a sigh. "It's likely no different than our relationships with the living, I guess. We have strong connections that build and take on the allusion of permanency and then, poof! The attraction disappears. The bonds that inspire us to devotion suddenly fade."

Mike pondered the intent of her statement but let it drop and asked, "I have a question for you, if I could?"

Juliet ignored him and continued. "The emotions that bind us are fragile. Do you ever marvel at the transience of our affections, Mike?"

"In my line of work, I see the worst of things. Permanency does not exist—family, work, friendships. I mostly see a world in search of now."

"It is hard on you, I can see. Your eyes have light, but they frown, and your smile is warm, but it is hidden. You're a hard man to get to know, Mike."

"Let's talk about Fannie. Why did you lose contact with her?"

"It could be on your account. Or it could be you that Fannie is waiting on."

"She may have to wait long time for me. I'm afraid I don't have your connections."

The two laughed in unison through the phone.

"You have the capacity for faith, but I sense that you have lost the need for it. You do not understand how it will help you or others around you."

Chief Callahan was above all humble. "I'm not sure what my faith has to do with anything, but maybe you can help me understand. In fact, the question I have for you is related."

"Out with it then."

"If I were to take you to a particular place, or show you an important photograph or scene, does an image like that strengthen your connection? Does it bring you closer to the Teleos?"

"Honestly, I don't know. No one has ever used my energy to solve a crime before. On the other hand, I invoke material objects all the time to create a context or framework for my meditations." Juliet thought deeply for a few seconds. The sarcasm in her voice was deep when she finally spoke. "You're testing me, Mike. You need to know so you can eliminate me as a suspect, am I right?"

"I promise you I'm not. I'm truly interested in what you can do. I need your help."

Juliet trusted Mike, perhaps not fully, but she trusted his motives. She knew he was skeptical, but he had theories about Walter Hayes' death, and he simply needed more proof.

"I will meditate about it. My success will depend upon how the energy is channeled, to whom it is directed and the degree to which Fannie perceives my effort to be just. Remember, she is not a vengeful person bent on retribution. She is a forgiving spirit."

"I understand. I have an idea that I think Fannie would approve of. But right now I have a hotel full of irritable guests who want to check out. Can we talk later?"

"Before you go, I must tell you this," said Juliet. "My hand was burned when I woke up from this session. It's never happened before. My left palm and index finger are burned. Something is upsetting Fannie. If I had to filter her message, I would say your victim is burned."

Mike stood motionless in the street and pondered the revelation, then smiled broadly and laughed. "There's no way I'm adding that to my briefing," he said to himself. By then, Juliet had already hung up.

When Mike arrived at the lab, Walter Hayes' body was under an ultraviolet camera used to enhance the image of damaged skin. A technician explained that the light would highlight changes in skin pigmentation caused by burning.

"Various body fluids fluoresce when burned and can leave invisible stains that the UV-detect camera will reveal," he began. "New technology can even detect irregularities in sub-epidermal layers of flesh and muscle tissue. What at first appeared to be a rash along his left hand and arm now looks to be from excessive heat, possibly caused by electric shock."

The technician had been about to open the chest cavity to extract the pacemaker for signs of malfunction when the chief had walked in.

"Look at the hairs on the back of his left wrist and arm. The ends are lightly singed and brown. Compare those to his right arm hairs, which are normal."

The technician handed the chief a 50x magnifying glass, which he used to closely examine the arm hair and follicles on the left arm. The infrared light suggested that heat from some source had traveled up the arm and into the chest where the redness dissipated. Mike turned the fingers and palm of the left hand upward, exposing a deeper redness and a pinhole-size blister.

"What do you make of this, Doc?" he asked pointing to the fingertips.

"It's too early to say, but it's quite possible that he touched something that produced an electrical shock. In the right conditions, current could travel through the arm and to the heart, causing immediate contraction of the heart muscle. The same current could conceivably cause a malfunction of the pacemaker."

"How much current are we talking about?"

"Surprisingly little. Less than a few volts can cause the heart muscle to contract. But you would need to consult with an expert."

"From the redness on his palm and fingertips, it looks as though he grasped a rod or handle of some kind."

The chief reflected on the scene of death and tried to recall anything fitting that description within arm's length of Hayes' body.

"Doc, do me a favor. I need to know if those marks would be consistent with grasping the end of a gun barrel."

He looked again at the hand and pictured a potential altercation through a bar-locked door.

"On second thought, maybe a doorknob. Check these burns and tell me if they could be from grabbing a standard metal doorknob."

"Sure thing, Chief, but I haven't got much time. They want him packed up by noon."

"Do what you can. Call Agent Fell and tell him you want clearance to retain the pacemaker here to run tests. Make up something if you have to; I want custody of that thing. Get me what you can on Hayes' history and why he needed a pacemaker."

The chief dialed Sergeant Graham.

"Morning, Graham. I have a 3C briefing with the FBI in thirty minutes. I need an update."

"Other than Hayes' prints, room 201 was clean. I have a positive match on the boot prints and glove fibers. We're about wrapped up with interviews. The only new information is that Ms. Windemuth reported to Mr. Van Oss what she thought was an electrical malfunction in room 202 when she checked in. According to Van Oss, everything was working fine when he checked on it. Other than that, we're waiting on your word to release the guests."

"Have we accounted for everyone who was checked in?"

"We have."

"Release the second- and third-tier suspects. Everyone else is on hold. What else do you have?"

"According to Chugach, the power was restored to the downtown grid, including the Van Gilder, at 9:52 P.M. Van Oss is certain it was just after ten when power was restored to the Van Gilder. He re-set the time-clock at 10:10 P.M., what he estimated was no more than five minutes after the power came back on."

"Interesting. We know the main shut-off was tampered with, and the timing places both Marcus Coble and Jack Randolph at the scene in a dark hotel."

"We're a step ahead of you, Chief. Fell is tracking down amperage draws from Chugach, which is measured every quarter hour."

"The lab is taking a close look at the cables from Randolph's car," said the chief. "I want to know if there are signs of use within the last twenty-four hours. I think they may have been cut for a reason, possibly to jump electrical current. If someone is trying to frame Randolph, there has to be a connection."

"Anything else, Chief?"

"Find me an expert on pacemakers."

"What are you working on?"

"Keep this quiet, Graham, but Hayes shows signs of possible electrocution. Have the guys check all switches, receptacles, every wire in Hayes' room—and just outside in the corridor—for signs of tampering or malfunction. Try to get a wiring diagram for the hotel."

"I'll get on it. Good luck with the briefing."

"Thanks for the reminder. I need you to represent the department at the press conference, Graham. Cause of death is cardiac arrest. He was found alone, behind a locked door, with no signs of struggle. No elaboration. Are we clear?"

"Damn, Chief, you know how bad I am at this."

"You'll do fine."

At precisely 10:30 A.M., Chief Callahan arrived at headquarters and was introduced to Governor Morris Thompson and Elliot Lawson, who had been the first to arrive. The governor's initial displeasure over Elliot's arrival in Seward had transformed into guarded relief when, at 11:30 P.M. the night before, Elliot awoke him and informed him of Walter Hayes' death. Since 5:00 A.M. that morning, Elliot had attempted to convince Governor Thompson to reject his resignation, which he had thus far not committed to do.

"I fail to see how Walter's death has improved our fortunes," he lamented to Elliot on the walk over. "It could just as likely fuel more cynicism and speculation about the depth of conspiracy among our ranks, at least until the cause of death is confirmed and exculpatory."

Elliot Lawson was a tall, lanky man of 6'6" with bushy eyebrows and a beak for a nose. He was known as "Hawk Eye" in Juneau, due to his likeness to the M*A*S*H character and his reputation for sarcasm. His Yale education and aloof manner earned him a reputation as an arrogant Ivy Leaguer among some. But no one denied that he was a very intelligent man, even if a bit green as a politician.

It was clear to the chief that Elliot Lawson insisted on the briefing for personal reasons; he wanted information that might help his case with the governor. Within a few minutes, they were joined by Agent Fell of the FBI, the Alaska attorney general, and the lead prosecutor for the U.S. Department of Justice, Asst. Attorney General Robert Morse, who assumed the role of moderator. After explaining the protocols of confidentiality, Morse stated that the hearing would be recorded and that as the officer in charge, Chief Callahan would conduct the briefing.

"It's all yours, Chief!"

"Gentlemen, I'll make this short," started the chief. "Walter Hayes was found in his room last night around 10:15 P.M., behind a barrel locked door, dead from what we believe now are natural causes—-cardiac arrest from ventricular fibrillation. Mr. Hayes wore a pacemaker and had a history of heart disease. The body was discovered by another guest from across the hall, who noticed the door was cracked open and went over to alert Mr. Hayes to that fact. There are a few unanswered questions that I won't elaborate on because to do so could compromise our investigation. I don't have much to add."

After a long and awkward silence, Governor Thompson was the first to speak up.

"That's it? That all you have to say? Chief Callahan, in a few hours I will be staring down a throng of media gorillas grilling me on what is arguably the highest-profile death in Alaska's history. The speculation out there is intense, particularly on how he died and whether there are indications of foul play. I won't ask you to compromise your investigation, but if there are unanswered questions about Mr. Hayes' death, I want to hear them."

After a short glance around the room for a show of support, the governor added quickly, "Surely you're aware that everyone in Seward, including every hotel guest, is feeding the media with live accounts of everything they see and hear. Why is there no gag order in effect?"

"We could not control the flow of information even if there was, Governor. We can't confiscate cell phones and computers; furthermore, a gag order would needlessly elevate public speculation."

"I think we should all know what you know, Chief Callahan."

"All I can tell you at this point is that Mr. Hayes' body showed signs of minor burns that at this time we can't explain. We don't know how they got there."

Morse interjected. "Agent Fell informed me that the main electrical shut off to the hotel was tampered with and that electrical cables were discovered in the car of someone scheduled to meet with Hayes last night. Is there any connection there?"

"We're investigating every lead, every connection, but it is not appropriate to publicly comment on any aspect of this investigation at this time. Some of the evidence we have gathered needs to be tightly controlled. Interviews in this case are critical."

Governor Thompson stood up and walked up to the chief slowly, positioning himself inches from Mike's nose and locking his eyes in a threatening glare.

"The people in this room are not the public. My reputation and that of my administration have been under attack, bolstered by testimony from a man who just died under mysterious circumstances—the very day he is meeting with the Justice Department to negotiate a plea bargain! And you expect me to tell the world he died of natural causes? You're setting me up to look like a fool."

The chief was an able negotiator, calm under fire, and was used to pressure tactics by politicians. He was not about to start bending now.

"With due respect, Governor, it is your decision to hold the press conference. Why not call for a period of mourning for Walter Hayes, cancel the press conference, and let me handle press communication on the investigation?"

"That sounds easy Chief. I have no intention of usurping your role in this, but I have no intention of canceling a press conference scheduled a week ago simply to avoid tough questions. I can see the headlines now: "Governor pleads the fifth!"

Elliot Lawson jumped in.

"Look, Chief, we'll talk this over and get back to you. At the least, we want an update before the press conference—if the governor decides to go through with it."

Elliot turned to Governor Thompson and quietly beseeched him to end the meeting.

"Let's talk outside," he whispered as he motioned the governor to the door.

Although there was no evidence directly implicating the governor, taped conversations between Elliot Lawson and Walter Hayes implicated them both in an illegal scheme to raise funds from the oil companies for the governor's re-election campaign, in exchange for official action by Elliot to promote tax legislation favorable to the industry. A federal indictment was pending, which is what precipitated the governor's decision to request Elliot's resignation.

However, Walter Hayes' death posed an entirely new set of circumstances, which was the subject of some urgency to both men now huddled in private outside police headquarters. Both men were now fixated on avoiding the embarrassment, not to mention the political upheaval, associated with a forced resignation. Elliot sensed an opportunity and he intended to seize it.

"Look Morrie, no one is the wiser. Let's reconsider your original plan. With Hayes gone, and no one to testify as to the authenticity or context of the conversations, the feds will drop the case. At the very least, my resignation now will be viewed as a sign of guilt, a confession. If you issue a statement denying the charges and stating our resolve to fight them, maybe the feds will back off. Alaskans believe in the right to a fair hearing, and how can we have that without the ability to question the government's main witness? I see no downside. We have the option of waiting."

Governor Thompson looked anxiously at Elliot. "I'm concerned about timing. There are a few unknowns, a few traps I want to avoid, not the least of which is appearing too anxious to capitalize on Hayes' death. On the other hand, if we have nothing to hide, the natural course of action is to stick with our plan. The fact that the press conference was scheduled a week ago is all the cover we need, agreed? You're sure there are no leaks on your end?"

"None, I assure you. We can speak honorably of Walter's service to Alaska, his tragic circumstances, and untimely death—but we need to be careful. We insist it was my resolve to clear myself of wrongdoing all along, after an open and full hearing of all the facts, which now may be impossible. We should avoid grandstanding, anything that might be perceived as self-serving or taking advantage of the circumstances."

"I'll hold the press conference, and I'm inclined to agree with you Elliot. Just remember this is your battle. If it turns on us, we have an understanding. Get me a draft by noon, and we'll go over it."

Clearly relieved at the outcome, Elliot heaved a sigh of relief and turned to go to his car. As he did so, the governor grabbed his arm and hauled him back into his stern gaze.

"Before you go, I want to be damn clear about something. Do you have any information about Walter's death that I should know about?"

"Nothing more than we both heard from Chief Callahan."

"I've heard that more than a few of Hayes' enemies are in town; and I heard Jack Randolph might be mixed up somehow. You have nothing more you can tell me?"

"Honestly, Morrie, that is news to me. As I told you last night, Jack's plan was predicated on Hayes being alive, not dead."

"Was it? From the way you explained it this morning, Jack was promising to make the problem go away, but he never explained how he would do it."

"Maybe true, but not by killing him."

"Robert Morse told me he had an appointment scheduled with Hayes for 9:00 A.M. this morning, and he fully expected Hayes to sign an immunity deal. Are you sure Jack didn't share any specifics about how he planned to influence Hayes' testimony? Morse hinted he knew something about your meeting yesterday with Jack in Juneau."

"I didn't question Jack about the specifics; it all seemed so far-fetched to me. I don't see how Morse could know any of the details unless ... I hope to hell that guy didn't screw me!"

"Has anyone questioned you about the meeting?"

"Not yet, but I'm sure they will. My flight from Juneau with Jack was supposed to be off the radar, but now look. My bigger problem is that I have no goddam alibi for last night. Jack and I parted at about 7:30 P.M., and I was in my room at the Orca Inn until 11:00 P.M. when he called me about Hayes."

"Jesus, Elliot, can't you come up with something?"

The governor's scowl left no room for negotiation. Elliot was not about to ask the governor to lie for him.

"Don't worry! Trust me, I'm clean!"

"The Endicott leases are worth millions to Jack, certainly enough to finance a hefty bribe—or worse— especially when you consider that Walter was threatening to bring down BOC."

"You're not serious?" questioned Elliot.

"Otherwise, why would Jack risk coming to Seward? He trusts Marcus with this business and asks him to set up a secret meeting with Hayes. From what you tell me, he hides his plans from his wife, attempts to bribe you, and flies through a damn blizzard to get here. It all seems a little desperate, even for Jack."

"I disagree. He always prefers to conduct business in person. He trusts Marcus, but I also think he senses Marcus may be mixed up somehow. He knows BOC is being watched, and he wants to keep a tight grip on things. That and he senses an opportunity to squeeze a little juice along the way."

"Nah, not Jack!" said the governor sarcastically. "I have your word, that's everything?"

"You have my word on it."

"Then let's meet in an hour and review your draft."

After the others had left the briefing, the chief received an update from Agent Fell. The description of the man who signed the folio for room 216 at the Orca Inn matched Jack's. But when a series of random photographs were presented to the clerk, his answers were vague.

Of far more importance, Fell had received an urgent voice message from Jason Wirum, an attorney who claimed to represent Jack Randolph. He made it clear that all future meetings or communication with his client be cleared in advance with him.

"I think we rattled him," said the chief. "Let's test the guy. Ask for cell phone records and credit card transactions over the last seven days on a voluntary basis. If we find anything, we'll ask for access to his home and personal computer. That may take a warrant."

"Agreed. All three want to check out of here, what should I tell them?"

"Not yet. I want a handwriting sample from each of them. Check their personal luggage for anything suspicious. I'm looking for electrical or chemical supplies, insulated gloves or work clothes—anything that strikes you as unnecessary for an overnight social visit."

"I'll get on it. I hear the press conference is on. Let's hope there aren't any shocking revelations!"

The chief grinned and smiled at Fell. They both knew what they dared not say out loud: that everyone in this growing circle of suspects appeared dirty, and the list of suspects was not narrowing.

# Chapter XIV
*Saturday, January 19, 1:00 P.M.*

**WHEN GOVERNOR MORRIS THOMPSON** walked up to the bank of microphones, the state of Alaska stood still for a moment. Aired live across Alaska and covered by the major networks, the governor's speech would have vast implications: to Alaskans; to the national political parties; to international gas line negotiations; and to the fortunes of many among Alaska's political and business elite. As he made his introduction, the governor sounded firm and confident but grave.

> Ladies and gentlemen, fellow Alaskans. We meet today at a crossroad. Just as Seward a century ago held the key to Alaska's promise, as an ice-free port with rail service to the vast interior, so today we are met by a far greater challenge, with far greater opportunity for our great state. I am speaking today of perhaps the largest and most ambitious private sector initiative ever undertaken in the history of mankind—a natural gas pipeline from Alaska's north slope through Canada to the hub of America's industrial center in the Midwest. The Alaska Gas Line Initiative is a partnership I have just concluded on behalf of Alaska with a consortium of Alaska's top producers. We met last week, after a series of tough negotiations, to conclude a contract that in my judgment presents the best and brightest hope for Alaska's

> future. The world's top experts on oil royalties and taxation, mineral leases, transportation, and profit sharing were representing our state at the table. I am pleased and proud to present the AGIA contract to the Alaska Legislature for ratification during the upcoming session and welcome a thorough review of the terms and conditions of performance.

The governor continued for more than twenty minutes, touting the merits of the contract and defending the "closed door" approach to his negotiations—which had been a point of considerable criticism over the prior weeks. He then turned to the subject on everyone's mind.

> I acknowledge the controversies that have recently surfaced with respect to my chief of staff, Elliot Lawson, here with me today. He will be holding his own press conference next week to address specifically the charges against him. Let me say that I maintain the utmost confidence in this man, and he has performed a pivotal role and honorable service to Alaskans throughout his tenure and, in particular, during the last several weeks in securing the AGIA contract. He and I are resolved to continue executing the trust and confidence Alaskans have placed on his office. It is my sincere hope that a full and complete airing of facts will soon be complete, allowing Alaskans to achieve an early closure and return to the work so vital to our future.
>
>   It is with a shared sense of loss for a great Alaskan that I confirm the passing of Walter Hayes last night here in Seward—I am told by natural causes. On behalf on myself and my administration, we wish to express our sympathies to his family. I understand that a more thorough briefing will be forthcoming by the officials conducting the investigation.

As was his practice, Governor Thompson ended with a short prayer and a promise to Alaskans that he would continue executing the trust they placed in him. Before he concluded his last sentence, throngs of hands shot up in a frantic scramble for recognition.

"Due to pressing business, I only have time for two questions."

"Governor Thompson, people within your own cabinet have predicted Elliot Lawson's resignation for weeks. How is he able to continue under this cloud of accusation, and how has the passing of Walter Hayes affected your decision to retain him?"

"My position with respect to Elliot's service and status has never wavered, notwithstanding the speculation by the media. I have not, to this point, entertained anything other than retaining his service, and so nothing has changed. As to my cabinet, I do not respond to hearsay and would ask that you refrain from attributing rumors to any member of my administration that you are not able to substantiate."

The governor pointed to another jutting hand. "Yes, Sir?"

"How can you invoke the trust Alaskans have placed in you, while at the same time conducting so much of our business out of the public eye, in Texas boardrooms and with such apparently low standards of ethical conduct?"

"Ethical conduct requires all of us, particularly an employer, to withhold judgment until we know all the facts. Recall that no formal charges have been filed yet. With respect to doing business in private, I would say that's the way it is done the world over. Deals of this magnitude are not negotiated in public or through the media. For Alaskans to get the best deal required delicate and carefully crafted communication, and, yes, some of it was in private. But I see no ethical conflicts when the entire contract is subject to legislative approval. The way we have acted maximizes the interests of Alaskans and reflects proper conduct by the executive and legislative branches of government."

To the loud cacophony of clamoring media, the governor and his chief of staff excused themselves from the room. Shouted questions chased them into a hasty retreat as they congratulated each other on what they mutually regarded as a solid performance. Sergeant Graham, who had been standing at the governor's flank, politely declined to comment on the case but indicated the department would have a formal statement once the coroner's report was complete. As the press conference came to a close, everyone involved in the case realized that the stakes had just been raised and that the pressure to solve the crime would intensify.

U.S. Asst. Attorney General Morse had successfully delayed the transport of Walter's body to Anchorage at the chief's request but only for two hours. The chief had skipped the governor's press conference in order to personally oversee the autopsy and lab analysis that would form the coroner's official declaration of the cause of death. The chief was now convinced that Walter Hayes' death was not accidental and hoped the cadaver would yield the evidence he needed. Every crime left behind clues, he knew, and none were more important to this case than confirming the precise cause of death.

When the chief entered the crime lab for the second time that day, the FBI's chief pathologist, Dr. Wang, was examining the pacemaker that had been removed from Walter's chest cavity. As the chief approached, Dr. Wang handed him the manufacturer's specifications, which outlined the basic operation of the Lifeblood Pacemaker and how its functions could be affected by electrical currents.

Portions of the report were highlighted, which the chief digested with acute interest.

> Even low-voltage of between 110 and 220 volts at 60-Hz AC current through the chest for a fraction of a second could induce ventricular fibrillation at currents as low as 60 mA. With DC current, 300 to 500 mA is required. If the current has a direct pathway to the heart, as with an electrode of some kind, a much lower current of less than 1 mA, (AC or DC) can cause fibrillation. Fibrillations are usually lethal because all the heart muscle cells move independently. Above 200 mA, muscle contractions are so strong that the heart muscles cannot move at all.

"Tell me, Dr. Wang, what makes electrical shock lethal? I know that both AC and DC current can cause death and that pathway is important. For example, if electrical current passes through the chest or head, the person can die. But I need to know more."

"What kind of current are you dealing with, AC or DC? It makes a difference. For example electrical shock from a main circuit or distribution panel leads to internal damage and cardiac arrest. Higher frequency AC current often follows a path along the surface of the skin rather than penetrating vital organs such as the heart. Alternating current will cause continuous muscular contractions ..."

"Let me stop you there, doctor. Hayes died while the electricity was out."

"In that case, you're talking about mains-magnitude DC, which interferes with the heart's natural rhythm and internal electrical pacemaker, leading to the risk of fibrillation."

The chief stopped taking notes and said, "Which in Mr. Hayes' case would likely be lethal, especially if his pacemaker wasn't operational."

"Something else you need to know," said Dr. Wang. "Hayes hadn't been in bed. He had just exited the shower. It's likely a small power supply as low as 32 volts could have caused his death."

"Dumb it down for me, Doc."

As a conductor, skin is highly variable. Dry skin is a poor conductor and normally carries a resistance of around 100,000 ohms, while moist or wet skin has a resistance of around 1,000 ohms. It's all in the report."

The chief consulted the paper in his hand, which summarized Ohm's Law (Voltage = Current × Resistance) illustrating just how critical conductivity is to causing death. The brief pointed out that while 9-10 amps were typically lethal, death can occur from currents as low as 30 milliamperes under the right conditions.

As the chief digested the information, his mind focused on the crime scene. He considered how a death by electrocution might have been perpetrated and by whom. The list of possibilities was narrowing and so was the list of suspects. It was now clear that any garage-style portable DC generator could produce enough current to interrupt Walter's heartbeat or to destroy this brand of pacemaker. The cables discovered in Jack Randolph's car were either used, he reasoned, or they were discarded after a power failure rendered them useless.

"This is all extremely helpful, Doctor," said the chief. "But tell me what you think caused his death."

"He was prescribed a pacemaker for ventricular fibrillation, a condition in which an uncoordinated contraction of the heart muscles in the lower ventricles causes them to quiver rather than contract. He likely died from an arrhythmia that interrupted blood circulation through the heart. The pacemaker is an implantable cardioverter-defibrillator called a Lifeblood II, a small battery powered electrical impulse generator. It works by detecting cardiac arrhythmias and corrects the irregular heartbeats by delivering a small jolt of electricity."

"I understand, Doctor. Was the thing working when he died?"

"Likely not. There was no signal when the body arrived, and death has no effect on the circuitry or battery. From what little I can gather about this model, the unit shows signs of what's called galvanic interference, which requires direct contact with a source of current. In extreme cases, when the interference is of a sufficiently high magnitude, it is possible for the pacemaker circuitry to be damaged, leading to a continued abnormal pacing behavior. I'm seeing signs of that here."

"It fits my theories about cause of death. Good work, Doctor. I want absolute certainty on this so I want a complete diagnostic."

"I just e-mailed their executive offices. According to their website, *electrical energy from direct current ablation can permanently damage circuitry and may lead to a no output response, sensing anomalies or erratic pacing.* I'll have some answers for you soon. You may be onto something."

"Thanks to your excellent work, I'm now convinced we're looking at a homicide," said the chief. "I'll inform Fell, but no one else is to know about this. Execute a chain of custody with top-level security clearances. We're dealing with some heavies on this."

The chief's next stop was to Seward's only heart specialist,

Dr. Bernhoff, who was waiting impatiently to learn of what possible assistance he could be to an investigation that now paralyzed Alaska with curiosity. In a short time, the chief could tell that Dr. Bernhoff knew a great deal about the investigation.

"I'm impressed with your knowledge of the case, but I'm curious where you're getting your information," posed the chief.

"Same place everyone is: www.ellenetal.com."

"Seems one of our guests is an efficient communicator," said the chief in mild exasperation. "I can't share everything with you, Doctor, but I can tell you that Mr. Hayes had a pacemaker." The chief consulted his notes. "An implantable cardioverter-defibrillator made by Lifeblood. What can you tell me about it?"

"I'm a cardiologist so I am very familiar with the device. It might be better if you ask me specific questions because I can talk for hours about things that likely have little relevance to your investigation."

"How would this pacemaker react to AC or DC electrical current that is introduced from a remote source—like an electrical outlet or portable generating device?"

"What you're describing is a source of interference. All manufacturers of pacemakers have design standards that are subject to rigorous testing before they are released. The tests are designed to investigate the effects of common exposures—say, for example, from household appliances such as microwave ovens. The Lifeblood model's response to AC or DC current would depend on a few variables, including the nature and strength of the current, the pathway and grounding characteristics of the receiver, the pacemaker's design, including the degree of shielding as well as its sensing and polarity characteristics."

The chief continued to scrawl his notes as the doctor

paused. Mike looked over his reading glasses with a facial gesture that encouraged the doctor to continue.

"The Lifeblood uses filters to attenuate electromagnetic interference outside the normal intra-cardiac range. Their design is effective when the interference is markedly different from electronic signals associated with cardiac activity, but these filters are not designed to resist direct electrical currents to the body of any magnitude."

"What would it take to fry one of those implants?"

"Very little I would think, given the circuitry. Typical household currents could fry one if the pathway was to the heart and resistance was minimal, for example over bare, wet skin. One hundred volts at minimal resistance levels—say 1000 ohms—requires only a half an amp to cause ventricular fibrillation and death. Defibrillators operate at 6,000 volts at 6 amps under similar conditions and definitely destroy the circuitry of a pacemaker. So that gives you a range."

"Are you aware of any other telltales signs of electrocution, particularly affecting the heart that might show up either internally or externally after death—say during an autopsy? For example, if an electrical current of sufficient strength was used to cause cardiac arrest, would you be able to detect this by looking at the internal organs?"

"Very likely, yes. The heart muscle is very strong and complex, but it also will retain many of the symptoms of death in its muscle structure."

The doctor pulled out a plastic model of the heart and proceeded in some detail to explain the various functions of the heart, its blood pathways and connections to the central nervous system.

Twenty minutes later, the chief was searching for a graceful exit strategy. "Doctor, you have been extremely helpful and I will very likely require your expertise in the near future. Thank you very much. Due to the obvious sensitivity of this case, I need to insist on strict confidentiality. It's important that you not repeat anything we discussed here today. Can I count on that?"

"You have my word."

When the chief left the hospital, he resolved to meet Fell at the Van Gilder. He was growing weary from the fast pace and long hours, but his mind could not rest. He needed to re-inspect room 201, and he could not escape a growing fascination with Juliet. Her reference to a burned hand was more than another unlikely coincidence. She was either involved in a murder or she possessed extraordinary powers.

As he drove the few blocks to the hotel, Juliet consumed the chief's full attention. He doubted Juliet's ability to commit murder or to abet such a crime. His quick research of her criminal past revealed only two charges: one nine years pervious for shoplifting and one for trespass, the latter for chaining herself to the Homer City Council chamber's doors in support of a nuclear-free zone resolution. On the other hand, Mike was trained to follow the facts and never to trust appearances. As innocent as she might appear, Juliet had questionable involvement in at least one piece of evidence and would remain a suspect.

The chief called Agent Fell.

"Fell, this is Mike Callahan. How's Morse holding up?"

"He's not happy. He had a ton riding on Hayes. Two years and a team of ten agents, and he's got little to show for it now. He's convinced we're looking at a homicide and is pressing me every hour for an arrest. I've got two more assigned to the team. How did your meeting go?"

"I'm getting close. I need to see you at the Van Gilder right now if you can make it."

"I can be there in five. What did you come up with?"

"Hayes' pacemaker was likely not working at the time of death. I believe a sudden shock of electricity damaged the circuitry. It ties with what we know about the condition of the body, the location of the body, and other evidence—such as the cables in Randolph's car. What did the lab have on that?"

"The cables are standard jumper cables. The size and shielding of the cables are typical of any heavy-duty brand. A thermal scan was inconclusive, but the cables had been outside for some time."

"Any wiring flaws show up in the room?"

"None; everything checked out."

"How about a wiring diagram?"

"I'll show you what we have. It's useless—hand-drawn pages. Put it this way, it's unlikely anyone other than James Van Oss could have used it for any purpose—even if they had possession of it."

"What did you come up with about the timing of power restoration?"

"Interesting finding on that point. The transformer stores data relating to power usage every half hour in order to calculate peak usage. But the data does not record usage by the minute. But, here's the kicker: downtown power grid was restored at 9:51 P.M. We're certain of that. And yet no power usage was recorded at all for the half-hour between 9:30 P.M. and 10:00 P.M. There is no doubt that someone killed the power using the main shut off during those nine minutes."

"Meet me at the Gilder, room 201 as soon as you can. I've got some ideas to run by you."

"See you in five."

When the chief arrived at the Van Gilder, he was greeted at the entrance by Juliet, who was holding a glass a wine in one hand and a cigarette in the other.

"Chief, we're having a party," Juliet said, gesturing to a collection of women and two platters of pizza. "You have to join us. You're not still working I hope."

"Maybe in a bit."

The chief turned away and peaked into the lobby long enough to identify the few guests who remained and then made a hasty departure for the stairs. As he entered the second floor landing, the chief visualized a dark corridor without emergency lights. The chief verified the ease with which a man of average height could unplug the emergency lights. As he progressed down the hallway, he carefully noted the location of every outlet and lighting fixture. As he approached room 201, he could see that the decorative end table at the end of the hall was pulled out from the wall, exposing a standard receptacle only a few feet from the doorway of room 201.

The chief pulled out his pocket flashlight and closely inspected the exterior brass-plated doorknob, which by now had been handled multiple times since the prior night. But a close examination of the soft-metal doorknob yielded telltale signs of clamping from a toothed devise, possibly the sharp jaws from the jumper cables discovered in Randolph's car. Just as the chief arose from his inspection of the doorknob, Agent Fell approached.

"What do you make of that, Fell?"

Fell dropped to his knees to get a good look at the doorknob from every angle.

"Not from normal wear. Marks look recent. I would guess it came from channel locks or a clamp of some kind. I notice some discoloration on the bottom here, black markings of some kind."

"Do you have your key handy?"

Fell unlocked the door and pushed it open, exposing the full room just as it was after the removal of Walter's body.

"Nothing's been touched, right?" asked the chief.

"Just as we found it, Chief. One curious detail my team uncovered this morning after looking over the interviews. You recall Ellen Windemuth's statement that she saw a man standing in front of room 207 when she ran downstairs in the dark. Well, that's a pension room that was registered to Dr. Strayer, who is female, and who was narrating the ghost story. There is no way it was her."

"I haven't found Ellen to be a particularly reliable witness. Don't forget, she was pretty liquored up," explained the chief.

"I'm thinking we should get that warrant for Randolph sooner than later. That attorney, Wirum, hasn't returned our call."

"Not yet, Fell. I'm looking for a portable welder or jumping device. Get your guys on it now, if you can. Check every nook and cranny on every level of this hotel. Have Mr. Van Oss help identify every possible stashing place in the hotel. There is no way someone would have risked taking it out of here. We find that and we find our killer."

Fell quickly assembled his team of investigators and directed them to sweep every possible hiding place within the hotel, with help from Van Oss.

"I'm looking for anything portable that can produce a current or that has wires coming out of it," Fell instructed.

The chief disassembled the doorlock and bagged it as official evidence.

Fell reached into his vest pocket and pulled a folded stack

of papers from his vest pocket and began to review them. "I've reviewed alibis for everyone in the hotel or who might possibly have a reason to kill Hayes. Of our eight primary suspects, only the Windemuths in 202 can account for each other between 9:00 and 10:00 P.M. We know Randolph was in the hotel at the time; what's your hesitation?"

"All true," responded the chief, "but I checked with Dale Minert, and Randolph was on that jet from Juneau when someone checked into the Orca Inn using his name. Why would someone register under Jack Randolph's name, unless he was either trying to frame him, or he was secretly meeting with Rachel? Furthermore, who other than Elliot Lawson knew Randolph was even coming to Seward, so how could someone know to frame him? And if Marcus Coble or someone else is sleeping with Rachel, he doesn't need to register as Jack Randolph to do it; it simply exposes him to unnecessary attention and risk. Last point: whoever posed as Jack Randolph is likely being protected by Rachel Randolph because he entered room 216 shortly after she did—with his own key!"

"What about the backpack and climbing gear in Rachel's room? Are you thinking they were placed there intentionally by her to throw us off, to make it appear as though someone is trying to frame Randolph?"

"That's what's bothering me," said the chief. "She's a smart woman, but I admit that's a stretch. She couldn't possibly know in advance that Jack was going to be a suspect in a murder investigation. There are only two explanations: she's involved herself and was caught off guard when we arrived unexpectedly, or someone else placed them there—but who?"

Agent Fell weighed in. "There's something about Mrs. Randolph that I don't trust. In my opinion, she's at least a co-

conspirator. If two are working together on this, a lot of pieces start to fall into place. Jack Randolph was parked in front of the Van Gilder, in plain view of everyone, with his keys in the car. Unless the guy is stupid, I can't see him committing murder and then carrying a murder weapon back to a getaway car parked in the most conspicuous location imaginable."

"Agreed," reasoned the chief. "Which leads us back to square one. Someone is trying to frame Jack, but who, and why? Why would someone choose him to frame? It makes no sense. Of all our potential suspects, Jack's motive is the weakest. Maybe we should focus on who might want both Hayes and Randolph out of the way."

"Rachel Randolph, if you believe she's obsessed with power."

"Maybe, but enough to kill for?" questioned the chief. "She has everything she wants now: money, status, stability. She doesn't strike me as someone eager to compromise the status quo."

"Maybe true, but what if she feared someone was threatening her perfect life?"

"Elliot Lawson is another possibility. He's about to lose everything—his job, his reputation, his life—and Walter Hayes held the key to everything. Elliot secretly flies to Seward the night Hayes dies. He is fully briefed on Hayes' whereabouts and the planned meeting. He has strong motive, opportunity, and no alibi. Furthermore, we know Lawson was being squeezed from every direction."

"True," said the chief, "but he arrived with Randolph around 7:15 P.M. and likely didn't bring electrical cables or a portable charger with him on the jet—unless we're really being played. He had no access to a car and no time to plan a murder. I believe whoever killed Hayes knew about the meeting, had some time to plan it, and yet was able to improvise. How else could he have responded to an unknown event like a power outage?"

"Unless the plan was to kill the power all along. Maybe the cables are just a distraction, a red herring. Maybe they were part of a plan to frame someone else, and Jack was just an unlucky bystander—maybe even mistaken for someone else. I agree that as desperate as he is, Lawson is not our man. Let's bring Coble in for a closer look. He strikes me as the one person with the most to lose from Hayes' testimony, and the most to gain by his death. He also has motive to frame Jack, since he would assume control of BOC."

"And he's smart enough to pull it off," agreed the chief. "I like your thinking. Go ahead and set it up for 4:00 P.M."

"Have you heard from Yushenko?" asked Fell.

"Nothing."

The chief turned to leave. "I'm going to go downstairs and join the ladies. Have your men track me down if they find anything."

Agent Fell knew the chief well enough to know that the extent of his social networking was with the boys over beer and a boxing match. No doubt he had a few ideas that he was keeping to himself.

The chief shuffled slowly down the hall and stairwell. scanning every possible hiding place as he went. He heard Inga's loud accented voice as he approached the library.

"Did you save me some wine, Ladies?" asked the chief. "Someone here has expensive taste. Silver Oak is my favorite."

"My one indulgence, Chief," said Inga. "We've had an exciting stay, but we hope to be on our way tomorrow morning. Are you going to let us go?"

"We're close to wrapping it up. I'm sorry you've had to experience this. Discovering a dead body is not exactly high on the list of recommended visitor activities. By the way, I hear you're quite an efficient communicator—or blogger," said the chief, turning to Ellen.

Ellen demurred, partly from acknowledgment of her website's popularity but also from a self-conscious admission that her content was purposely sensationalized to gain an audience. Ellen's blogs had gone "viral" in less than twenty-four hours, generating thousands of hits. Her homemade video footage that re-enacted her discovery of Walter's body through the bar-locked door had made YouTube's top ten list. Her favorable reviews of the hotel, which were accompanied by a flattering collection of photos, had caused a flood of internet inquiries and phone calls to the hotel.

However, it was Ellen's treatment of Fannie the Ghost that was generating the most curiosity and attention. She recounted Dr. Strayer's reading the night before in masterful detail, creating a historical context from an actual murder that few outsiders were aware of. Her stories were reconstructed from guest interviews, all of which were posted on Ellen's blog, where would-be crime stoppers could evaluate clues and construct their own theories. Ellen's colorful sketch of Juliet, accompanied by a detailed account of her ghost-like appearance the night before, placed Juliet on center stage in a public drama that Ellen was clearly directing.

One photo in particular accounted for the web-frenzy that consumed Ellen: a beautifully captured facial portrait of Juliet's candlelit face against an opaque background. Her penetrating eyes glowed from behind a veil of vapor, creating a soft but captivating stare that asked for help.

The image of Juliet had inspired chat-room comparisons to the Mona Lisa. Juliet's quirky combination of inner peace and mild angst captured perfectly the melancholy of a mystic shunned by modernism. Entire networks of mystics and faith healers were reporting their own connections with Fannie and were prepared to crown Juliet their spiritual leader. It was precisely this frenzy of attention that had the four women now assembled in the library whipped into lively conversation about the case and their immediate fortunes. When the chief arrived, they turned their attention to him in unison.

"I enjoy it, Chief," admitted Ellen. "It's more than a hobby. I was actually a travel writer for seven years, and I maintain my web site as a sort of 'rambler's guide.' Three-thousand hits in the last twenty-four hours, can you believe that! We were just talking about it."

"I have to admit I barely know what the internet is," said the chief. "I know when I need fingerprints, I go onto a computer. That's about it."

"Everyone is dying to meet the chief," teased Ellen. "I mean, how cool would it be for me to post a blog from you. I think you're the only one missing."

She turned to her laptop, which was connected to the hotel's wireless network and pulled up the piece on Juliet.

"Juliet's famous, look at this."

The chief inched forward and put on his reading glasses. He sat down and read Juliet's page as Ellen scrolled through the collage of photos, text, and links to other media. At once, and for the first time in his life, the chief was able to witness first hand just how powerful this form of communication had become. He realized the medium existed, but he had never witnessed anything this immediate, this professionally rendered—and it connected events to a world audience in such a personal manner. The degree to which his investigation could be manipulated by such a forum, and the extent to which public opinion was shaped by it, was unsettling to him.

"You mean to tell me three-thousand people have read this just in the last day?" he said.

"Yep, but that's nothing. The YouTube video alone will have four thousand hits today. Look here, Juliet has an invitation to be on Late Night with Conan O'Brien."

"No idea who he is, but it sounds impressive."

"So whaddaya think, Chief, can we do an interview? The world is dying to know if you believe in Fannie the Ghost."

Ellen scrolled to her mother's page and clicked the interview link. She played a short audio clip and explained to the chief how easy it was to use her computer as a video recorder. The recording they all heard of Inga was an unabashed criticism of "fakes and fortune tellers" who believed in ghosts:

> These so-called sightings are dreams and fantasies. We all have them. Those who believe in ghosts create them from their own imagination and fears. It makes me think of the witch hunts of the seventeenth century. We conjure spirits to promote our self-interest, to create tyranny and submission. We need to admit that the evils and injustices perpetrated by mankind on itself are of our own making. We should lend no ear to those who would shift from man himself the blame for evil inspiration or who suggest that anything but humanly imposed justice is really just. Fannie may be real in someone's mind, but that does not make her real ...

Ellen stopped the audio clip, and turned to the chief. It was her turn to place him on the spot.

"So, Chief, what do you believe?"

The chief glanced at Juliet, who studied his face intently. She lifted her eyebrows in a widened stare, then cocked her head to one side as a reminder that Fannie was listening and was easily offended.

"I have the advantage of being able to stare my enemy in the eyes, Ellen, and the burden of proof that a jury will find convincing. I do not pretend to have any powers that put me in touch with spirits or events of another world, although I admit that would come in handy in my line of work."

Juliet was determined to provoke the chief and press the point. She was now familiar with his smooth tongue and was resolved not to let him off the hook. If Fannie was trying to reach him, she believed, any insult here would surely quash the opportunity.

"Whether or not you have the ability to reach Fannie is not the question," she said. "After all, it is rare even for me, and I actually put effort into it. The question is: Do you believe Fannie exists or not? I think Ellen is seeking a straight answer."

Ellen knew the answer before it was delivered. The chief of police would never admit to the presence of ghosts, in spite of how popular or widely accepted that theory was with respect to the Van Gilder Hotel. The chief, on the other hand, was not always predictable or politically correct in such circumstances, perhaps the singular reason he had been passed over for Alaska's Commissioner of Public Safety.

"I admit I don't believe in ghosts," he said. "But I do believe in spiritual connections that inspire certain people to perform miracles."

"Here, Chief, I need a photo of you to go on the blog," offered Ellen by way of distraction.

She positioned the chief squarely under the shoulder-mounted deer on the wall above and clicked. She quickly e-mailed herself the shot, downloaded it, pasted it to a homepage template, labeled it "Chief Callahan," and linked it to her homepage. Within five minutes, the chief was an active player on a world stage.

The chief had decided to accommodate Ellen for two reasons. He needed to learn more about this business, and he also knew he could not effectively limit it, let alone stop it. He preferred that the information come from a source that he enjoyed a dialogue with, but the chief was a cop. Even after a few sips of wine, he never let his guard down. Furthermore, Ellen had never cleared herself of complicity in this entire affair.

"This is all very interesting, Ellen, but it strikes me as a lot of work. Who pays you to do all this?"

The chief could see that Ellen enjoyed the near-celebrity status and attention, indeed thrived on it, but that alone would not present a motive to murder.

"I do it for fun. But people pay me to send them stuff all the time: photos, quotes, or reports I've written. I was offered $500 for non-exclusive use of the photo of Walter's room," said Ellen as she pointed to a bright, full color digital photo of room 201 taken from the entryway. "I have people calling me for exclusives on this one, but I'm having too much fun."

"Well at least someone is," said the chief. "I'm curious, what do you write about?"

"Everything and anything. I don't try to guess anymore what people find interesting. Blogging is really best if it comes across as spontaneous, unedited, even unpolished. So I just write. In this case, I am writing about the hotel, the storm, the lights going out, the story of Fannie the Ghost, all the important people who are in Seward for some unknown reason. The entire scene strikes everyone as surreal."

"And do you discuss evidence or theories about how Walter Hayes died?"

The room fell suddenly quiet, and Ellen almost laughed at the perfect round-robin progression of glances around the room and their synchronized convergence on her. Juliet was the least conscious about hiding her complicity, as she rolled her eyes toward the ceiling, smiled broadly and turned her head in a mock gesture of "who me?"

"Of course, Chief, that is half the fun. We're not serious. I hope you don't get the wrong idea. It is not promoted as factual in any way. It's editorialized fiction, what I call Rambo journalism."

"In that case, I have concerns about appearing on here," said the chief.

"I generally don't allow editing of any kind, but in your case I understand the sensitivity involved. Anything you don't like, I'll remove. How's that?"

"So if your blog is editorial, why do media people pay for it?"

"You're joking, right? Media is not about facts, Chief, it's about what sells. But I have a tab here labeled 'Evidence and Clues,' and I try to keep that as filtered as possible."

Mike asked Ellen to open the tab, which he scanned with intense interest. Ellen's account of her initial discovery was accurately rendered. Somehow she had learned about the cables found in Jack's car and the key on the fire escape. Ellen sensed the chief's discomfort as he read through the blog, and she used the opportunity to raise a controversial subject.

"You must know that there isn't anyone anywhere who believes that Walter Hayes died of a heart attack. At least among the bloggers, the Seward police look pretty foolish at the moment."

The chief chuckled. He knew the truth of the observation, particularly after the ill-conceived press conference earlier that afternoon. He was not intimidated by the remark. In fact, it was at moments like this that he earned his reputation for straight talk.

"Damn politicians. I don't write the rules, Ladies, but I do have to live by them. I can't condone your blog, and I can't control it. But if any of you become aware of evidence that might shed light on this case, it is a crime to withhold it."

Juliet was insulted by what she perceived as a warning singularly directed at her. How can she be accountable for withholding clues she obtains from Fannie, especially when the chief refused to classify any such information as evidence. In fact, he would immediately discredit anything revealed by Fannie, and yet he was saying now it would be a crime to withhold it! She rose to her feet and spoke directly to the chief.

"You're just like the rest. You want it both ways. You want someone else to find a solution, but you'll never admit you're part of the problem," she said as she exited the room.

Mike watched Juliet steam down the corridor and slam the door to room 106. He turned back with a quizzical look. "What did I say to make her so mad?"

"Don't worry, Chief. She was on edge when we arrived," said Inga. "She's convinced she healed that diseased killer whale and complains incessantly about her lack of recognition. Personally, I think she is just a bitter person. This business about a ghost is nonsense. When Ellen interviewed her, I thought to myself, 'This is crazy and she actually believes it!' Let it go, Chief. Have some more wine."

The chief was visibly uncomfortable. He didn't want to divert his attention from Ellen's website, but he feared he might have committed a transgression greater than simply offending Juliet.

"I'm sorry if I offended anyone. Ellen, may I see Juliet's page please?"

Ellen opened Juliet's page, the most fully developed of the website.

"She's becoming famous, Chief!"

He scrolled down the page, scanning Juliet's ideas and the evidence she had obtained. Everything that Juliet had shared with him was there for the world to see. The chief felt blindsided and cheated, but he reminded himself that he never took Juliet's stories seriously enough to demand confidentiality. Trust was a two way street, he admitted to himself. If he was to make progress with Juliet, it would have to be on other terms.

After his brief tour of the website, the chief was intrigued by the possibility that the killer was monitoring events through Ellen's blog.

"Do you know who is accessing your website at any given moment, Ellen? Do people who visit you get tracked somehow?"

"My IP provider tracks the pathway, I think, maybe even for each visitor. Someone must have it, but it's nothing I can produce."

"So if I access your blog and open this page on clues and evidence, someone would know I did that?"

"Someone can access that data, Chief, but I can't. I could use some software to track what portal or search engine you used, but I don't know how to obtain your address."

The chief nodded in understanding, then shuffled over to the doorway and craned his head down the hall.

"Ellen, Ladies, thank you very much for the glass of wine. I learned a lot about Rambo journalism. I should check in on Juliet. Excuse me, please."

Juliet met the chief at the door, as though she knew he was approaching. She had changed into her evening gown and seemed to relish the role of a celebrity ghost-model.

"Come in, Chief, I've been expecting you. And don't tell me you came to apologize."

"OK, but why the cold shoulder?"

"You really don't get it ... Mike. You think I'm nuts, just like that Nazi in there, don't you?"

"No, I don't. I trust you, Juliet. You have great wisdom and powers of observation."

"But you don't believe Fannie exists do you?"

"No, I admit I don't. But don't take that to mean I don't believe you. I've been wrong in many things before, and I could be wrong about this too."

"There you go again. You believe me when I tell you I have met Fannie. And yet you don't believe she exists. Your father would call you a man of forked tongue."

Above all else, the chief had pride in his word, and he pondered the implications of Juliet's accusation.

"Let's give this a chance. I'm learning."

"I'll talk in your language because you will never understand mine. You have a theory about how Mr. Hayes died. In fact, you believe he was murdered. You even know how he was murdered. You have several suspects but none that you can connect to the crime. You are missing key evidence, which you believe is hidden in this hotel that will link the killer to the crime. All you need is to find that evidence and you will solve the case. Am I right so far?"

"You're right. You have been since the beginning. I need evidence."

Juliet's eyes locked onto Mike's in a cold, hardened vise that lasted an entire minute. He shuddered under her trance, anticipating a sudden case-breaking disclosure.

"People of our age who ask for second chances generally don't deserve them. If everyone would simply act as though there may never be another chance, our world would be a more wonderful place."

Mike stared blankly at Juliet.

"I know more about you than you think, Mike. About your son's death; about why you and Diane divorced; why you have been stuck in the same job for twenty years. Second chances don't exist in some cases."

"Can't we continue as we have, Juliet? Let's not make this personal."

"That's the problem, or more accurately, you're the problem. Five minutes ago, you offended Fannie by denying her, and now you're saying you want her back. Well she's gone! Poof. Vanished like a ghost. And the irony is that you leave with the confirmation you came for, that Juliet is a loon, a fraud. Well screw you! There's no second chance in this case."

Mike lowered his eyes, and his voice softened in a way Juliet had never heard before.

"When I lost my son, my only child, he was only fifteen. He trusted me. We were crossing a lake on snowmobiles, and he broke through the ice and disappeared before my eyes. I have been asking for a second chance ever since. And you were right about me before. I lost a part of myself when that happened. It cost me everything, my wife, my faith, maybe even my ability to love. But you are wrong about something else. I have never given up, and I am not about to now. Teach me what you know."

"Have you ever read the Bible, Mike?"

"Not extensively, no."

"I'll read you a favorite quote of mine from St. James. Maybe it will serve as a starting point."

Juliet picked up her King James Bible and located the bookmarked passage.

> Who among you is wise and understanding? Let him show his works by a good life in the humility that comes from wisdom ... But the wisdom from above is first of all pure, then peaceable, gentle, compliant, full of mercy and good fruits, without inconsistency or insincerity. And the fruit of righteousness is sown in peace for those who cultivate peace.
>
> Where do the wars and where do the conflicts among you come from? Is it not from your passions that make wars within your members? You covet but do not possess. You kill and envy but you cannot obtain; you fight and wage war. You do not possess because you do not ask. You ask but you do not receive, because you ask wrongly, to spend it on your passions.

Both sat in silent reflection waiting for the other to speak. For the first time since meeting Juliet, Mike felt a growing sympathy and respect for her. He checked himself as he admitted it was impossible to imagine her committing a crime or even tampering with evidence. For her part, Juliet felt a growing bond of sympathy for this man, but it was Mike who spoke first.

"Juliet, let's think about this. Fannie hasn't gone. She lives here. She's waiting for something. What else could account for her disappearance?"

Juliet glanced skeptically toward Mike but smiled warmly.

"You're coming along, Mike, that's a good first step. Recall that Fannie does not haunt the crime committed but the passions I just spoke of that lead to such things. The energy she emits is before an act of evil intent, not after, and it dissipates with time. That is why she has vanished."

"If that is true, then pressure exerted on the killer might arouse enough fear to force a second act of desperation. All we need is enough negative impulse to stimulate an evil thought, such as a plan to cover up a crime already committed or to frame an innocent person."

Juliet could discern the effort Mike was making and could not deny her growing affection for him. He would not betray her as others had done. She sensed Mike was close to discovering Teleos, but his awakening was a private matter. The problem was that he could not use private revelation for his public mission and so he could not cross over. He could not solve a crime or admit to solving a crime by communicating with spirits.

"What can I do to help you re-establish your connection?" asked Mike. "I will trust you, but I have to know that everything we discuss won't end up on a blog. I can't risk my credibility or this entire investigation over a misplaced report about ghost sightings."

"On the other hand, you can't have it both ways. Fannie may only reveal herself to a person of faith, to one who openly professes to it. History is full of opportunists who attest to their faith when advantage is pressing but who denounce the demon once the award ceremony has passed."

"Juliet please, give me a break. I'm really trying hard to work with you."

"*Me* give *you* a break? Unbelievable! I can hardly believe I'm here. Do you know how many breaks I have been given by people just like you, who pretend to need me and to trust me only to dump me when the tide turns. Don't you get anything? It is not me from whom you need to beg forgiveness! Start with your wife, and then maybe you'll have a chance with Fannie."

"You're hitting below the belt with that one, Juliet. I'll be leaving now."

"Yes, please go now!"

Mike shuffled sheepishly to the door and walked silently down the corridor to the library.

"How'd it go, Chief?" boomed Ellen. "Care for another glass of wine?"

Mike tightened his face and stared at the ceiling in a contemplative pose. He looked blankly around the room, then up to the ceiling again.

"Something wrong, Chief?" asked Ellen.

"Another glass of wine sounds perfect right now, Ladies."

As Ellen poured, the chief turned to her, smiling to himself as he formulated his confession in his head.

"Ellen, get your blog pencil out. I have something for you."

Ellen eagerly grabbed her laptop and prompted the chief to begin.

"You talk, and I'll write. Don't forget, you can edit the copy before I publish it. So don't worry too much about getting it perfect the first time."

> Chief Michael Callahan here folks, with breaking news from
> the Van Gilder Hotel, where our able host, Ellen Windemuth,

> keeps our minds alert and imaginations stirring with the latest evidence, theories and yes, even ghost sightings surrounding the death of Mr. Walter Hayes.

The chief knew he was breaking the rules, but he also reasoned that there was little official about the forum. His statement went on to compliment Juliet's "rare gifts and insights" and invited all "ghost whisperers" to contribute.

> The purpose of this blog is to ask for your help. Juliet needs a focused concentration from all energy sources to gather any evidence she can. She reported receiving a communication from Fannie that suggests we are looking for a man in his early sixties and who exited the hotel with a portable generator just before Mr. Hayes' body was discovered.

Mike assessed the risks of such a bold and unorthodox disclosure. The solicitation amounted to an open invitation to every publicity-seeking miscreant on the planet. But Ellen assured him that she would filter the responses, although she never indicated how. Nevertheless, Mike reasoned that the blog was the best forum to communicate with the killer and to bait a hook. He was sure the killer was tracking the investigation on Ellen's website and was one of the 3,372 hits the site had received in the last twenty-four hours. If nothing else, the blog would reassure Juliet that that he was shedding a bit of armor.

> If anyone knows anything about such a machine, please contact us at info@ellenetal.com.

# Chapter XV
*Saturday, January 19, 3:00 P.M.*

"**MR. BRADY,** this is Police Chief Mike Callahan from Seward. I'm in charge of the investigation into Walter Hayes' death. Do you have a few minutes to discuss the case?"

"I do. How can I help you?"

"Well, I understand he was a client of your firm, and I have a few loose ends, some of which involve your partner, Marcus Coble. I'm not sure how much he's told you, or what you've heard through the media, but I'm hoping you can help me."

"I'll sure try, but I know almost nothing about it. From what I heard, he died of natural causes," said Bill.

"I can hardly believe the frenzy this has caused. All this Twitter and Facebook stuff has me running in circles. You're not a blogger I take it?" inquired the chief.

"No, quite the opposite actually, one step beyond a feather quill, I'd say."

Immediately, the chief knew Bill Brady was being less than truthful. "This case has attracted quite a cast that's for sure. Did you know your partner was attempting to meet Mr. Hayes in Seward?"

"No, I didn't. Is Marcus implicated in any way?"

"No, but he was inside the hotel at the time of Hayes' death. When was the last time you spoke with your partner?"

"Yesterday around noon. To be honest, he made me

nervous. He said he was involved in things that I wouldn't approve of and that it was time to dissolve the firm. It struck me at the time as hasty, almost panicked."

The chief was surprised by Bill's volunteered disclosures that did less to protect Marcus than to expose him to greater suspicion.

"What do you think caused him to say those things?" said the chief. The open ended question was designed to test just how far Bill Brady would go to discredit his law partner.

"Marcus is under intense pressure. He's engaged in some questionable stuff, and now he's trying to clean up his mess. It's all over the papers, so I'm sure it's no mystery to you. I have no doubt Marcus was trying to obtain Walter's loyalty."

"So you have been reading about the case?" asked the chief.

"A single instance: some on-line report that my secretary brought to my attention."

"Do you recall the web address?" the chief asked.

"No, I don't, but where is this going?"

"I just find it interesting where people get their news. Nothing important. So why do you think Mr. Coble wants to quit the firm when it's doing so well?"

"He's been treading a fine line for years, acting as counsel to himself, in effect, as vice president of BOC. Until recently, Jack Randolph ran the entire show, and Marcus was just a name on the annual reports. Since their strike in Kuparak, BOC's growth has been meteoric, and Marcus is taking over all operational duties—and making a fortune in the process."

"So would it be fair to say Mr. Coble is betting his future on BOC; he's giving up his law practice to become an oil executive."

"Absolutely."

"Could Walter Hayes have been blackmailing Mr. Coble or BOC?"

"Given the deals those two have brokered, sure it's possible. Three weeks ago, Walter came into my office and outlined a payment scheme allegedly set up by Marcus that had surfaced in connection with the FBI's investigation of Representative Van Fleet. Ostensibly, Walter wanted to disclose a potential liability to the firm; but in truth he was looking for help. He never came out and asked for anything, but it was clear that he was starting a negotiation. Walter got pretty sideways with Marcus over that."

"If Walter Hayes told you this in confidence, how did Mr. Coble find out about it?"

"Walter knew that I would have to verify his information with Marcus, which I did."

"So fair to say that Mr. Hayes was applying pressure on you and Mr. Coble to help him—maybe even to the point of fabricating an invoice!"

"Sure, although I never heard any direct threats. On the other hand, Marcus' reaction was pretty hostile."

"Does Mr. Coble's departure from the firm concern you?"

"I have to question the timing of it. I'm not looking forward to the paperwork. Our office building, pension, and receivables are all jointly owned. Hundreds of hours of attorney time at grossly inflated rates!"

Both men shared a hearty laugh, at which point the chief decided to shift gears.

"Has your firm ever represented Victor Yushenko?"

Bill paused but responded firmly. "No, I don't believe we have."

"Has Mr. Yushenko ever approached you about working together on Russian projects?"

"Not me personally, you'd have to ask Marcus about that."

The chief's sixth sense was at work. Although he had never met Bill, something in his answers sounded less than forthcoming.

"That's curious because I understand the two men are not the best of friends."

"That may be, I don't know. I recall speaking briefly to Victor a few months back. As I remember, he wanted Marcus to review the status of oil leases in the Russian Chukchi."

"Does BOC have any oil leases in Russia?"

"None that I'm aware of. What does all this have to do with me, if I may ask?"

"It really doesn't concern you directly, but it does concern Mr. Coble and his relationship with BOC. Is Mr. Coble a paid officer and employee of BOC or just their attorney?"

"Some of these questions border on confidential. I don't think I should go into much more depth until I speak with my partner. I hope you understand."

"I understand, but it seems to me if my partner was in trouble, I'd want to know about it."

"I definitely do, but you haven't suggested Marcus is in any trouble. In fact, you said he wasn't implicated."

"This is a complex and ongoing investigation, and Mr. Coble is squarely in the middle of it. I'd like to tell you more, but I prefer to do it in person. I think it's fair to say that Mr. Coble will need you here. And if he doesn't, there's a good chance I will."

"What are you asking me to do?"

"Is it possible you could come to Seward tomorrow? I would deem it a favor. How long has it been since you've been to Seward?" asked the chief light heartedly.

There was a long silence that the chief half expected.

"Way too long, Chief. I'd be happy to come down, but I can only spare a day."

"Fine, we'll see you tomorrow then, say around 11:00 A.M. at the Van Gilder. Oh, one more thing. Do you know if Mr. Hayes suffered from heart trouble of any kind?"

"No, I don't," said Bill with more than a hint of impatience.

When Mike hung up, he immediately called Agent Fell to brief him on his conversation with Bill Brady.

"It's curious that he hadn't talked to Coble once since Hayes' death," the chief said. "I detected a little resentment there, for sure. He didn't ask any questions about Coble and sure didn't rise to his defense. When I mentioned Victor Yushenko, he went cold on me."

After a brief consultation, both men agreed that it was time to turn up the heat, and they would start with Marcus Coble. If Jack Randolph was indeed being framed, which appeared likely, Marcus had sufficient motive and opportunity. No one knew Jack better than he did; he was in love with Rachel and was poised to take over BOC in the event of Jack's incapacity.

"Get him in here, but first contact Brady's secretary and find out when he left the office on Friday. I'll see if I can't put some of Ellen Windemuth's coaching to work."

The mobile command center parked on Adams Street was a recycled, stripped down AATCO trailer on wheels. The only redeeming feature of the poorly insulated, leaky-roofed fiberglass container was the new wireless communication center, which even the chief found reliable and easy to use. In the few minutes before Marcus was expected to arrive, the chief and Agent Fell conducted their research on Bill Brady and carefully reviewed the field of potential suspects.

The chief was ticking down the list when Fell interrupted. "Don't forget about the unidentified man who was present during the reception and ghost reading. Van Oss is certain the man was not a registered guest and was wearing a Chugach Electric jacket. He drank straight Jack Daniels and wasn't particularly sociable. According to Van Oss, he left sometime during the ghost story."

"Do we have a physical profile?"

"Long, black hair and beard, about six-feet-one, maybe 220 pounds, mid-forties. He struck Van Oss as an odd duck."

Within ten minutes, there was a knock on the mobile office door and Marcus stepped inside. He greeted Mike with a genuine smile and a handshake.

"Hello, Chief. I'm sure you understand I was just trying to do my job last night. I hope there are no hard feelings."

"Absolutely not; I understand. We all have our jobs to do. Please, have a seat. You've met Agent Fell, FBI."

"I have, thank you. I need to disclose up front that Jack and Rachel Randolph have secured other legal counsel on this matter, so I no longer represent them, at least until my name is cleared."

"Which leads directly to the point of this meeting and a disclosure of our own. You need to know you're a prime suspect in what is now a murder investigation."

"Jesus Christ! You can't be serious."

"You know the drill. The more you tell us, the more we know. If you don't cooperate with us, we'll know it, and you can expect your life will be miserable for the foreseeable future. If you lie to us, we'll know that too. We assume you're OK to continue?"

"Sure."

"We'll be asking you tough questions, so we want to be sure you're ready. Can we get you anything first?"

"No. I'm as ready as I'll ever be."

"First, I want to ask a few questions about your law partner," said the chief. "Would you consider him adept at using a computer?"

"Above average for a man his age, I would say."

"And how does he usually get his news?"

"All on-line. He's a junky."

"Describe his build. This picture we have is old," said Fell as he tossed a file in front of Marcus.

"Tall, maybe six-foot-three, 220 pounds, black hair, brown eyes, youthful baby face. Why, what's up?"

"Why hasn't he called you about Hayes' death?"

"He's not particularly enamored with me at the moment."

"Because of your association with Walter Hayes and your decision to leave the firm?"

"Precisely."

"Does Mr. Brady know that Walter Hayes had a heart condition?"

"Let me think." After a long silence, Marcus looked almost surprised. "He did … he must have. Walter kept it pretty quiet, but he participates in our firm's health plan. I recall discussing the disclosure with Bill a few years back."

"And what's his favorite drink?"

"Straight scotch or bourbon whiskey."

"I'm going to switch gears on you," said the chief. "Mr. Hayes was very likely murdered. Do you have any idea who might have done it?"

"No clue."

"Really, I find that hard to believe," Fell interrupted.

"Everyone seems to have a theory about it."

"I'd rather not engage in speculation."

"Then let's start with what you know and aren't sharing with us," said the chief.

Marcus stared blankly at the two without an answer.

"Are you withholding any information that could prove helpful in our investigation, yes or no?"

"There is one thing. The articles you found in Rachel's room are likely mine. I have no idea how they got there."

"That's a good start. We were going to ask you about that. The backpack, boots and climbing gear—all yours?"

"I only saw the boots and coat. I don't own any climbing gear," said Marcus despondently.

"We'll come back to that. When did you learn Rachel was coming to Seward?"

"I never did. It wasn't until I met her at the Orca Inn with Sergeant Graham that I knew she was here."

"Did you ever visit Rachel in her room?"

"No. I just told you I didn't know she was coming."

"Last night, Mrs. Randolph stated that you told her Jack was coming to Seward. Is that correct?"

"Actually, no. I had no idea Jack was coming to Seward, but I told Rachel it was likely he would end up here sometime over the weekend."

"Have you ever done business with Victor Yushenko?"

"What does that have to do with Walter Hayes?"

"Answer the question, please."

"We've talked but never transacted business."

"Does BOC have any Russian oil leases?"

"No, it doesn't."

"Why did Mr. Yushenko come see you a few months ago?"

"He's a big shot. I don't trust the guy, personally. He's nothing more than a front for Russian oil companies trying to steal western technology—who, as soon as they acquire it, turn around and screw us out of everything."

"Sounds like you've got a burr in your saddle over it."

"Not really. BOC is unique. We're small, and yet we own the best drilling and extraction technology in the world. We're also the best at what we do: negotiating leases and drilling rights on marginal fields. Victor doesn't have any expertise. He's simply a middleman. I'll be honest, I don't like people who insert themselves into transactions but bring little value to the deal."

"I understand. But you still haven't answered my question," said the chief.

"About a year ago, we negotiated a technology swap with a Russian firm, Extron Oil. They hired Yushenko to get them out of the deal. He was leaning on me to relinquish our control over the extraction technology, but I said no. That was the purpose of the visit and the end of it."

"Did Walter Hayes have any dealings with Yushenko?"

"Everyone in our business likes high oil prices, right? I'm not certain, but I believe Victor paid Walter to keep things quiet with Alaska's governor and legislature."

"Dumb it down for me, Mr. Coble," ordered the chief.

"In 2004, the U.S. State Department feared the global effect of Russian nationalization of their oil industry. Our government doesn't like high oil prices because we import so much oil. Therefore, any international crisis that de-stabilizes supply is a bad thing. Big Oil, on the other hand, loves high prices. But the bigger threat to them was the loss of their Russian investments and the wholesale rip-off of western technology, which is the competitive edge that allows Big Oil to leverage these deals in the first place. It's actually pretty simple. Our government struck a three-way compromise. The U.S. would not resist nationalization if the Russians compensated Big Oil and enforced trade restrictions of western technology."

"It sounds like politics as usual."

"A delicate compromise involving billions. If the Russian people knew what President Martov paid to buyout Western Big Oil, he would face a firing squad. If the American people knew that we caved into communism, our president would be skewered. But here's the key, as an oil-producing state with a growing stake in the Russian far-east, Alaska stood to gain from high oil prices but to lose big from the withdrawal of Alaskan-based oil contractors from Russia. So there was resistance from the start. Walter's job was to keep a lid on things."

"I think I get it. Yushenko was working to implement the compromise, which worked against the interests of Alaska."

"Exactly. Here's another tip for you. You've met Inga Windemuth, I assume. I bumped into her this morning. You probably believe her story about retirement and ski vacations. Bullshit! BOC did a background check on her; the Russian government sent her. This Venezuelan free oil we're allowing—this Chavez giveaway—it's all part of the same scheme: keep oil prices high and divert attention and blame from the Russians. Inga is monitoring U.S. compliance with the deal, I have no doubt. You did *not* hear that from me! There's your motive!"

"Not sure I follow."

"Other than I, Walter was the only person in Alaska who knew that Yushenko was fronting for the Russians on this. Can you imagine if that was leaked? It would affect world oil markets and threaten his life. The Russians were monitoring Walter's status a lot closer than we were."

"I thought you said the plan was sanctioned by the State Department."

"Secretly, maybe, but no one would ever admit to it publicly. Yushenko would be hung out to dry!"

"Was Walter Hayes actually accepting money from the Russians through Yushenko?"

"I'm sure he was, but I can't prove it."

"Did Hayes ever complain to you about any threats or coercion from Yushenko?"

"No, but I'm sure Walter knew he was flying solo on that deal. I'm sure absolute secrecy was a condition of getting involved. But that's what Yushenko does best. He's damn good. I have no doubt Hayes was on his secret payroll."

"And you believe Inga Windemuth is an active spy? She's definitely who she says she is; I had Fell run her through Immigration, but it never crossed my mind to check with CIA. If she were conducting a hit, I would think she'd be a little more circumspect."

"Trust me, she's a spy. If you think about it, her daughter is perfect cover. There's more to this blogging business than you realize."

Mike thought about his recent experiment on Ellen's blog and thought to himself, "Dammit! Where is this trail going to end? One step forward, two back."

He turned to Agent Fell and asked him if he had any more questions for Mr. Coble. The chief's ploy was common among detectives. He was playing the role of the good cop who was all-to-ready to let Marcus go. Fell, however, would hit hard.

"I don't believe a goddam word this guy is saying, Chief. He confesses to recognizing some clothing in an attempt to gain our trust and then bamboozles us with a bunch of bullshit. I think he's in love with Rachel Randolph and screwing her. He's the damn VP of Beaufort Oil for Christ's sake; he knew exactly when the company jet would arrive and with whom!"

Agent Fell turned back to Marcus.

"You checked into the Orca Inn as Jack Randolph, dropped clothes and equipment off with Rachel, and planted your key on the fire escape. It took you both to pull this off, one on watch and the other on the trigger. Walter Hayes was about to take you down. You recruited Rachel by convincing her that BOC was in jeopardy and that you could keep her husband clear of the dirty work. Secretly, however, you plotted to frame Jack and to make his frame appear as an accident to Rachel. Walter Hayes had enough incriminating testimony to sink both you and BOC. He was probably blackmailing you over it. You saw an opportunity to save your ass and to grab two other trophies you've wanted for a long time: Rachel and BOC."

"Nice theory, but it doesn't hold up. What about the ... ?"

Fell quickly interrupted. "It's no theory, and it will hold up. I'm just getting warmed up. Maybe I can save you some breath. The items discovered in Rachel's hotel room were yours, and you knew it last night, so why didn't you report it? Why didn't Rachel report it when they mysteriously showed up in her room?"

"I would have to be the dumbest sonofabitch to leave ..."

Fell pounded away.

"We have an eyewitness placing you in the second-floor hallway just moments before Ellen Windemuth discovered Hayes' body."

"That's impossible; who is it, Ellen? She's a lying drunk who probably killed Walter herself!"

"You told investigators that you were in the lobby when

Ellen came screaming down the stairs and that you had just come in from outdoors, correct?"

"OK."

"You also stated that it was pitch-black outside, and the power had not been restored at that point, did you not?"

"I did. In fact, that's why I decided to come inside."

"Well, we know you are lying because the entire downtown power grid was restored at least ten minutes before Ellen's trip down the stairs. So I'm curious, the only reason you would have to lie is if you are guilty of something. And the only basis you could have for stating that power was still out when the body was discovered is if you were inside the hotel, which was still without power when Ellen discovered Hayes' body. So I'll say it again. Our eyewitness swears she saw you in the second floor hallway at the exact moment Ellen ran downstairs."

This was new information to the chief, who did not entirely agree with Fell's tactics, but he kept quiet, carefully observing Marcus' body language, which was now beginning to talk.

"That's impossible. I never … . It's a lie."

"It's no lie, Mr. Coble! It's testimony that will convict you, that is, unless you start telling the truth."

"You're full of shit. No one saw me on the second floor of that hotel, and you know it."

"Have it your way, Mr. Coble! We've got enough to arrest you right now. I'm just giving you one last opportunity to come clean. It's really that simple. If you choose not to tell the truth, we'll hand you over to the DA. But frankly, I think you're holding back a lot of information, and it makes me wonder why."

"Look, this is two-way street, and I don't appreciate you telling me you have a witness when you don't."

"And how are you so damn sure!" Fell shouted, his red face now thrust to within inches of Marcus. "Tell me where you really were when the body was discovered because I'm about through with you. The media will have a heyday with this, big boy!"

"Because it was pitch black in that hallway, OK? There was no witness, and you know it."

"Now we're getting somewhere. The only way you could possibly know that is if you were on the second floor sometime prior to the murder. The power was not on to the hotel when you arrived as you stated, and it was not on when you were upstairs looking for Mr. Hayes. The emergency lights were intentionally unplugged on the second floor hallway, and it was pitch black, just as you say. In fact, it was the only totally dark area of the hotel. But the only way you would know that is if you were there."

For the first time since meeting Chief Callahan and Agent Fell, Marcus had no response.

"Power was restored outside the hotel but not inside because Rachel Randolph shut off the main disconnect to ensure that you would have the cover of darkness to do your work. When Ellen screamed, you panicked and went out the fire escape. That's when you dropped the key. You hid long enough to ensure the coast was clear, and you flipped the main back on. Then you immediately went back in to join the party."

"I was in the hall, OK, and I did see Ellen run downstairs screaming. It was dark. I admit I panicked, OK? I left via the fire escape and then came around and entered the lobby from Adams Street. I knew I would look suspicious if I remained in the hallway. But I swear, I didn't touch the power, and I didn't kill Walter." Marcus paused and then glared at Fell. "Don't lie to me again, Sir! I don't appreciate it."

"That makes us pen pals, doesn't it," said Fell. "You planned to shut off the electricity to the hotel even before the power outage, and you killed Hayes by electrocution using a portable welder, likely the Craftsman unit you bought from Sears last year. I'll wager the cables stashed in Jack's car have your prints all over them."

"I'm being framed, goddam it!" Marcus Coble suddenly looked like a caged animal. He shot up from his chair and started pacing the small office in frantic half-circles. His vengeful scowl and intense concentration reflected a mounting desperation.

"You see what's coming down now?" said Fell. "Unless you decide to cooperate fully, we can't help you. If you think someone's trying to frame you, we're all ears," said Agent Fell.

Marcus turned sharply. "Look, dammit. I didn't do this. I'm not a killer, and I'm not screwing Rachel either."

"I think you'll have to convince a jury of that at this point. Unless you can come up with something convincing, we're going to arrest you right now."

"Look, I need time. You have my word that I won't leave Seward. Give me twenty-four hours to help you piece this together. Please, I'm begging you! I could save a lot of unnecessary grief for everyone."

Fell looked squarely at the chief. "Your call, Chief. I say we take him in. At the least, I want him to volunteer a DNA sample."

"You report to me every hour and surrender a DNA sample, and I'll give you twenty-four hours," said the chief. "If I hear about you digging a little too hard, I'll arrest your ass faster than you can unzip your fly."

"I can't believe this is happening. You'll get a match on those clothes. I just need to figure out who and how someone got into my house and stole them."

"You've got twenty-four hours, Marcus, no more. By the way, I figured you would need a lawyer, or at least a friend, so I called Bill Brady and asked him to be here tomorrow."

"Jesus Christ, a lot of help he'll be," said Marcus as he turned to leave.

The chief smiled at Fell.

"You're getting pretty good at this, Fell. How the hell did you come up with that?"

"You're not the only one talking to Juliet," responded Fell smugly. "And I read your blog. Nice piece by the way. Actually, I figured you were getting a little desperate, so I went on a fishing expedition of my own. Central's receiving e-mail and calls from every imaginable quack out there, mostly in response to your request for 'focused energy.' They forwarded one anonymous lead from someone claiming to know Mr. Coble and who saw a new portable welder in his shop a year ago—a Craftsman he thought. I tried it on, and it fit."

"What about the jumper cables? Do they have his prints?"

"They do in fact have prints, inconclusive but enough to convince the lab they're his."

"We have our man, Fell, but I want to be sure. There's some risk, but I'll hold tight to the hourly reporting. At the least, I figure we have a desperate man with the connections and the incentive to solve this case. I'm sure he has a few theories of his own."

"What do you make of his Inga Windemuth story?"

"Inflated I'd say, but possible. It hinges on Yushenko. Let's see if we can get him on the phone."

Mike had to consult his "black book" for the private number, but within a minute he had the man on the phone. This was *the* Victor Yushenko, perhaps the most high-profile defector from a Soviet eastern-bloc country in history.

"Victor, this is Mike Callahan. How are you doing, old friend?"

"I've been great. I've got lots of fishing stories to tell you when I see you."

"Well, I hope that's soon, but right now I have my hands full with Walter Hayes' homicide."

"I heard about that, a bit of a shocker even given everything else that's going on. It's now officially a homicide?"

"Not officially, but listen, I just met with Marcus Coble. Between you and me, he's got his back up against the wall. I need to ask you some questions. I need it straight, but I have to keep it on the record."

"Fair enough, Mike."

"I understand Walter Hayes was working for you."

"You aim to get me in big trouble, don't you?"

"I just need you to shoot straight, Victor."

"He was for a short while, but he withdrew months ago due a perceived conflict of interest. He had two missions: One was to quash opposition to importing Venezuelan oil to Alaska. The other was to keep the Alaska Legislature from taking action against the Russians. My role was to broker the silence, if you will, of the major firms having interests in Russia. It was hoped this would stabilize the oil markets and eliminate the likelihood of a technology embargo."

"Mr. Coble made it sound like you're working for the Russian mafia. Who else knows what you do?"

"Mike, I'm a registered international broker. Everyone

knows what I do. Some of my clients require discretion and a certain degree of anonymity, but I'm under a microscope. I don't always sleep too well, but I've managed not to make too many enemies."

"Victor, you're a high-profile guy always flying at mach-10! Mr. Coble alluded to pressure on Walter coming from overseas, particularly Russia. What do you know about that?"

"It's true but not necessarily sinister. The Russians keep a close watch on me too. It's nothing more than a hedge. The Kremlin still has remnants of the old guard from East Germany doing some of their dirty work; they make sure we know that they're watching their investment. It wouldn't surprise me if they had someone working Walter Hayes in Alaska."

"Without your knowing."

"Entirely possible; in fact likely. It's not about nukes anymore, Mike, it's all about oil."

"And what if Hayes doesn't perform?"

"We send him to Siberia … just kidding. Seriously, Mike, we cancel the contract. It's that simple."

"Have you ever heard of Inga Windemuth?"

"Sure, she's one of them, former East German, I believe. But she's a network intelligence officer—we call 'em gobees—not an assassin. Trust me on that."

"I'm not so sure. Inga Windemuth checked into the Van Gilder just hours before Hayes was killed. We found some evidence in Hayes' room that suggests they were at least in contact."

"No shit! Well, I'll think about that, but I can't think of any reason the Russians would have to kill Walter Hayes. The truth is that their plan worked much better than anyone imagined. In fact, nationalization was a non-event—and over a year ago!"

"What if Hayes' testimony at trial threatened to expose his connections to you and to the Russians? What kind of shit would that stir up?"

"Maybe some embarrassment to both sides, nothing more. It's yesterday's news, and no one got hurt—no laws were broken. And listen, I move around in these circles. This is chickenshit stuff. The feds are not going to bat an eye at the fact that the Russians hired an Alaskan lobbyist to help maintain the flow of technology to their country. It happens every day."

"Good enough, I don't mean to get you excited. I also need to know what business Mr. Coble has in Russia."

"This one's off the record, Mike. Coble has an interest in Extron, which he obtained by trading technology software. These are "off-the-books" OK, because neither he nor BOC is licensed to market the technology overseas. The contracts are in his name, I believe, since he insisted BOC not be involved."

"I'm following you. Go on."

"I'm brokering buyouts of all non-Russian interests in the Russian Chukchi. Bottom line, Coble wouldn't sell his Extron interest. From what I understood, it was a tax and disclosure matter that would have caused him exposure. My advice to him was to walk away from the deal, but he wouldn't listen."

"Did you guys ever trade blows?"

"Never, but he and I have never been friendly for some reason."

"Victor, I thank you for the information. It's helped a great deal. If I really need you, what are the chances you can make it to Seward tomorrow?"

"Happy to be there, my friend, but I have to clear a few things from the flight deck. I hope you nail your killer!"

## Chapter XVI
*Sunday, January 20, 11:30 A.M.*

**EVERYONE IN SEWARD** could tell the time by the bells that sounded Sunday mass at the Catholic Church just north of the hotel. Inside the Van Gilder, Chief Callahan had created a strikingly familiar scene. Instead of tiny offices there were small hotel rooms, but everything else about the setting was reminiscent of Alaska's legislative offices during session—the narrow halls and mahogany doors, the bright red carpet, the historic fixtures and photographic exhibits. Everything seemed strangely like the hallowed halls of Alaska's Capitol.

But beyond all this, the aura of Alaska's political headquarters was created by the collection of faces: Governor Thompson and his chief of staff, Elliot Lawson; Jack and Rachel Randolph; Marcus Coble and his senior law partner, Bill Brady. Stuart Bond was there with Rick Fulton; Ellen and Inga Windemuth had extended their stay voluntarily, and even Victor Yushenko made a surprise showing. Agent Fell, U.S. Asst. Attorney General Robert Morse, and several other Justice Department representatives all huddled around impatiently to hear the chief's rendering of events.

"I've assembled you all here for good reason," began the chief. "You have all been most patient and cooperative throughout this investigation, and I promise not to waste your time. I realize we're all a little cramped in here, but I thought it would be important to locate where the events that resulted in Mr. Hayes' murder occurred."

This was the first time anyone in the room had heard an open declaration from the chief that Walter Hayes was murdered. An audible restlessness resulted from the disclosure. There was more to Mike's awkward choice of venue to bring closure to his case than he admitted, however. The truth was, he still had loose ends. He needed someone to break, and that could only come from intense pressure applied in a public yet highly controlled setting. And finally, there was Fannie, whom Mike now privately acknowledged was as real as any woman, and as hard to get to know. But he was making every effort to secure her favor—and assistance—to create the pressure he hoped would provide the break he needed.

"I'm glad we finally have an acknowledgment from you on what all of us knew long ago," said the governor. "Let's have it."

Agent Fell turned to Sergeant Graham. "I hope the chief knows what the hell he is doing," he whispered. "This had better work, or we're all going down hard."

"Governor, with all due respect to you and your office, I need to start at the top," began the chief. "Your administration could be spared a great deal of embarrassment, perhaps even several indictments, on account of Mr. Hayes' untimely death. Perhaps you can explain to everyone here what you meant when you e-mailed your chief of staff a week ago and said that you wanted Mr. Hayes out of the way."

The chief handed the governor a copy of the e-mail.

"You are taking that out of context," said the governor. "I was simply saying he was no longer welcome in my office."

"Implausible and careless wording if that is what you intended to communicate," said the chief. "It seems you also owe us an explanation about yesterday's press conference. I have here a draft of your speech prepared last Thursday accepting the resignation of Elliot Lawson."

"Where the hell did you get that?" the governor snapped. "This is outrageous! I had two separate statements prepared by my team prior to my meetings here in Seward, which is not unusual when daily events influence my decisions and when I haven't made up my mind. In this case, my decision hinged on the evidence against Elliot, which I needed to hear directly. If you have a point to make, I suggest you make it quickly."

The governor and his chief of staff retreated into a side room to confer in private, which only served to heighten everyone's curiosity. The chief was forced to raise his voice to keep the attention of the retreating men.

"Governor, excuse my boldness, but I am simply calling it as I see it. You both had substantial motive and opportunity. Neither of you can confirm your whereabouts at the time of the murder. In fact, you both took extraordinary precautions to conceal your arrival in Seward and your subsequent movements. Mr. Lawson's pending indictment was bad enough, but you figured you were next, didn't you, Governor?"

The entire crowd of people was dumbfounded by the shocking turn of events. Even the investigative team was surprised by the blunt, unanticipated attack. The audacity of the chief seemed nothing short of suicidal. Turning to the governor, who had come back into the room, the chief resumed his argument.

"Mr. Hayes' testimony would ruin your chances for re-election, possibly even implicate you directly in the royalty tax vote, which we know involved bribing votes with campaign contributions. And to top it all off, Walter Hayes threatened to expose your duplicity on the subject of free oil from Venezuela, didn't he? If Alaskans knew you were allowing the oil imports to placate the Russians and to stifle protests about artificially inflated oil prices, you would have killed any chance for re-election."

Governor Thompson could no longer contain his anger; his red face and clenched jaw thrust itself to within inches of Mike's nose. But before he could summon any words of reproach, the chief continued his well-planned attack.

"Your chief of staff, however, had even greater motive, and the secrecy surrounding his arrival in Seward makes his lack of alibi all the more suspicious. We know about his pending indictment and the obvious motive behind silencing Mr. Hayes. What most people don't know is that a felony conviction would strip Mr. Lawson of all his future benefits, his lifetime health insurance, pension and retirement account—over two million dollars in future benefits accumulated during thirty-five years of government service."

"I don't know what you're trying to accomplish, Chief," said Elliot, "but it seems to be nothing more than a fishing expedition bordering on trash talk. Unless you're placing me under arrest, I'm through here. I've heard enough mudslinging for one night."

"In fact, Mr. Lawson, you *are* being placed under arrest."

Elliot stiffened and turned suddenly pale. He looked around the room in horror. The expected gasps were momentarily stifled as everyone held their breath in anticipation of what would follow.

"Although not for the murder of Walter Hayes. No, you are being arrested for conspiracy to obstruct justice and for violations of state ethics laws. Your conversation with Jack

Randolph Friday night at the Goldmark Hotel was recorded. It's all here," the chief said pointing to a hand held recorder. "And while it doesn't clear you of complicity in Mr. Hayes' death, it supports a motive for keeping him alive. Unfortunately, you were all too willing to trade the public trust for your personal gain.

"Which leads me to the next casualty of this sordid mess," the chief continued. "Mr. Randolph, you are also under arrest for attempted bribery, extortion, and obstruction of justice, based on the same conversation. As soon as I am finished here, Agent Fell will read you your rights and take you both into custody."

"None of this will stand up in court!" shouted Jack from down the hall. "My lawyers will have a field day with this. Offering Mr. Hayes an incentive and opportunity to defend himself is not a crime and certainly not obstruction of justice!"

"To Mr. Lawson's credit, at least he acknowledged the law," responded the chief. "You, however, can't distinguish between a request and a threat. It's precisely the kind of unscrupulous business behavior that led to Walter's death, as we'll see."

Rachel moved to place her arms around Jack, but he flung them off, electing to stand alone peering into the darkness of Adams Street. He stood waiting to learn the identity of Walter's killer, all signs of which pointed to Marcus, who was pacing nervously at the outer fringe of activity at the end of the hallway. Marcus had produced no new evidence in his allotted time and now feared the worst.

"Tell us Ms. Windemuth, why are you here in Seward," said the chief to Inga.

"I am on vacation, as I told you."

"You are visiting, but in fact you are hardly on vacation.

We've tracked your so-called vacation itinerary, and you have an amazing propensity to turn up wherever Mr. Hayes happens to be. In fact, you have been following him for three weeks, haven't you?"

"That's absolutely absurd!"

"Is it? I'm sure everyone here will find it fascinating that you worked for the East German secret police for twenty years, until the wall came down, and since then as a Russian field operative specializing in tracking the whereabouts of missing persons. I rather suspect you are here on assignment for the Russian government, which had an intense interest in Mr. Hayes."

"Seems you're full of conspiracies tonight, Chief," said Inga. "It makes for a great international thriller, but unfortunately there is no truth to what you say."

"Well, let's talk about motive. Mr. Hayes was one of several individuals with enough knowledge to expose the duplicity of Russian President Martov's policies, the secret payoffs being made to the oil companies for huge profits, and the illegal exchange of protected drilling technology. The Russian government was not about to let Hayes' testimony on these subjects see the light of day."

"If Mr. Hayes knew about these schemes you talk of, I am sure many others knew about them too," said Inga. "After all, he made a living from selling information."

"I believe Mr. Hayes was afraid to tell anyone what he knew out of fear for his life. And yet, as desperate as he was, I believe Mr. Hayes regarded his silence as negotiable, to be maintained at a price. In fact, he was receiving considerable sums of money from the Russians through you, was he not?"

"I have no idea where you're getting this, or more importantly where you're going."

The chief pulled a tight roll of $100 bills out of his pocket and counted them one at a time. The effect was dramatic and convincing.

"Mr. Hayes was blackmailing you, wasn't he? Among his personal possessions was $5,000 in cash, traced to a London bank and issued to you three weeks ago before you left for the U.S."

Inga was stone-faced. "That is preposterous!" was all she could muster in the way of a defense.

"In fact, you made contact with Mr. Hayes through a local intermediary just before his death. You arranged for a time and place for an exchange of money, did you not?"

"I did no such thing."

"And in fact, Ellen was more than just a little curious about a cracked door when she approached room 201 and discovered Mr. Hayes' body, wasn't she?"

After a few seconds of silent stares, the chief continued. "Now let's talk about opportunity. You were directly across the hall from Mr. Hayes when he died and could monitor his activities fairly closely, couldn't you? The three of you had in fact met, maybe even argued—which you lied about. Did Mr. Hayes attempt to extort more money from you? Was that it? Or maybe after taking $5,000, he informed you that he was turning himself in."

"Pure speculation!"

"Is it? Here's a copy of a statement from a Ms. Laura Beckett, confirming that she received instructions from you to contact Mr. Hayes last Friday night at the Van Gilder Hotel and to direct him to room 202—which, coincidentally, was directly across the hall from Mr. Hayes. That was 9:20 P.M. Friday night. Ms. Beckett did not expect to be an accomplice to murder and when she realized her facial portrait was circulating around town, she panicked and turned herself in. Her statement is all here. You lied to me more than once, and you had the motive and the means to kill Walter Hayes!"

Ellen blurted out: "Mr. Hayes was dead when I found him. We did not kill anyone!"

"Your travel blog was excellent cover, Ellen. You used it to steer my investigation and to avoid suspicion, didn't you? It was a perfect communication tool to relay progress to your government. Is that not the truth?"

Ellen began to sob.

"Misreporting the purpose of your visit to the Immigration Office invalidates your passport, at a minimum. Obstruction of justice, bribery, and extortion may not be enough to extradite you, but murder is. I can promise you that any one of these offenses is enough to keep you from returning to the U.S. ever again. Directly after this meeting, you both will be escorted to Anchorage for immediate deportation. I'm afraid I do not have enough evidence to hold you for murder."

"I can hardly believe this!" volunteered Bill Brady. "You're running out of suspects, Chief. Who the hell killed Hayes?"

At that instant, Juliet Castellani jolted her head around and looked squarely at Bill. She had never heard him speak before, but his voice sounded strangely familiar. Her fixed stare was unnerving to Bill, and he recoiled in momentary fear.

"Can I help you, Ma'am?" Bill asked.

"No, I'm so sorry. I thought I recognized you, but I was mistaken."

The chief tracked Juliet intently as she slunk to the back of the hallway and inched closer to room 106. Until now, Juliet had been silent and motionless, observing intently every minute expression and gesture of the participants. Suddenly, she was distracted and visibly shaken.

"Excuse me folks for just a second," said Mike as he approached Juliet.

"What's going on Juliet? Are you OK?" he whispered.

"That man standing behind me, who is he?"

"That's Bill Brady, Mr. Coble's law partner. Why?"

"I'm not sure. I've heard that voice before, but I just can't place it. If you don't mind, I'd like to be alone."

Mike turned to the crowd and apologized for the interruption as Juliet ducked into her room.

"Apparently, all this business is making her ill," said Mike.

"No doubt, I think we all are slightly nauseous at this point," said Marcus. "But I really need to interject. Everyone in this room assumes we are here to learn who killed Walter Hayes. All of your meanderings border on intimidation and harassment. Everyone here is certain I killed him. Let's get that out in the open. You're waiting for me to crack; is that what all this is about, because you don't have the evidence you need to arrest me? Well, bullshit, you and I both know I'm being framed."

"You're right about one thing, Mr. Coble. I may not have enough evidence to convict you, although maybe enough to arrest you until a few minor pieces fall into place. But no one is holding you here against your will. I invited you here as a courtesy to help you exonerate yourself."

"Well, you might start by asking who would want to frame me. Who besides Jack and Rachel knew I was coming to Seward?"

"Good questions, and I'll get to them in a minute. Everyone here is aware of the evidence we have collected in this case, thanks to Ellen's blog. But there are a few things you all don't know about Mr. Coble. For example … "

Mike's story was interrupted by an event so freakish and well timed that it was regarded as staged by everyone in attendance, the latest scene in a play about a mystic and a murder. The chief, a recent convert among a crowd of skeptics, watched carefully as Juliet emerged from her room carrying a vase over her head. Her sheer gown obscured the skin-tone body suit underneath, giving the appearance of full nudity that stunned the ogling onlookers. Juliet glided trance-like up the stairs. Un-humored and yet intrigued, no one could decide whether to follow Juliet or to ignore her.

"Let's just hope she doesn't drop that candle," said Mike intent on giving Juliet her space. "Where was I?"

"You were about to share new information about me, Chief, not that I'm anxious to hear it," said Marcus.

"It seems you have some personal business interests in Russia that you haven't disclosed, Mr. Coble. Is now a good time?"

"I'd rather not."

"Well then, let me do it for you. Most of you have heard of Victor Yushenko, although you have probably never met him," said Mike, pointing to Victor seated at the kitchen table and hidden from view.

"I invited him here to help us sort a few things out—and to clear his name.

"Mr. Yushenko is the Russian fighter pilot who defected to the U.S. in 1968. He has devoted twenty years of his life to helping this country win the cold war. Now that it's won, he's made a good living consulting with Russian businesses, including oil companies, and occasionally this leads to big deals involving the Russian government. When Russian President Martov moved to nationalize the Russian oil industry, Mr. Yushenko became involved in a complex international plan designed to stabilize oil markets and to prevent black-market exchange of U.S. technology.

"President Martov wanted Russians to think he was protecting the motherland by kicking out foreign profiteers. Secretly, however, he was buying off foreign companies and reassuring the international oil markets that production would remain steady and foreign investors would be compensated fairly. Mr. Yushenko was the man to accomplish this."

"Sounds great, but what does this have to do with Marcus?" asked Bill.

The chief faced Marcus directly and continued his story.

"You were a major thorn in Mr. Yushenko's butt because you held substantial interests in several Russian oil leases, which you obtained in exchange for access to highly sophisticated mapping technology. You refused to negotiate or to sell your interests, knowing you held a key component to developing those fields.

"Two months ago, Mr. Yushenko met with Bill Brady, your law partner, in an effort to get you to cooperate. As it turned out, Bill didn't know anything about your secret Russian transactions. Furthermore, it became clear that the leases were all in your personal name in spite of the fact that the technology is owned by BOC."

"Marcus! This better not be true," barked Jack from in back of the room.

"Jack, don't play dumb for Christ's sake, and let's not discuss our business here."

Chief Callahan turned to Marcus, altering his tone.

"And to top it off, the technology you were trading is a protected class of technology outlawed by the FTC. It's no wonder you didn't want Victor Yushenko or anyone else sticking his nose into your business. If you didn't murder Mr. Hayes, which remains in doubt, you are guilty of international trade and SEC violations. I'd be surprised if the IRS doesn't prosecute you on charges of tax evasion."

"All of the business I conducted was as an agent on behalf of BOC, and the technology was never actually transferred. Besides, these deals were brokered long before the embargo was in effect. We were well within our rights to negotiate foreign leases using technology we pioneered and owned exclusively. Don't deceive people, Chief. Ninety percent of the leases BOC has signed in the last ten years have been executed by me alone. This hardly gives me a motive to kill Hayes."

"Mr. Hayes was the only person who knew about your illegal trades and you knew the federal investigation and eventual trial would put enough pressure on Hayes to expose everything. Of course, you had motive … substantial motive, enough to kill for I believe."

"I will admit to one thing. Whoever is framing me for Hayes' murder did a damn good job."

"You lied about your presence on the second-floor corridor minutes before Mr. Hayes was murdered. You clearly intended to meet him Friday night, and yet you elected to surprise him. We know that Mr. Hayes was not expecting you. None of these actions were staged by someone trying to frame you. You committed them yourself. Electrical cables with your prints on them were discovered in a parked car shortly after the murder, cables that were likely used to electrocute Mr. Hayes. Work clothes with your hair fibers were found in Mrs. Randolph's hotel room, and you have no alibi. Every piece of evidence we have in this case points to you!"

"It all sounds so neat and tidy, doesn't it? Maybe a little too perfect? But not everything fits, and you know it, or I would be in jail. Why the hell would I stick around the hotel after killing someone? Why would I put cables in someone else's car, or plant my clothes in someone else's room that I know can be traced back to me?"

"Maybe you're just not all that smart a killer; maybe your plan was interrupted by a power outage and you panicked. Or maybe someone knew you planned to kill Mr. Hayes and simply wanted to be sure you didn't get away with it. Instead of framing you, maybe someone just wanted to make sure you were caught."

Bill Brady had heard enough. Silent and intent on obscurity up to this point, Bill now felt the urge to speak, but whether it was out of indignation or the need to defend his partner was unclear, especially to the chief, who scrutinized every detail of Mr. Brady's remarks.

"As your friend and partner for twenty years, Marcus, I have to admit I'm a little shocked by all this. While I can hardly imagine that you are capable of murder, I do think you have a lot of explaining to do. But I don't think this is the time or the place to do it. I strongly advise you to remain silent until you can retain good legal counsel."

"Well, I'll say it again, I didn't kill Walter Hayes. I have nothing to hide."

"Speaking of which, Mr. Brady, you have been hiding a few things yourself, haven't you?" said the chief.

"What in God's name are you talking about?"

"One thing I learned this morning from Rachel," interjected

Marcus. "You knew both of us were coming to Seward, knowledge you conveniently failed to volunteer."

"She called me out of fear because she was worried for her life. No doubt she had cause to, since she was following you. No one knows you better than Rachel, Marcus, and yet even she didn't trust you! She obviously trusted me, so don't go there. I was protecting you and honoring Rachel's request by keeping it confidential."

"You're the only person in the world with access codes to the security systems at my house," said Marcus. "I had the chief call the alarm company to query the system. Someone entered my house at 2:57 P.M. on Friday. Now how could I enter my house if I'm on the road to Seward?"

"Marcus, think for a minute. You could have given your access codes to anyone. Listen, don't do this. You know from experience that the worst time to defend yourself is when you're under this kind of pressure. I highly recommend you don't say anything more."

"It may be the only opportunity I get for a long time to clear my name," responded Marcus.

At that instant Juliet emerged from the stairwell, absent the vase and meditative pose she departed with. Juliet approached the chief and placed her lips gently to his ear, cupping both hands to ensure complete privacy.

"You need to come with me now. I have something important to tell you. Look into my hand," Juliet whispered. She stepped back and slowly retracted her fingers. In her palm was a perfectly formed periwinkle sea shell. She clasped her hand quickly to hide the evidence and pulled herself back up to the chief's ear. "I believe Fannie is ready to reveal herself to you. You need to come with me."

Mike looked momentarily puzzled. He turned to Agent Fell, who offered a nod of understanding.

"Folks, I have to apologize. This may seem a bit untimely, but I have a possible emergency … at least something that demands my immediate attention. It may take some time. I'm turning things over to Agent Fell here. It's 1:00 P.M. now. We'll reconvene here at 4:00 P.M. when I expect to wrap this up, for better or worse. You are all free to go; the only restriction is that no one is to leave Seward."

Anxious to avoid the embarrassment and conflict that would inevitably ensue from personal interaction, every participant in the chief's unfolding indictment quickly disbursed. As the hallway cleared, the chief followed Juliet into room 106.

As the chief entered the darkened room, he recognized the distinct fragrances and the familiar flicker of candlelight emanating from the bathroom.

"Sometime after I turned to meet Mr. Brady, I looked down on the floor and spotted this at his feet. I picked it up as I was leaving."

Juliet handed Mike the perfectly formed shell, which he carefully inspected and then placed into his vest pocket.

"Ok, but what are we to do with this?"

"You know what this means," said Juliet. "This means that Bill Brady could be your man; at the least that he could be contemplating something sinister."

"It also means that Mr. Brady has been visited by Fannie, or can expect to be soon, would you agree?" asked Mike.

"I would, and I see where you're going with this. I will pay the man a visit soon, maybe set the stage so to speak. But first, we have something far more important to attend to."

Juliet led the chief by the hand into the large, ornate

bathroom, the centerpiece of which was an old-fashioned claw-footed tub. The tub was filled with water. Fragrant votive candles were floating under a large pane of glass, which Juliet had propped upon the rim of the bathtub. Pointing to a pillow on the floor, Juliet asked Mike to sit down and look closely into the glass. He seated himself and peered into the glass. Immediately, the chief recoiled at the eerie images in front of him. His expression seemed opaque, and yet distinct against the fluttering light. His eyes lost all depth perception against the multiple dimensions of light and dark.

"Look closely, Mike. She is waiting for you. Close your eyes and release your mind. Open your soul and let the light shine within you."

Mike hesitated and then placed his face up to the glass. He stared blankly at the screen, not completely sure of his purpose.

"After I discovered the sea shell, I came directly here. I didn't know what to expect, but I realized right away that Fannie was asking for you. Right where you are sitting, I saw her leading you by the hand to a deserted beach that fronted a magnificent ocean. She was pointing to a small dory, where a single man was rowing calmly out to sea."

"What does that mean?"

"It is a mystery, Mike, a journey of discovery. Do not be afraid. Go! Go now!"

Mike seemed confused and disoriented as he stood up to leave in reaction to her command.

"No, silly, sit here! Close your eyes, and listen to me. I want you to focus on breathing for a few minutes, nothing more. Just control your breathing."

Juliet waited for several minutes until she was sure that Mike was completely relaxed.

"Fannie is waiting for you, and you must find her. It's not easy, but it starts with a simple acceptance that Fannie is present with you here at this moment. You believe in her, but more importantly you *need* her."

The flickering candles stilled themselves as a sheen of light illuminated the panel of glass.

> On a pane of glass reflections drew pictures only the worthy will see right through...

"Do not allow your conscious mind to control events. Erase your memory. Feel nothing but peace ... peace." After a pause, she said, "When I leave, you will be alone with Fannie. You will open your eyes and you will see her, and you will be home."

With imperceptible motion, Juliet opened the door and exited the room. Agent Fell was waiting patiently on a bench just outside the room.

"Agent Fell, how are you?" Juliet asked in a calm voice. "Mike asked to be alone for a few minutes. Everything is fine."

"What is all this about? Did you discover something upstairs?"

"I think it's best if you ask the chief. I am hopeful that he will have some answers to that question when he emerges, but I would give him all the time that he requires. Where did everyone go?"

"We let everyone go for now, but I asked them to return at 4:00 P.M. Why?"

"Oh my! I fear that may be a mistake. Something tragic is likely to happen."

Agent Fell looked at Juliet intently; even if he was not convinced himself of her premonitions, he was sure that his boss would want him to take Juliet's warnings to heart.

"What? To whom?"

"I suspect it may involve Mr. Brady, but I am not …"

Agent Fell quickly placed a cupped hand over Juliet's mouth.

"Shhhh! He is in the library and can hear you."

"Then please excuse me. He's just the person I am looking for," said Juliet as she turned down the hall.

☙❧

Bill Brady was sitting alone in the library, typing into his laptop when Juliet entered. He ignored her until she closed the door in a clear indication that she wished to engage him directly and in private.

"What can I do for you, young lady?" Bill asked politely.

"When I said earlier that I thought we had met, I was not mistaken."

"Well, I apologize. You'll have to remind me of the occasion."

"Did you recognize the woman with the vase and candle over her head who came out of my room a while ago."

"That was you, and, yes, I recognized you."

"Ah, but you were fooled. In fact it was not me, it was Fannie."

"And who might Fannie be?"

"Fannie Guthry-Baehm is a spirit, Mr. Brady."

"Hah, a spirit! OK. Am I suppose to be afraid or something?"

"If you have a reason to be afraid, then you should be. On the other hand, if you are at peace with what you have done, then there is no reason to fear the consequences."

"Consequences! What consequences?"

"You have met Fannie, and recently, I believe. So you understand that her spirit is real and has the power to possess you in life and even beyond. You have witnessed first-hand the consequences of evil intentions, and I doubt you are prepared to live with Fannie for the rest of your life."

"This is all nonsense. Could you please excuse me?"

Bill Brady was visibly agitated, pacing the library and smacking his tongue and lips together in a nervous chirping sound. Juliet knew she had discovered Fannie's most recent victim.

"I'm happy to leave you alone. I just want you to know that it is never too late to repent. Fannie is a forgiving person. But absolution is only possible if confession occurs before the case is made, not after the evidence has been gathered."

"So you are the chief's interrogator, sent to solicit my confession? And your leverage is Fannie, a ghost who is supposed to haunt my conscience for eternity. Lady, I'm entertained but not interested."

"Fine, Mr. Brady. I am not surprised. Many people have written me off as crazy, but you should know that Chief Callahan is with Fannie right now."

"With a spirit? The chief of police is talking to a ghost, and I am suddenly expected to spill my guts out of fear? Wait until I report this to the media. The chief won't have a job!"

"On the contrary; your deepest secrets, your darkest desires are known to Fannie. Your conscience is your curse. Fannie hopes to save you from suffering—the same kind that afflicts you now. You now hope to compound your sin by making others pay for it. Fannie is asking you to reconsider your plan."

Bill Brady rolled his eyes and threw up his arms in mockery of Juliet's point.

"Don't play dumb, Mr. Brady. We both know you have met Fannie. What you do *not* know is that Chief Callahan has established communication with her as well."

"Well I appreciate your … observations, but I have nothing to hide and nothing to fear. So if you'll excuse me, I have some mail to return."

"That's ironic because you do have something to hide, something you hid once, but not well enough apparently."

"What are you talking about?"

"I'm talking about the murder weapon, the device you used to electrocute Walter that you hid on the second floor."

Bill Brady went suddenly comatose. He stared hard into Juliet's eyes in a vain attempt to discern the degree of speculation in her words. He grabbed her arm almost instinctively in an effort to frighten her into further disclosure. His narrowed eyes and tightened jaw revealed an intensity that Juliet instantly perceived as guilt. Juliet calmly reached down and removed his tightened grip from her forearm and replaced it gently to his side.

"Think hard about this, Mr. Brady, but please don't do anything stupid. This will all be over soon, I am sure. Your time is short."

When Juliet left the library, she passed Agent Fell pacing the corridor outside room 106. It had been close to twenty minutes since she left Mike alone with Fannie, and she was as curious as Agent Fell to learn of his progress.

"That's your man in the library, Agent Fell. I suggest you keep a close eye on him."

"I won't ask you how you know that, but I will remind you not to interfere with the investigation. We're close to nailing this case, and we can't afford to lose it on a technicality."

Juliet ignored him and cracked the door to 106.

"Did you hear me, Juliet? No meddling!" he whispered as he peered over Juliet's head into the room.

"Yes I heard you. Now if you'll excuse me, I need to check on the chief."

Agent Fell was about to register his protest when the chief stumbled out of the bathroom doorway. He missed the half-step down from the elevated bathroom floor and careened onto the bed, jolting him from his stupor. He looked blankly up at the two, then around the room as if to confirm his whereabouts.

"I'm sorry. I ... I'm not sure ... . How long have I been in here?"

Juliet turned to Agent Fell and with firm reproach gestured to him to back off and let her handle Mike.

"Time is not important, Mike. Just relax for a minute. It's important that you immediately process your connection, that you evaluate the message before it becomes clouded by other things. Did you reach Fannie?"

"I did. I don't know what ... She ... she was so real. She knows who I ... everything about me ... I need to go."

"Mike, please listen to me carefully. You are crossing over, and you need to focus on your purpose here, on your job as the chief of police. You are conducting a murder investigation here at the Van Gilder. You have several suspects, but you are missing key pieces of evidence. Something bad is about to happen, and Fannie is trying to help us stop it. What did she tell you?"

Mike stood erect, his eyes closed, and his head tilted back for a long minute. When he opened his eyes, he appeared disoriented.

"What did Fannie reveal to you, Mike?" repeated Juliet.

"Nothing, really ... but in a way everything." Mike reached

into his pocket for his notebook and pen. He scribbled some notes and handed them to Agent Fell.

"That should tell you everything you need to know." Agent Fell and Juliet anxiously deciphered the scroll.

"Any idea who hid the machine there?" asked Fell.

"I know who put it there and who killed Hayes. Just locate that welder, and I'll worry about the rest. Go now!"

"I'm on it, Chief. If it's there, we'll find it."

"Hold on!" said Juliet. "Let's think about this first! We may find what we're looking for, but how are we going to link the evidence to our killer? Chief, listen to me. I've been through this before. You're not going to convince anyone, let alone a jury, that a spirit revealed to you the identity of the killer. What if the machine has someone else's fingerprints all over it, with no other means of tying it to the real killer?"

"Good point, Juliet. Good goddam point."

"I've got an idea, Gentlemen. But it will take all of us working together, and no one else can know about our plan. Fannie and I are about to pay a visit to our friend, Mr. Brady. Can I count on you, Mike?"

"I'm in your hands, Juliet," said Mike.

# Chapter XVII
Sunday, January 20, 3:40 P.M.

**WHEN MIKE ENTERED THE LIBRARY,** Bill Brady was slouched over in one of the olive-cushioned oak chairs pretending to be asleep. Mike sat down at the round table across from him and made his presence obvious enough to bring Bill to attention.

"Mr. Brady, good afternoon. I'm sorry to disturb you."

Bill feigned a yawn and shook his head vigorously. "No problem, I just dozed off in the sun here. How's the investigation going?"

"Very well in one respect. We have identified our killer."

"And?"

"As soon as he arrives, I'll be placing your law partner Mr. Coble under arrest for Walter Hayes' murder."

"I don't know what to say; I'm shocked and at the same time relieved. It wasn't too long ago that some crazy woman was in here telling me you had found the murder weapon and that you were communicating with a ghost."

"When I started this case, Bill, I didn't believe in spirits. I do now. I absolutely do. The truth is, we do … ."

"What was that?" Bill shot up from his chair and looked around. "That noise."

"I'm not sure what you heard, but I didn't hear anything. It's just you and me here. I need you to focus for a minute."

Just as Bill sat down, the TV flickered on and then off. At the same time the lights darkened.

"Oh my, not again," said the chief. When the lights came back on almost immediately and the TV screen re-appeared, this time accompanied by deafening volume, the chief explained that Fannie was not happy with someone. "I admit that Fannie has played a role in solving this case. I think initially she had you confused with Jack Randolph because you two look so much alike. But eventually she led us to the evidence."

"What evidence?"

Just as Bill asked the question, a curious image passed in front of the library entrance. He pushed himself half out of his chair, craning his neck to see through the sheer curtains on the French doors of the library and out into the corridor, which had gone suddenly dark.

"There's that weirdo Juliet again," Bill said. "She's still carrying that candle; she still wants me to think she's a ghost, hah! Is all this some kind of charade?"

The chief rose from his chair and opened the door to the hall.

"There's nothing out here, Mr. Brady. You're welcome to see for yourself."

Bill decided to pursue the challenge and stepped into the hallway. As he peered into the darkness of the corridor, he saw the billowing gown and trailing train of hair as it glided out of sight and evaporated into the darkness of room 112.

Determined to expose the hoax, Bill darted down the hall and turned into room 112 just as the lights came back on. He was greeted by emptiness. His almost hysterical search of the room yielded no evidence of anyone—or anything. He checked the shower, under the bed, behind the curtains, in the closet. He even observed that both windows were locked tight from the inside. When the chief entered the room, Bill was stripping the bed of pillows.

"Go easy, Mr. Brady, or the hotel might have to charge you a cleaning fee."

"This is crazy!"

"It was hard for me to accept at first. Something is stirring up Fannie, and I admit it has me a little nervous. But as I was saying, she led us to the evidence we needed."

Bill Brady had a look of confusion on his face that bordered on hysteria. He kept turning his head into the room, refusing to give up his search.

At the far end of the corridor, Agent Fell came lumbering down the stairs dragging a large metal box. He stumbled into the hallway just in time to intercept the chief as he and Mr. Brady were returning to the library. The chief motioned to Bill to stop as he approached the machine.

"Look what I found, Chief," said Agent Fell, "exactly where you said it would be—or should I say where Fannie told you it would be. We need to give the lady her due, I guess. A rather ingenious hiding place if I do say so. This matches the model on Marcus' Sears account. We have our evidence, and we now have our killer."

"This places Marcus Coble at the scene and ties him to the murder weapon," said the chief. "Good work, Fell. Get it over to the lab."

Bill Brady looked at the machine and with feigned curiosity bent down for a closer inspection.

"Marcus used this to electrocute Walter? I can hardly believe it."

"That's exactly what happened. Don't touch the machine, Mr. Brady," warned Agent Fell.

"Unbelievable! And you said a tip from a ghost—this Fannie—led you the hiding place? That is crazy!"

The hotel erupted into pandemonium as a half-dozen participants in the chief's unfolding drama streamed through the entrance of the hotel: Marcus, Inga and Ellen Windemuth, followed by Governor Thompson and Elliot Lawson. Even Dr. Strayer was among the curious who insisted on witnessing the finale to one of Alaska's most notorious crimes. The group ran headlong into Agent Fell and the red box that was the subject of their rigid attention.

"And what have we here?" asked Dr. Strayer, the inquisitive and always blunt investigative historian.

"I'm afraid it's what they've been looking for all along, Dr. Strayer," said Marcus in resignation. "I'm sure you've matched it to the portable arc welder I purchased from Sears a year ago. I have no doubt the serial numbers match. It's the last piece of your puzzle, I suspect?"

"Indeed it is, Mr. Coble," said the chief. "Indeed it is. I'm officially placing you under arrest for the murder of Walter Hayes. Agent Fell, please read Mr. Coble his rights and escort him to headquarters."

Over the loud protestations of Marcus, Agent Fell could be heard reciting Miranda Rights as the two disappeared down the hall.

"Where in God's name did they find that thing?" inquired Dr. Strayer, once again showing her ageless curiosity. "I thought they had ripped this place apart looking for it."

"Follow me and I'll show you" said the chief as he turned toward the stairs. "I don't think we ever would have found it had it not been for Fannie."

The chief's casual disclosure amused the crowd as they

bounded enthusiastically up the stairs.

"Take my advice, Mike, and keep that to yourself or you'll find yourself without friends," said Juliet.

"You'll have to elaborate on that one a little later, Chief," said Inga.

The climax of witnessing first-hand this case's conclusion consumed everyone's attention as they herded up the stairs. Suddenly, a loud shout came from down the stairwell.

"Chief, I've got a problem down here. I need you now!"

The chief turned and bounded down the stairs without excusing himself.

"That doesn't sound auspicious. I hope everything is all right," said Juliet. The tight circle of faces was full of disappointment as everyone lingered on the landing. Only Juliet knew that the distraction was planned, her cue for what Juliet hoped would be the final act. "Where could Marcus possibly have hidden such a machine?" asked Juliet. "Agent Fell described the location, but it didn't make sense ..."

Juliet stopped mid-sentence as the lights went out. The complete darkness and silence that enveloped the small assembly was unsettling. Juliet grabbed her prop—a small framed piece of glass—and held it up against the distance dimness.

"It is Fannie. She is here. I see her. Everyone look!" Juliet held the frame against the darkened tunnel that formed the hallway. Faint reflections of their faces peered back at them as they searched the emptiness for Fannie.

"She is searching for something. She keeps pointing at us," said Juliet.

Behind the glass an image appeared to traverse the hallway between two rooms. Suddenly out of the 212 emerged the vaporous outline of a young woman in a white apron. Her hair was rolled into a high bun, and she seemed to be carrying a serving tray on her shoulder. A soft and feminine voice could be heard repeating the words, "It is never too late; never too late." The angelic face of the ghost was mesmerizing as it strode purposefully toward Bill Brady and offered him the empty tray. Juliet could feel the vacuum behind her as the small crowd inched backwards in retreat.

Suddenly the lights snapped on. Looks of confusion and bewilderment were quick-frozen on everyone's face. Bill Brady, however, was noticeably agitated and sweating as Juliet bent down to pick up a perfectly formed periwinkle at his feet."

"Look at this," said Juliet. "It appears as though Fannie has some unfinished business. What do you make of this, Mr. Brady? Is there something you want to share with us?"

"No … why would … maybe I …" Bill stuttered as he looked around in fear.

"She has told us everything, Mr. Brady. The chief has the killer in custody; you have only Fannie to fear now. She just wants you to acknowledge her, to share with us what she has revealed to you. Where did Marcus hide the machine?"

Bill Brady shuddered; he was nearly hyperventilating as a wave of cold blood seemed to infuse his body. Deep paranoia gripped him as his eyes widened into a psychotic stare.

"I heard Agent Fell describe … everything. This ghost … this … this … She told the chief … and now I … The machine is in here," said Bill. He seemed to be in a drunken stupor as he led the group of would-be sleuths into the pension bathroom. There, behind the shower, was a compression fit, removable panel leading to a hidden closet. The panel was perfectly formed and trimmed in oak in such a manner as to hide the seams and to appear part of an adjacent room. Bill carefully pried the panel away and there, for everyone to see was a bright red portable arc welder exactly like the one downstairs.

"What the hell ... how could ... ?" said Bill. In a panic he could not conceal, he attempted to thrust the panel back in place.

"How indeed?" thundered a deep voice from behind the mass of heads gathered in the tiny shower room. Chief Callahan motioned to everyone to move back.

"Step on out here, Mr. Brady. In fact, Agent Fell never once revealed to anyone the precise location of that machine. The only way you could have known it was there is if you placed it there yourself. And as we all witnessed, you led us right to it."

Bill looked around in panic.

"Juliet, you were there when Agent Fell described to us where the machine was found."

"I was there. In fact, I recorded the entire conversation. It's all right here."

Juliet held up a small recording devise and played back a portion of the recording for everyone to hear. Before Bill Brady had time to recover from the shock, the chief launched into his closing argument.

"When Mrs. Randolph called you and told you in confidence that she was coming to Seward but feared for her life, she simply validated what you already suspected. Your recent discovery of Marcus' hidden Extron deal and the Van Fleet payoff confirmed your worst fears about the man. You pondered the extremes of deception and injury to which your law partner might go. Mrs. Randolph's call was the proof you were waiting for: a warning from a trusted source that confirmed you were not alone in your fear and distrust of Mr. Coble. You knew the damage Mr. Hayes' testimony could cause to your firm, and yet it was your partner, Marcus Coble, whom you loathed the most. Framing Marcus was in many ways better than killing him, wasn't it?"

Dr. Strayer was not satisfied with the fast-moving pace of the chief's explanation.

"I don't understand; who is this man? And why does he detest his own law partner enough to commit murder and frame him for it?"

"Have you ever heard the advice 'follow the money'? Mr. Coble was leaving the law firm he had built up with Mr. Brady and was taking a million-dollar contract with him. Furthermore, if Mr. Coble were to become incapacitated, Mr. Brady would succeed Mr. Coble as lead counsel for BOC. However, Mr. Brady went one step farther. If Mr. Coble and Mr. Randolph were both out of the way, he would assume control of Alaska's largest independent oil company. I believe Mr. Brady felt so thoroughly betrayed by Mr. Coble, so jealous and resentful of his success, that he could no longer control himself."

The chief turned to Bill for rebuttal; when none was forthcoming, he continued.

"The devastation Mr. Hayes' testimony could cause to your firm's reputation was a plague to you, wasn't it, Mr. Brady? You saw everything working out for the dishonest deal makers while you got stuck holding the bag. The loss of revenue when Mr. Coble left the firm would be financially crippling. Even Governor Thompson and Elliot Lawson wanted something done about Mr. Hayes and openly questioned whether Mr. Coble was the man to take care of it. Did Governor Thompson put you up to it, Bill? What did he promise you?"

"Nobody set me up to do anything; this is all conjecture and

I'm not going to dignify any of it with a response."

"When Victor Yushenko came to you and exposed Mr. Coble's duplicity and self-dealing in Russia, that was the last straw for you, wasn't it? You knew you could no longer trust him. So you devised a way to eliminate your firm's legal exposure, to gain the favor of Yushenko, Elliot Lawson, and Governor Thompson, all while elevating yourself to a position of immense power, isn't that true? By killing Walter Hayes and framing Marcus, you could finally have it all!"

"Spirits and ghosts seem to be your primary witnesses, Chief Callahan. I hardly think your investigative methods will stand up to public scrutiny—let alone a court of law."

"Interesting defense, Bill, but a ghost didn't lead us to the murder weapon, you did."

"I'm invoking my right to silence at this point, and to an attorney."

"Fine, but I'll finish my story."

After nods of encouragement from the others, Mike continued.

"You speculated that Mrs. Randolph was being blackmailed by Mr. Coble over their affair—or that possibly they were conspiring together to assume control of BOC. So you followed her to Seward. You half-suspected you would catch them in the act. When you arrived in Seward, you decided to pose as Jack Randolph to gain access to Rachel's room, which you suspected she was sharing with Mr. Coble. You used a BOC credit card and forged Jack's signature to obtain a key under his name. You had no idea how perfectly it would play into Rachel's circumstances—her lack of credit at check-in and her explanation that her husband would be arriving soon after her.

"You disguised yourself, waited in the lobby for Mrs.

Randolph to leave the hotel and then checked-in as Jack Randolph. You were issued a key to 216, which you used to access Rachel's room, the same key you left on the fire escape of the Van Gilder."

Agent Fell arrived and handcuffed Mr. Brady.

"I'm officially placing you under arrest for the murder of Walter Hayes," said Agent Fell.

To compound Bill's embarrassment, Marcus trotted up the stairs and joined the crowd of confounded actors, smiling and relieved at the successful outcome. After the brief interruption, Mike continued.

"Your plan was brilliant, Mr. Brady, and it almost worked. You suspected Seward might experience a power outage, or if they didn't, a momentary outage would not raise suspicions. So when you arrived at the Van Gilder to plan the murder, you located the main disconnect and unplugged the emergency lights on the second floor. The footprints and materials on the roof would match the articles you staged in Rachel's room. Finally, you located a convenient hiding place for the welder—a perfect solution that allowed you the option of exposing the evidence if it became necessary to frame Mr. Coble or alternatively to conceal it for a long time. The entire time, you had a perfect disguise: a Chugach Electric lineman on standby. You knew exactly the voltage that would be lethal to someone with Mr. Hayes' heart condition, which is the voltage setting we see here. Everything took only minutes. Sometime thereafter, you recognized Jack Randolph when he entered the hotel and tracked his movements to his car across the street. You assumed that Mr. Randolph and Mr. Coble were there together, so you planted the cables just in case suspicions arose as to the cause of death."

At the conclusion of Mike's rendition of events, everyone was convinced of its accuracy, if not by its logic, then by the expression of guilt it created on Bill's face. The chief had intentionally assembled the makeshift jury as a referendum on his theories and in preparation for his public pronouncements. He felt satisfied by the favorable reaction he witnessed among the innocent, as well as by the telltale signs of defeat and resignation among the guilty.

"Is there any connection to the earlier events at the Waterfront Bar, Chief Callahan?" asked Sergeant Graham.

"None, according to Mr. Bond here and others I interviewed. It all started with a couple of drunken, pissed-off pool players. No one was hurt."

The short round of applause that ended the ghostly drama was a fitting conclusion to the case, for the chief had recently resolved that this was his last assignment. He bowed, not out of any sense of accomplishment, but out of respect for his companions. This was his curtain call, his final act, and he gave a respectful nod in honor of the occasion. The uncharacteristic action was not lost on those who knew the chief, who was smiling broadly, and the several who understood the significance of his gesture bowed respectfully in return.

In spite of the emotional climax, the chief retreated from the celebration with unusual haste. Surrounded by his comrades in such a moment of triumph, Mike Callahan would normally be the first to break out the cigars and begin the backslapping debrief that would build on his legend and resumé of success.

But not this time. His smile faded as quickly as his footsteps, and he appeared distant, even sad as he passed James Van Oss in the hallway without acknowledgment. Ever since his experience in the bathroom of 106, Mike had been preoccupied with bringing the case to closure—but not for the reasons one would suspect.

In fact, Mike himself did not fully comprehend the impatience and sense of urgency that overcame him. He almost felt haunted by Fannie himself. But hers was a welcoming intervention, and Mike had a burning desire not to run but to reconnect with something that was missing from his life—something he had ignored and almost forgotten over the last twenty years: Diane, his former wife.

## Chapter XVIII
*Monday, January 21, 9:10 A.M.*

**THE NEXT DAY** was a bright and sunny day in Seward and the throngs of media who descended on the small coastal town all insisted on meeting the chief and the new celebrity mystic they now referred to as the Ghost Girl. The four high-profile arrests and two deportations were nothing short of miraculous, and there were offers pouring in for exclusive interviews, publishing rights, and speaking engagements of every sort. The chief and Juliet were instant celebrities, and their seemingly opposite character and incompatibility only heightened public interest in what the *Seward Sentinel* referred to as "The Fannie Affair."

Those on the losing end of the weekend's events, however, were already plotting revenge. Elliot Lawson and Bill Brady, in particular, were intent on destroying the chief's credibility by portraying him in the media as a drunk, a whacked-out, washed-up police chief whose only evidence was conjured by spirits. For his part, the chief shunned all the attention, content to take the day off with the one person he credited with solving the ugly crime and for awakening him to things he had not thought about for most of his adult life.

"So, Chief," began Juliet, "you had me a little nervous after your communication with Fannie. Our plan worked perfectly, but when you told me that Fannie didn't reveal anything to you,

I have to admit I panicked a bit. Now you understand what I go through. Sometimes a communication is clear, but the purpose of it is not; other times it is like a dream and nothing is clear. We were lucky to have Fannie is all I can say. She works hard to reform her subjects right up until the moment for reconciliation has passed. Watching Mr. Brady crumble before my eyes was powerful. It makes me wonder how an open confession from Mr. Brady might have changed things."

"Well, it was all a gamble, and it paid off. If I learned anything from you, I learned to trust a little bit more. I'm not sure if I've figured out exactly who or what I'm supposed to trust, but somehow I knew that everything was going to work out."

"We are helped along by pure hearts and unselfish intentions, Mike, I know that much. But, I admit I don't have all the answers. I can't tell you where it all comes from or when the help will appear. Lord knows we are all tested. But I am a witness to the presence of a higher power."

"I once felt as though I was, but now I am not sure."

"You never told me anything about your experience with Fannie, Mike. Did you reach her?"

"I did, and to be honest I am still trying to understand it all. I'm not sure what to think anymore."

"Let me help you. What did you see?"

"Well, I can tell you what I didn't see. I didn't see a darn thing relating to the Van Gilder Hotel or anything connected to Walter Hayes' murder or to Mr. Brady. Not one thing."

"You're serious, aren't you? You really weren't kidding?"

"No I wasn't. I can't entirely explain how it all came together, Juliet. Somehow I just knew. It was like someone took my hand and wrote that note to Fell. You deserve all the credit."

"Hah, credit! Funny thing about that; it's never there when you want it and finally when it comes, you really want nothing to do with it! Thank you, though. So tell me more, Mike. I know there is more to your story."

Mike paused and took a deep breath. His soft eyes were filled with trust and at the same time a great deal of anxiety.

"I guess it all started when you told me that sometimes we don't get second chances."

"Unfortunately, it's true, but go on."

"As I stared down into the glass, I heard a voice say, "You *need* her," but I remember being confused. I remember saying, "I need *you*" into the glass, and that's when everything happened and I ... I went into ... went rowing out ... ." Mike's voice trailed off. "It turned out to be my former wife I was talking to."

"Amazing things happen when we admit to ourselves we need others."

"I didn't tell you this, Juliet, but when my son drowned, it was my fault. I led him across what I thought was a frozen reservoir. He was riding right behind me one minute, and then when I looked back he was gone. There has not been a day in my life that I have not relived that moment. I see his panicked face as he searches for the hole in the ice to come back to."

"Mike, you need to let it go. It was not your fault."

"My wife has never forgiven me, and I have never forgiven myself. Diane did not speak to me for months. She could not touch me without losing herself in grief. It was as if my presence was unbearable to her. We drifted apart piece-by-piece over several years. It was as if I was drowning a slow-motion death right beside my son, gasping for air. Losing my son was the hardest thing imaginable, but losing Diane cost me my life. We divorced, and to be honest I have never been the same since.

Until yesterday, I had never understood what happened to me. You were right, Juliet, there is nothing here. I need her."

The chief patted his heart as his large brown eyes glistened with tears. He lowered his head and began to weep.

"Mike, this is an amazing story. Something happened to you at that moment. What was it? Fannie shared something with you. What happened, please tell me."

"Fannie introduced me to my wife again, Juliet. Diane was there for me to see, and to smell. I felt the warmth of her breath on my face and the tickle of her hair. It was almost like a slide show of her life over the last twenty years, how lonely she has been, how sad. But also how beautiful she still is, how full of life in so many ways."

Juliet began to sob herself. She pulled Mike into her body and wrapped her arms tightly around his expansive chest.

"And the greatest thing about this was the moment I realized that Diane is still alive, that there is still time. I was able to talk to her and tell her I that miss her, that I have always loved her, and that my life has not been the same without her. I know that she heard me and that she is waiting."

"You need to go, Mike! You need to go to her now. Find her and marry her again!"

"I am still not convinced that Fannie is not guilty of a little matchmaking," said Mike, choking back his tears. "It could all be a dream maybe, a cruel illusion. But Diane held her hand out and asked me to come with her. The light was so bright I couldn't see where she was taking me, but her smile told me everything. I sure miss her smile."

"Go to her! Do not look back, Mike. Go now!"

"I plan to, Juliet. I'm quitting the force. I'm not sure they want a chief who believes in ghosts anyway."

"Celebrate the love and the life that was lost because you have found it again. Go in peace."

"That's exactly what I aim to do. I'm off to Homer today. Wish me luck, loonie tunes!"

"You are a wonderful man, Chief, and you deserve so much in life. I will miss you."

"It's funny that you say that, because it is you who has brought new life to me. Do you remember that vision you had with Fannie of the man in the dory rowing out to sea? Well, I had that same vision with Fannie, only I was not alone in the dory. I can't be sure who it was with me, but you were waving to me from shore, shouting to me never to lose my capacity to love, and never to lose my faith in God."

Juliet finally loosened her grip and pushed Mike away.

"Off you go, before I lose it completely."

Juliet turned to walk down Second Avenue on her way to the Sea Life Center. Mike walked uphill to the Van Gilder. When they both turned in a perfectly synchronized last salute, they raised their arms and waved a final goodbye, less than a block from where Fannie Guthry-Baehm had waved a final goodbye to her kids seventy years before. As he lowered his arm, a sudden warmth came over the chief's body as he had never felt before.

"Thank you, Fannie," he said audibly as he crossed Adams Street.

The End

# Afterword
*A Short History*

**IT WAS A BRIGHT AUTUMN SUNDAY** in the year 1915 when Mr. E.L. Van Gilder emerged from a Salt Lake City church with his family and declared his wish to conquer the last frontier. Alaska afforded unlimited opportunity, he boldly proclaimed to his wife and family. Mr. Van Gilder vowed to construct Alaska's finest commercial office and retail building in what was sure to become the economic hub, indeed the capital, of this gold-struck land to the north. Streams of people would flood into this land of glacier-clad mountains and endless wilderness, he reasoned. New railroads were punching into the interior from Seward. If history were any lesson, this ice-free coastal port with limited real estate would become the next San Francisco.

There was one significant wild card: a competing company was punching a railroad through from Whittier to Portage and from there to Anchorage and the interior of Alaska. Mr. Van Gilder speculated that huge profits would be made by the company that completed the first rail connection to tidewater and by those investing in its success. The town that hosted the winner of this rail race would prosper while the other would fail.

It was this frontier land-rush fever that possessed Mr. Van Gilder in 1915. If he developed prime real estate in this keystone community at the terminus of the rail system that would control access to Alaska's vast interior, then Van Gilder would become a rich man. Just that day, Van Gilder had clipped an article from the San Francisco Chronicle detailing the spectacular opportunities in Alaska, and he pulled them out to show his family.

Protesting rather vociferously, however, was Mr. Van Gilder's sister, Ruth Cartright. "Why in heaven's name would you uproot your family, forsake the land you love, and risk everything for such a scheme? Have you lost your marbles?"

"Why indeed," replied Mr. Van Gilder, "Call it intuition if you will. My destiny is there. The land calls to me as the Lord called upon his disciples."

"Well, Brother," replied Ruth in a discreet manner intended to be hidden from the children. "It is good you have a fine wife in Sarah, since you have suffered the lack of 'calling' as you put it for a good many years. Perhaps it is for the best."

And without much further discussion the Van Gilder family headed straight home and began packing for Alaska—a journey they all assumed would be one way.

In February of 1916, E.L. Van Gilder purchased a small plot of land behind the Bank of Seward from T.W. Hawkins, owner of the popular Brown & Hawkins store, for a total of $4,000—a high price in those days. From Kellogg, Idaho, Mr. Van Gilder arranged for shipment of his building supplies and furniture and then boarded the steamer Evans with his wife and daughter on May 27. Soon after arriving in Seward, Mr. Van Gilder began construction on one of Seward's only concrete structures, a two-story office building.

Not more than two months into the project, with encouragement from local businesses as to his certain success, Van Gilder decided to add a third story to accommodate lodging rooms. William Kingsley, a local architect, drew up the plans for the addition, but the added unbudgeted costs doomed the project almost as soon as it was built. Lacking adequate capital and the credit to borrow more funds, Mr. Van Gilder was forced to sell the building to Charles E. Brown of Brown & Hawkins Bank on December 29, 1916, less than a year he started the project.

Van Gilder remained in Seward long enough to allow his daughter, Florence, to complete her school year, after which the family of three reluctantly departed Seward. A letter from Florence Cutting (Mr. Van Gilder's daughter) from 1964 read:

> I don't know why I should care so much about Seward. I lived there only one year when I was thirteen years old. My father had become interested in the town by reading about the building of the railroad; and many people at that time thought Seward was certain to be a big city. We lived in Kellogg, Idaho, at that time. Father spent everything he had in putting up that building. It was originally planned as a two-story office building. While it was under construction, local lodge members persuaded him to add a third floor as a lodge room. Well, the development of Seward was very slow, particularly when Anchorage (instead) began to build up. And my father—having exhausted his assets—could not wait. So he sold the whole thing for less than he paid for the lots. We picked up and took the boat back to the states. At Ketchikan, while looking over the town, my parents were both offered jobs. So we hastily removed our belongings from the ship and stayed there a year. I worked part time too. We made enough at Ketchikan to invest in a small business in St. Helens, Oregon. That is my total experience in Alaska ... I can see now that had my father been able to wait awhile, his Seward venture would have been successful.

Newspaper accounts of the day reported that the town welcomed Mr. Van Gilder with open arms, declaring him a man of vision who deserved "a tremendous lot of credit for giving a building like this to Seward" and who "set to work unostentatiously to erect 'The Office Block.'" The banker, Mr. Hawkins, described Van Gilder as a reverent man, hard working, but perhaps naïve and too quick to befriend strangers.

The Van Gilder opened in late 1916 to considerable fanfare, including a three-piece brass band and bonfire across the street, carefully monitored by the Volunteer Fireman's Hall. A three story reinforced concrete building with 12" thick exterior walls and a full basement, the original building measured 34' x 85' and totaled 11,560 square feet. Railroad ties were used to reinforce the basement slab and are representative of the structural integrity of this survivor of North America's greatest earthquake in 1964. A framed newspaper article in the lobby of the hotel today contains a description of the building when it opened in 1916:

> The first two floors contain twelve office suites with hot and cold running water and lavatories in every suite. The hall partitions and doors are of non-transparent glass. The third floor is being fitted up for Lodge purposes and will be second to none in Alaska. All exterior doors and windows are to contain wired plate glass. The windows are the celebrated Whitney windows and the building will be heated by an "ideal" down draft boiler of 3,750 feet capacity, with a Honeywell automatic temperature regulator. The radiators are of the "peerless" screw nipper type. On the whole the building is one of the finest in Alaska.

Today, the Van Gilder Hotel is the second oldest surviving hotel in Alaska and the most celebrated. The late Georgian architecture with its flat parapet, ornate cornice, formed window sills, and stucco exterior presides over the historic district of downtown Seward like a crimson bow-tied innkeeper, a dominant but subtle persona that binds generations by age and tradition, a repository of legend and genealogy, of secrets both honorable and dark. Its face is stern, expressionless, and yet beautiful in its innocent simplicity.

A "Statement of Significance" used to determine eligibility of the Van Gilder for registration on the National Register of Historic Places in 1980 calls the Van Gilder "a vital part of Seward life for 64 years, a landmark structure significant both in local, and state history." The Van Gilder has long been associated with persons and events that made a significant contribution to local and state history, and "it possesses integrity of location, setting, materials and workmanship that represent a distinguishable entity in Alaska's past, present and future."

It is this long and colorful history that ensures that every Alaskan knows about the Van Gilder Hotel and has a favorite story to tell. A recent vice-mayor, Willard Dunham, talks of the days in the late forties when he was the night clerk; when the Van Gilder was the social center of town and daily pinochle games occupied the cities elite; when the famous "Lounge Lizards" dispensed wisdom and political advice for those who would buy them coffee.

He talks about the night Fannie was shot. He was there, a witness to a murder, which some insist was never solved but which others argue was an open-shut case. One thing everyone in Seward knows and agrees on, in spite of the controversy over the murder trial, is that the Van Gilder Hotel is occupied by a spirit.

The changes in use and ownership over the years have been noticeable to residents of Seward. They know, for example, that the hotel once acted as the housing quarters for Seward's vocational training center, called AVTEC, and they remember vividly the colorful and somewhat controversial character of Frank Irick, who entertained influential men during the pipeline boom from all over Alaska and the oil fields—men who counted on Frank for entertainment and anonymity. In those days, the entire ground floor of the hotel was a restaurant, and the bar in the present day lobby was the town's liveliest watering hole. The get-rich-quick, rough-and-tumble of Alaska's frontier-meet-Texas fast lane was alive and well at 508 Adams Street under Frank Irick's tenure.

After a decade of neglect following Mr. Irick's bankruptcy in the late 1980s, new owners revived what was clearly a lost soul, a ghost of its former self one might say. A knowledgeable curator might detect the presence of non-period antiques or take exception to the Devonshire Cream painted mahogany stair rails and trim so prevalent in the original structure. But a haunted building has a character of its own and the cold stare of the street-side elevation reveals no secrets.

Jonathan Faulkner, a lifelong Alaskan, was born in Anchorage and now lives in Homer with his wife and five children. He graduated from Harvard University in 1983 with a degree in history and literature, interests he now pursues by restoring historic properties in Alaska, one of which is the Van Gilder Hotel, and writing. This is his first novel.